GUESS AGAIN

Books by Charlie Donlea

SUMMIT LAKE

THE GIRL WHO WAS TAKEN

DON'T BELIEVE IT

SOME CHOOSE DARKNESS

THE SUICIDE HOUSE

TWENTY YEARS LATER

THOSE EMPTY EYES

LONG TIME GONE

GUESS AGAIN

Published by Kensington Publishing Corp.

GUESS AGAIN

CHARLIE DONLEA

KENSINGTON
PUBLISHING CORP.

kensingtonbooks.com

KENSINGTON BOOKS are published by

Kensington Publishing Corp.
900 Third Ave.
New York, NY 10022

All Kensington titles, imprints, and distributed lines are available at special quantity discounts for bulk purchases for sales promotion, premiums, fundraising, educational, or institutional use. Special book excerpts or customized printings can also be created to fit specific needs. For details, write or phone the office of the Kensington Special Sales Manager: Attn. Special Sales Department, Kensington Publishing Corp., 900 Third Ave., New York, NY 10022. Phone: 1-800-221-2647.

Library of Congress Card Catalogue Number: 2025934261

KENSINGTON and the K with book logo Reg. U.S. Pat. & TM Off.

ISBN: 978-1-4967-5396-0
First Kensington Hardcover Edition: August 2025

ISBN: 978-1-4967-5398-4 (ebook)

10 9 8 7 6 5 4 3 2 1

Printed in the United States of America

The authorized representative in the EU for product safety and compliance is eucomply OU, Parnu mnt 139b-14, Apt 123
Tallinn, Berlin 11317, hello@eucompliancepartner.com

To Murf
Leader, brother, friend

The tragedy of life is not that man loses
but that he almost wins.
—Heywood Broun

Summer 2015

Cherryview, Wisconsin

WHEN HE UNCLASPED THE BUTTON ON HER JEANS, SHE KNEW SHE would lose her virginity that night.

His aftershave was stronger than she ever remembered. She'd smelled it before, like the first time they kissed in his car. But tonight, in his apartment when he was on top of her with his lips on her neck, it was intoxicating. Hyperaware of every sensation and emotion, she tried to calm herself as she took in his scent. She wasn't nervous about losing her virginity. She was in love and wanted this badly. Her anxiety came from inexperience, and she worried that whatever the act of sex was supposed to be, she would get it wrong.

She felt his hand slip inside her underwear. The moment intensified when he gently pulled them down. She lifted her hips and was suddenly lying naked on his bed. It was the first time she'd been naked with a man. It was happening. It was real. And she had never been happier in her life.

He pressed his hips against her pelvis and slid inside of her. She inhaled sharply at the shock of it. But the pain was overshadowed by a thought. It dawned on her, as she wrapped her arms around his shoulders, that she should whisper his name into his ear. But she couldn't. As a star player on the high school volleyball team, all she'd ever called him was Coach, and to refer to him that way now seemed wildly inappropriate and even more awkward. Instead, she closed her eyes and settled on a soft moan as he pushed himself deeper inside of her.

PART I

Un-Retirement

CHAPTER 1

Madison, Wisconsin
Thursday, May 22, 2025

ETHAN HALL HAD BEEN THE OLDEST STUDENT IN HIS MEDICAL school class. He was thirty-six when he walked into gross anatomy lab during his first year of med school. Today, he was a forty-five-year-old emergency medicine physician. Although he was without the years of experience other physicians in their forties sported, Ethan was more than competent. He had finished first in his class and could have gone into any specialty. He chose emergency medicine because his previous occupation had conditioned him to chaos, and somewhere along the way bedlam became imprinted in his DNA.

Years earlier he was a special agent with Wisconsin's Division of Criminal Investigation and in charge of investigating crimes against kids. For a while it was satisfying to put away the subhumans who committed such atrocities. But the job had taken a toll. He saw too much violence directed at society's most vulnerable. A "win" in his old profession still left a kid dead, a family grieving, and a perp getting three meals a day and a warm pillow at night. During the ten years that he worked for the DCI, he'd lost faith in the human race. He fell so far adrift that he had started to lose touch with the human condition. It had been a decade-long slippery slope and dangerous spiral he needed to escape before the void swallowed him whole. He decided a career change was necessary to keep his sanity. So, he put in his notice and applied to medical school.

Now, as an emergency room physician, he was able to help his patients *before* they died. It was a refreshing change, and something his life desperately needed. For the first time in many years, Ethan Hall was a happy man.

He pulled the curtain to the side of ER Room 3 and found his patient sitting in the bedside chair. This was unusual. Patients were typically lying in bed when he entered the room. Also odd was that this patient was not wearing a hospital gown. The thirty-eight-year-old male, according to the chart, sat in the chair wearing a T-shirt, shorts, and flip-flops. Taken together with the man's long blond hair that nearly reached his shoulders, he could have been on the cover of a surfing magazine. Ethan smiled.

"I'm Dr. Hall."

"Hey, Doc. Christian Malone."

"Are you the patient?"

"I am. I just can't do the whole gown and the bed thing. I mean, unless something was tragically wrong with me. Then it's fine. But otherwise, it just takes away my dignity and makes me feel like shit."

"Fair enough," Ethan said, tapping on the computer keyboard to bring up the man's file. "You're having abdominal pain?"

"I *was*. Not anymore. Listen, I don't want to waste your time. I had a nasty pain in my back, so I came in this morning. Your nurse told me it was a kidney stone. She said the doctor ordered pain meds, shot me up with morphine, and hustled me down to have a CT scan. But just before she gave me the morphine, the pain went away. Like from a ten to a zero in a matter of seconds. She insisted on giving me the morphine anyway because she said the pain had subsided only because I had found a comfortable position. But the pain never came back."

Ethan pulled up the CT scan on the computer and saw that his patient had a kidney stone sitting in his bladder, indicating that it had already made the painful trek through the ureter.

"Yeah, see? It passed into my bladder," the man said.

"You a doctor?" Ethan asked.

"No, just a tech guy from California."

"California? What are you doing in Madison?"

"I escaped Silicon Valley and live here now."

"Welcome to the Midwest. I'm assuming this isn't your first kidney stone."

"Nope. I've had two others. Hurts like hell until it gets to the bladder, then I pee it out a couple of days later. I tried to tell the nurse, but she shot me up with morphine anyhow. Gotta admit, the buzz is pretty phenomenal."

Ethan smiled. Christian Malone, the thirty-eight-year-old Silicon Valley transplant, suddenly sounded like a Californian.

"Did you drive yourself to the ER this morning?"

"Yes sir."

Ethan tapped on the keyboard as he entered notes into the chart. "I can't let you drive after we gave you morphine. We'll have to keep you for a few hours before I can discharge you."

"I'll call an Uber."

"I'd have to watch you climb in the car. Otherwise the hospital would be liable for discharging you while you're under the influence of a narcotic."

"Come on, Doc. I feel fine."

"Morphine is like that. One moment you're good, the next you're high as a kite."

"Can you make an exception? I've been here for three hours already."

Ethan checked his watch.

"You're the last patient of my shift. How about I buy you a cup of coffee? If you're still feeling woozy, I'll drive you home myself."

"Sure thing, Doc. As long as I can get the hell out of this room."

CHAPTER 2

Cherryview, Wisconsin
Thursday, May 22, 2025

T HEY SKIPPED THE CAFETERIA COFFEE AND OPTED FOR A STARBUCKS drive-thru, both ordering venti black coffees. Back on the road, Ethan commented on Christian's coffee choice.

"No skinny vanilla with soy for the California transplant?"

Christian smiled. "Black coffee all day for me."

"All day?"

"It's all I drink."

"If you want to avoid another kidney stone, I'd suggest adding some water to your diet."

"I'll take it under consideration." Christian pointed. "Take a right up there."

Ethan twisted his Jeep Wrangler onto a winding road that snaked through a tree-lined area along the water until he emerged a mile later at the edge of Lake Okoboji.

"There I am," Christian said, pointing.

Ethan looked across the lake to where a massive home sat at the water's edge. The morning sunlight reflected off the large windows that made up the back of the house. A set of stairs spiraled down from each side of the back patio and cut through the emerald-green grass to meet the man-made beach area that sprinkled down to the water's edge.

Ethan had seen the house before. Everyone had. It was the largest on the lake.

"That's your house?"

"Yes sir." Christian pointed through the passenger-side window. "Head around to the north, it's easier to get in through the back entrance."

Ethan hesitated a moment before turning the wheel and heading around the lake. Ten minutes later he pulled through the gate at the rear entrance of Christian's home and parked in the driveway, counting five bay doors on the garage.

"You feel okay?" Ethan asked.

"Unfortunately. My buzz is just about gone. Come inside and finish your coffee. I'll show you the house."

Ethan followed Christian through the massive double-doors at the front and shook his head at the enormity of the home. The interior was a combination of cutting-edge innovation and Northwoods Wisconsin.

"We'll sit out back," Christian said.

Ethan walked through the home, noticing the tablets on the walls throughout that put everything from the thermostat to music at Christian's fingertips. Lights came on as they walked, although he never saw Christian touch a light switch. The back of the home was an uninterrupted sequence of floor-to-ceiling windows that offered a majestic view of the lake.

"This is pretty amazing."

"You should see it when it snows. The only time I like the snow is when I'm sitting in this room and every window is filled with falling snowflakes."

Christian pushed through a tall glass door and walked out onto the patio. Ethan followed and they sat at the patio table.

"The heat this year is nearly unbearable," Christian said.

"It's only predicted to get worse," Ethan said.

"The heat is okay. It's the humidity that's killing me."

"So how does a tech guy from California end up in Wisconsin?" Ethan said. "You've got to tell me that story."

Christian took a sip of coffee and looked out over Lake Okoboji. A few sailboats tacked at different angles, the morning wind filling the sails. A speedboat hauled a water skier behind it.

"I founded an online file storage and sharing company. It started out primarily as files but expanded to include photos and videos and basically anything you want to store securely in the cloud, share with other users, and have access to across all your devices."

Ethan squinted his eyes. "Like CramCase?"

"Yeah, that's it."

"CramCase is your company?"

"It was. I sold it."

Ethan slowly nodded his head and raised his eyebrows. "I read about that last year. Didn't it sell for . . ."

Christian nodded. "Billions."

There was a short pause before Christian made a slight correction.

"Well, billions and billions."

"Damn. And you owned the whole thing?"

"No, just fifty-one percent. I wrote the code for it in my college dorm room. Back then it was just my roommate and me. He's still at the company. But I couldn't take it anymore. Everyone thinks they want to be filthy rich, but there's this threshold of wealth not many people know about. Once you reach it, especially through a publicly traded company, you *lose* freedom rather than gain more of it. I got sick of stuffy, Ivy League nerds telling me what to do with my money and my company. The whole situation beat me down and stole my passion. So I sold my portion and got the hell out of Silicon Valley."

"And landed in . . . Cherryview, Wisconsin? How did that happen?"

"By way of Chicago, but that's a whole other story."

Ethan nodded. His life had taken a similar trajectory, minus the billions. He once had a job he loved, but lost his passion for it.

"You look like you're doing fine," Ethan said. "Both in life, and since my nurse shot you up with morphine. If you want us to analyze the stone when you pass it, we can. Tell you what it's made of so that you can change your diet and try to avoid another one."

"Yeah, I think I'll just let it slip out to sea after it exits my body. But thanks."

"Add some water into your daily routine. Trust me, it'll help."

"Got it. Thanks for the ride home, Doc."

"Sure thing."

"You headed back to the hospital?"

"No. I'm heading out of town. I've got a few days off for the long weekend."

"Safe travels. And when you get back, stop over someday. I don't know many people in town yet, and this big house scares everyone away."

Ethan smiled. "Maybe I will."

CHAPTER 3

Madison, Wisconsin
Thursday, May 22, 2025

THE MAN LIMPED THROUGH THE HALLS OF THE HOSPITAL. THE FLAC-cid leg was new and had come on quickly. Despite the doctor's warning that such symptoms were imminent, the deterioration still came as a surprise. There was no pain, just the refusal of his right leg to follow what his mind commanded it to do. So he limped and used whatever was around to help with balance—the door he pushed through to gain access to the ER. A gurney in the hallway. And, on his final approach to the nurses' station, a patient's vitals monitor, the pole of which he grabbed at the last minute when he was sure he was about to topple over.

"Sorry about that," he said to the patient lying in the bed and waiting to be transported somewhere.

He made it to the nurses' station and placed both hands on the countertop.

"Did you check in at registration?" a nurse asked.

"They told me to just come back here."

"No. They need to collect your insurance information and put you in the queue."

He wasn't surprised by her confusion. He looked like any other injured Joe gimping into the ER.

"I'm not a patient."

He reached into the breast pocket of his sport coat and produced his badge.

"Special Agent Pete Kramer with Wisconsin's Division of Criminal Investigation. I'm looking for Ethan Hall."

The nurse hesitated a moment.

"Tall, good-looking guy. Mid-forties. Works out and stays in annoyingly good shape."

"I know who Dr. Hall is."

"Ah, perfect. He around?"

The nurse tapped on her computer. She took a quick moment to read the screen.

"Dr. Hall's shift ended at seven this morning."

"He *finished* work at seven in the morning?"

"Yes. He was on overnights this week. Eleven to seven."

"So he'll be back here at eleven o'clock tonight?"

"No. He's gone for a few days now. On vacation for the Memorial Day holiday."

"When will he be back?"

The nurse paused, and Pete saw the suspicion on her face.

"Don't worry. The good doctor's not in trouble. We're old friends and he owes me a favor."

Pete put the badge back into his pocket.

The nurse offered a reluctant smile. She double-checked the schedule on the computer. "Dr. Hall will be back next Wednesday. The twenty-eighth."

"Thanks. Have a good weekend."

Pete Kramer limped out of the ER. He'd come back next week.

CHAPTER 4

Madison, Wisconsin
Friday, May 23, 2025

O N FRIDAY MORNING, ETHAN SECURED THE BOSE HEADPHONES OVER his ears, ran through his final flight check, and fired up the engine of the Aviat Husky A-1C-200 amphibious seaplane, which was capable of taking off from the private airstrip in Madison, and landing on the lake up north where his cabin was located. The propeller began to rotate until it was only a blur to the human eye. He looked at his passenger next to him and reminded her to take a deep breath.

Maddie Jacobson was relaxed only when they were cruising at eight thousand feet. And then, just barely. During takeoff and landing she was a mess. She hated flying commercial, let alone in a two-passenger floatplane.

Ethan adjusted his mouthpiece. When he spoke, his voice echoed through Maddie's headset.

"Piece of cake," he said to her.

Maddie closed her eyes and nodded.

He taxied the small two-passenger plane onto the runway and waited for clearance from air traffic control. Once he had the all clear, he advanced the throttles for takeoff and started down the runway. When he achieved the proper ground speed, Ethan pulled back on the controls and lifted the Husky into the air. The ragged bounce of the runway disappeared, replaced by the smooth transition of being airborne. It was his favorite part of flying—the moment he left the earth. It had always filled him with a feeling of freedom. He reached over and squeezed his girlfriend's hand. Maddie responded by keeping her eyes closed and ignoring him.

They flew north out of Madison, climbing to eight thousand feet. With the flight plan programmed into the Garmin GPS on the north-northwest heading and confirmation that weather was clear for the next two hours, he engaged the autopilot and switched on his music—Jimmy Buffett came through his headphones. "A Pirate Looks at Forty." Maddie finally opened her eyes and exhaled.

"Good news, bad news," Ethan said through the headset. "Bad news: We've got two hours left in this plane. Good news: When we land, we've got five days all to ourselves."

Maddie attempted a smile. "I'll appreciate the days in front of me when you get us safely back to earth."

"Roger that."

One of the perks of emergency medicine was Ethan's ability to arrange his schedule in such a way that allowed him to work seven straight days of eight-hour shifts in exchange for seven days off. The down time served as a recurring battery recharge that prevented burnout, and for the past two years he had followed the schedule without interruption. He spent the days off up north, and Maddie joined him whenever her schedule allowed.

Ethan owned a cabin on Lake Morikawa in northern Wisconsin, east of Duluth, Minnesota and not far from the shores of Lake Superior. The lake itself was the property of the Bad River Reservation, and specifically the Bad River Band of the Lake Superior Chippewa tribe. Ethan's cabin was one of only eight homes on the lake. It had been built in the 1920s by his great-great-grandfather after a land cession treaty was signed that awarded the acreage to the U.S. government. Ethan's ancestors had been the last vestiges of Hall Copper, a mining company that rose to prominence during the copper boom in the late 1800s before going bankrupt during the Great Depression. All that remained from that once prominent empire was the Halls' fishing cabin planted on the shores of Lake Morikawa.

A government-sponsored buyback program in the mid-1900s allowed the Chippewa Tribe to purchase the land back from homeowners for a handsome sum. Ethan's grandfather, along with only seven other Lake Morikawa residents, turned down the generous offer and kept the cabin in the family. The result was that the lakeside cabin belonged to the Halls, but the surrounding land—including the lake itself—belonged to the Chippewa.

Many stipulations came with owning the property. The greatest of which was that repairs and improvements could be made to the cabin's structure, but the property's footprint could never be enlarged because the surrounding land belonged to the Native Americans. And it was only because of the Chippewa's generosity that Ethan was able to fish the lake. Despite the restrictions, there was a benefit to the arrangement. Since the lake and the surrounding land were the property of the Chippewa Reservation, it ensured that no other homes or cabins would be built. Ethan had back-doored his way into having Lake Morikawa nearly to himself.

To show his gratitude, he'd worked out a quid pro quo with the reservation over the last few years. After graduating medical school and starting his emergency medicine residency, Ethan had offered free healthcare to the Chippewa Tribe. Three times each year, Ethan set up shop and spent a week at the reservation performing general medical exams, prescribing medications for diabetes and hypertension, diagnosing disease and dental issues, and setting up referrals when necessary. In exchange, Ethan had fallen into the good graces of the Chippewa, and no one ever bothered him when he was at his cabin. The tribe knew him as the nice doctor who kept to himself and took care of them three times a year.

After two and a half hours and three hundred miles, Ethan spotted Lake Morikawa in the distance and began their descent. There was a subtle chop on the water, which aided his visuals. The wind was from the north and he cut into it as he made his approach. He cleared the tops of the tall pine trees and reduced his air speed to just beyond a stall before touching down in the middle of the lake. The engine was at idle as he taxied toward the dock in front of the cabin. Standing at the end of the pier was Kai Benjamin, the local Chippewa elder, who held up his hand as Ethan approached.

Ethan guided the Husky alongside the dock and set the engine to neutral. Climbing from the cockpit, he tossed Kai a rope that the

Chippewa man wrapped around the pylon to slow the plane and bring it to a stop. Ethan reached back into the cockpit and killed the engine. He helped Maddie out of the passenger's seat and they both stood on the plane's float and enjoyed the sounds of the surrounding wilderness.

Ethan's cabin sat at the intake of Heaven's River, where the rapids raged into Lake Morikawa. He and Maddie listened now as the water gushed over stones and echoed through the lodgepole pines that surrounded them. A loon crooned from the middle of the lake, and birds chirped from the dense foliage all around them. Kai stood silently to allow his friends the peaceful moment of their arrival to this majestic place.

Ethan smiled and inhaled the fresh air. "It doesn't get any better than this."

"This place is even more beautiful when you bring your better half. She's prettier than you, and much better company."

Maddie smiled and jumped onto the dock. "Good to see you, Kai."

They hugged in a warm embrace.

"Let me help you with your gear," Kai said.

"Thanks." Ethan opened the door to the cargo area. It took three trips for them to haul Ethan and Maddie's gear—two Yeti coolers, duffle bags, several tanks of gasoline, food, and water—up the long flight of stairs to the cabin. Kai was somewhere in his seventies with dark skin leathered by the sun. Ethan had stopped protesting when the man offered his help. Kai was strong as an ox and always eager to assist.

Ethan and Maddie stowed their gear while Kai disappeared to his truck.

"I have something for you," Kai said when he returned. He was holding a long fishing spear.

"I sharpened it and reaffixed the head so it's tight and strong."

"Kai," Ethan said, "you didn't have to do that."

"I wanted to."

During the first week Ethan ran his makeshift clinic for the Chippewa Tribe, he had noticed abnormal results in Kai's blood-work. Further workup revealed a mass on the man's intestine. Had it gone undiagnosed, it would have been fatal. Ethan had arranged

Kai's surgery with a gastroenterologist colleague down in Madison. Kai was now healthy and strong. He and Ethan had grown close over the years.

To show his gratitude, Kai gifted Ethan an ancient fishing spear that had passed through three generations of Chippewa. The long bamboo pole was tipped with a harpoon carved from walrus tusk. So moved by the gesture, Ethan had hung the spear decoratively on the wall in the main room of the cabin where he saw it every time he entered. On Ethan's last trip to Lake Morikawa, Kai had noticed that the walrus tusk was loose.

"May I?" Kai asked now.

"Of course."

Kai lifted the spear and set it back onto the wall hooks, which were made from ivory tusks and also gifted from Kai.

"Maybe this weekend you will finally use it."

"I've used it," Ethan said. "All I've ever hit with it has been the bottom of the lake, which is probably why the tip was so loose."

"It takes patience and practice. Eventually, though, you'll find the spear more effective than the cheating poles you use. And I don't need to remind you that, to date, you've never out fished me."

"Is that a challenge?" Ethan asked.

They both looked at Maddie, who rolled her eyes.

"Just go."

"You sure?" Ethan said.

"If you promise to bring back walleye for dinner."

"Promise," Ethan said before bolting for the door.

Like two kids who managed an early release from school, Kai grabbed the spear off the wall while Ethan pulled his Loomis rod from the rack of poles near the front entrance. A few minutes later, the 50hp Mercury outboard was shooting them across the water in Ethan's Crestliner. They pulled into their favorite bay—one that was usually teeming with northern pike and walleye.

Ethan took his spot on the casting deck at the bow of the boat and tipped his rod with a Mepps #5 bucktail spinner. Kai took his spot at the stern, studying the water with the ancient fishing spear over his shoulder. It took just a few minutes. Ethan felt a fierce strike jolt through the Loomis and set the hook with a confident tug of the pole. He looked to the back of the boat wanting to offer a one-upmanship smile to Kai. But he saw that his friend was tracking the shadow of a northern pike behind the boat. Just as Kai launched the spear into the water, Ethan's reel screamed as his fish took a long run that demanded his attention. He got back to work, lifting the rod tip high in the air to pull his catch closer, then dropping it back down while he spun the reel to regain line the big fish had taken.

And just like that, Ethan relaxed. After a few minutes on the water, and amidst the hunt, his anxiety about the upcoming parole hearing for the man who killed his father, and had nearly taken Maddie's life, drifted away.

Ethan Hall was, for at least the long Memorial Day weekend, a man without a worry in the world.

CHAPTER 5

Madison, Wisconsin
Wednesday, May 28, 2025

ETHAN WORE BABY-BLUE SCRUBS AND SAT AT A COMPUTER BEHIND the nurses' station—a large, square reception area that took up the middle of the emergency department. He was one hour into his first overnight shift since returning from his cabin and the long weekend with Maddie. He pulled up charts to check lab results and complete those of patients he had already discharged. He worked through the list of names until he came to Christian Malone's chart, the tech guru from California. To prevent the man from driving home while under the influence of morphine, Ethan had failed to finish his chart before leaving for the holiday weekend.

He pulled up the chart now and added Christian's previous history of kidney stones and lifestyle choices of drinking only caffeinated coffee throughout the day with no water intake.

"You left the DCI to be a doctor, but here you are chugging away on a computer at midnight just like the old days."

Ethan didn't have to look behind him to know who the voice belonged to. He'd been Pete Kramer's partner at the DCI for a decade before he decided to retire. He smiled and slowly swiveled his chair around. Pete was leaning with both elbows on the counter of the nurses' station. He wore his customary sport coat over a button down, no tie. It was all Ethan had ever seen the man wear.

"You look cute in scrubs. Just like Dr. McDreamy from *ER*."

"I think that was *Grey's Anatomy*, but thanks," Ethan said.

"I thought you stopped being a special agent so that you could treat patients and save the world. But here you are playing solitaire on the computer."

Ethan continued to smile. No one could shovel shit better than Pete Kramer.

"And, I remember," Pete continued, "you also left because the hours were terrible. But my recon tells me that you're barely an hour into an overnight shift that's surely going to screw up your melatonin output and circadian rhythm. So I guess you make more money now, but you still got the short end of the stick."

"I *choose* to work overnights because they buy me time after I work a straight week of them."

"You've got some gray in your temples that you didn't have when you and I were working together."

"Ten years will do that."

Ethan stood up and broadened his smile. "What the *hell* are you doing here, Pete?"

"Can't a man come see his old friend without ulterior motives?"

Ethan knew Pete Kramer was in his ER *only* for ulterior motives. Once best of friends, their relationship had soured since Ethan abandoned their partnership to pursue a career in medicine.

"I just started my shift, Pete. And we've got an ER full of patients. Is this an emergency or can it wait until tomorrow?"

Ethan watched his old partner straighten up and take his elbows off the counter. He took a few steps to his left, and Ethan noticed the profound limp Pete carried. And now that he looked more closely, after the surprise of seeing his old friend after so many years had worn off, he noticed the ashen tone of Pete's face.

Ethan slowly lifted his chin. "Are you sick, Pete?"

"Worse than that, pal. I'm dying, and I need a favor before they put me six feet under."

CHAPTER 6

Madison, Wisconsin
Wednesday, May 28, 2025

"ALS?" ETHAN REPEATED AS HE SAT WITH PETE IN THE DOCTOR'S lounge. It explained the limp and subtle slur Ethan heard when his old friend spoke.

"Good old Lou Gehrig's Disease. Every specialist I've seen has said it's a real son of a bitch. Most people don't make it three years after diagnosis. What do you know about it, E? And don't sugarcoat it."

Ethan knew too much about amyotrophic lateral sclerosis. It was a progressive nervous system disease for which there was neither a cure nor any great treatments. Receiving an ALS diagnosis was akin to being handed a death certificate. The only variable was how long it took to kill you. Pete's limp and slur were likely the first visible symptoms. Ethan knew there were others quietly creeping inside Pete's body that would soon rear their ugly head.

"It's not good," Ethan finally said.

"How fast does it move?"

"It's different for everyone. You breathing okay?"

Pete shook his head. "I'm short of breath all the time. And not from exerting myself. Sometimes I'm just watching television and suddenly have a hard time catching my breath."

Ethan considered holding his tongue for a moment, but knew his old partner would call him out.

"That's bad, Pete. When it gets to the lungs . . . it's nasty and it's fast." Ethan paused. "Sorry."

"Ah, you're not telling me anything I haven't read. I guess I just wanted to hear it from someone I trusted."

If his friend made it a year, Ethan would be stunned.

"Any wacky stuff out there?" Pete asked. "Eastern medicine, or stem cell, or experimental crap?"

"It's not my area of expertise, Pete. But I can put you in touch with some specialists I know. See if they tell you anything different."

Pete shook head. "Been to the best in Milwaukee, Chicago, and Cleveland. Even spent a week up at Mayo. They all told me the same thing."

"They give you a timeframe?"

"None were that blunt, but looks like about a year. Nine months until the shit hits the fan if my breathing keeps declining—ventilator and all that crap."

"Sorry, Pete. I didn't know you were sick, or I'd have reached out."

Pete took a sip of coffee. "Don't get mushy on me, kid. I didn't come for your tears. But full disclosure, I hope my situation helps sway your decision."

Ethan lifted his chin. "Decision about what?"

"The favor I need from you."

CHAPTER 7

Madison, Wisconsin
Wednesday, May 28, 2025

ETHAN RAISED HIS EYEBROWS.

"What's the favor, Pete?"

"The year you left the DCI, I was assigned to a case. Young girl named Callie Jones went missing. Vanished without a trace from Cherryview. You remember it?"

Ethan left the DCI in 2015. He had been in his first year of medical school at the time. He remembered little from that year other than anatomy lab.

"No."

"The case was all over the news. You don't remember it?"

Pete's disdain for Ethan's career change was still palpable, even a decade later, and Ethan didn't care to rehash old arguments.

"Give me some details, maybe it'll ring a bell."

"Girl's father was a wealthy businessman turned state senator. She was a star volleyball player about to enter her senior year of high school. Pretty, charming, was gonna be a doctor. Had the world by the balls. Then, during the summer of 2015, she disappeared."

Ethan slowly nodded his head. "I do remember that."

"Glad you could take your head out of the textbooks at . . . thirty-however-old you were back then, to notice what was going on in the world."

"I started medical school that August. What's the favor, Pete?"

"I worked that case hard. Went at it from every angle, but never caught a break. The case went cold. I worked it as my primary for over a year until my boss assigned me to a different case. Still, though, I kept digging. Dug for five years. And even after that, every so often when I was between cases, I'd go back to the Callie Jones file and review things because I knew there was something I was missing."

Ethan nodded "Head scratchers are hard to let go of."

"You don't understand head scratchers because you never had one. You and I were partners for ten years, which constituted your entire tenure at the DCI. During that time, you had a one-hundred-percent solve rate. So don't pretend you understand what it's like to have a head scratcher, Dr. Full-of-Shit."

"What's the favor?" Ethan asked again.

"Callie Jones is back."

"Back, like you found her?"

"No. She found me. I got so involved with the case that this girl seeped into my psyche. Back when I was working the case, I knew her so well that I started dreaming about her. Then those dreams turned to nightmares, and before long Callie Jones started haunting me. She'd show up every time I slept, begging for my help. It took years for those dreams to finally end."

"And now they're back?"

Pete cocked his head. "Every time I close my eyes. The girl probably knows I'm dying because ever since they slapped me with my diagnosis, Callie Jones is there every night I go to sleep. It's almost like she knows I'm the only one on this planet still looking for the truth. And after this damn disease takes me, no one else will lift a finger to find it."

"What's the favor, Pete?" Ethan asked a final time.

"I need you to look at the Callie Jones file and put your one-hundred-percent solve rate to the test. And keep it perfect."

CHAPTER 8

Madison, Wisconsin
Thursday, May 29, 2025

THE DAY AFTER PETE KRAMER SHOWED UP IN HIS ER, ETHAN ENTERED the Edgewater Hotel in downtown Madison. He had no idea what he was walking into, only that he had agreed to meet his old partner and hear him out about the Callie Jones case. Had Pete not mentioned the ALS diagnosis noosed around his neck, Ethan wouldn't have entertained the idea of helping him with a ten-year-old cold case. But here he was, partly intrigued, mostly annoyed, and still racked with guilt over his broken friendship with Pete Kramer.

He walked into the lobby and saw Pete sitting on a couch. It took effort for Pete to stand. Ethan thought about suggesting a cane, but knew his hardheaded former partner would rather bathe in lava than be seen using a cane.

"What are you wearing there, sport?" Pete asked as Ethan approached.

Ethan looked down at his scrubs. "I just finished my shift."

"We're meeting someone, kid. Couldn't you have put on some real clothes?"

"Your message was pretty cryptic, Pete. All it said was to meet at the Edgewater. I was running late so I came right over. Want me to go back and change?"

Pete shook his head. "No, but do me a favor? Be an investigator today and give up the save-the-world doctor thing for just this one meeting? Can you do that for me?"

"Pete, I'm giving you some leeway to be an asshole only because I still carry some irrational guilt for deciding to make my life better by leaving the DCI. You've been dealt a shitty hand with the ALS thing, and I'm trying my hardest to help you out here in any small way I can. But I'm not going to say this again. Get off my ass about my life and my career or I'm walking out the door and you're not going to see me again."

Pete began clapping. "Well, lookie there! It's my old partner. Took you long enough to show up. That's the attitude I need you to have for this morning. Let's go."

"Where?"

"Upstairs. We've got a room reserved."

"Let's just talk here, Pete."

Pete limped off toward the elevator. "It's not me you'll be talking with. Come on."

CHAPTER 9

Madison, Wisconsin
Thursday, May 29, 2025

T HE ELEVATOR DEPOSITED THEM ON THE THIRD FLOOR, AND ETHAN followed Pete down the hallway as his old partner used the wall to aid his balance. Pete stopped at room number 349 and knocked. A man in a suit and tie opened the door and stepped into the hallway. Pete pointed at Ethan, and the man nodded. He pulled a badge from his breast pocket and held it out for Ethan to see.

"Jon Grace, DPU. I need to pat you down before you can enter."

Ethan raised his eyebrows. Wisconsin's Dignitary Protection Unit was in charge of protecting the governor and his family. These guys were akin to the Secret Service. Ethan looked at Pete.

"See why I wish you hadn't worn your doctor costume?"

Ethan put his arms out to his sides while the DPU agent checked his body for weapons.

"Go ahead," the agent said when he was finished.

Ethan followed Pete into the hotel room and, sure enough, was suddenly face-to-face with Wisconsin's newly elected governor. A woman was also present who Ethan did not recognize.

"Ethan?" the governor said, extending a hand. "Mark Jones. Thanks for coming."

"Yes sir," Ethan said, shaking the governor's hand. "I'm not really sure what's going on here."

Still holding Ethan's hand in a firm alpha grip, Mark smiled. "We'll get to all that. This is Geraldine Feck, our state's attorney."

Ethan finally got his hand back from the governor and offered it to Ms. Feck, wanting to ask Pete Kramer a thousand questions about what the hell he was doing in this hotel room with the governor and the DA. He felt awkward standing in the hotel room in scrubs, and wished he'd changed into his civilian clothes before hustling out of the hospital for this meeting.

"Let's have a seat so we can talk," Mark said.

They sat around a table in the suite that overlooked Lake Mendota. The governor lifted a box from the ground and pulled bound folders from it, distributing them around the table. When one of the packets reached Ethan, he looked at it and read the title page.

CALLIE JONES

MISSING 7/18/2015

Ethan looked at the girl's name and it finally registered.

Jones.

Mark Jones had been the wealthy businessman turned politician whose daughter had gone missing in the summer of 2015. Callie Jones was the governor's daughter. Winning the gubernatorial election the previous year was the catalyst for reopening his daughter's case.

"Ethan," Mark said once the packets had been distributed, "I know you're a busy man, so I'll get right to the point. My daughter went missing a decade ago. Agent Kramer worked the original case and, even after chasing some promising leads and zeroing in on a few potential suspects, came up short. Despite some exhaustive investigative work, no hard evidence was ever found. Eventually, those in charge believed the case was unsolvable and moved on."

"But since the 2024 election," Ethan said, "you and a new group of law enforcement officials have come into office."

"I see you're starting to put the pieces together," Mark said. "But it wasn't my idea to assemble a team to look into my daughter's disappearance. It was Agent Kramer's. We all know about Pete's recent diagnosis, and it was his request that we take one more look at Callie's case. Pete has served the state of Wisconsin for thirty years, and we owe him a debt of gratitude. He presented this idea to me. I obviously have a personal connection to the case, and then we both ran it past District Attorney Feck."

There was a pause, and Ethan felt the need to fill the silence.

"How, exactly, do I fit into all this, sir?"

The governor pulled another file from the box.

"I dug into your background and looked closely at your time in the DCI." Mark looked down at the packet and turned a page. "You sported a one-hundred-percent solve rate on the cases you were assigned while you were an agent with the Division of Criminal Investigation. Impressive."

Ethan nodded but said nothing.

"You were a special agent for ten years, specializing in kid crimes. You were Agent Kramer's partner for your entire tenure."

Another nod.

"Pete believes, and I agree, that you represent our best chance at figuring out what happened to Callie. And although reopening the case was not specifically my idea, I would very much appreciate your assistance."

Ethan pulled his brows together as he began to understand the situation.

"Sir, as I'm sure Pete told you, or maybe it's in that file you have on me"—Ethan pinched the collar of his scrubs—"I'm an ER doctor, not an investigator with the DCI."

"Yes," Mark said, looking down at the file. "You left the DCI in 2015 to attend medical school at UW Madison. Finished first in your class and took an emergency medicine residency in Milwaukee where you were chief resident in your final year. It appears that you excel at whatever you do in life."

"If you know all that, sir, then you know I don't investigate crimes anymore."

"I'm hoping you'll make an exception." The governor cleared his throat. "My daughter went missing ten years ago, and I've never gotten any answers to what happened to her. Pete has become a close friend over the years and has never stopped looking for Callie, even after the DCI brass discouraged him from doing so. But with my election, there're new people in place now, and I would consider it a personal favor if you'd take a look at my daughter's case."

"Look at the case?" Ethan said. "As in, what? Review the file?"

"To start, yes. But I'm hoping you'll put your boots on the ground and actually investigate it, too."

"Investigate it how, sir? I'm a doctor. I don't have any jurisdiction or authority to investigate a missing persons case."

Mark nodded at Geraldine Feck, who took over.

"Governor Jones is willing to formally make you a consultant to the DCI, and my office will grant you the authority to investigate the case. That means anything you turn up can legally be used to move the case forward."

Feck reached into her briefcase and slid a badge across the table. Ethan saw that his name was engraved on it.

"You'll get creds, but no weapon," she said. "And for as long as you work the case, you'll be on the DCI payroll."

Ethan lifted his hands and smiled. "You all know I have a full-time job, right? And a contract with the hospital that requires me to actually show up to my full-time job?"

"Look, E," Pete said. "We didn't come to you on a whim. We didn't decide yesterday to ask for your help on this. We looked at this from every angle. We know your work schedule. And I've got to admit, you do it the right way. You work seven straight eight-hour overnight shifts, followed by seven days off. They call you a 'nocturnist.' Sometimes, you go rogue and work twelve-hour shifts for a week straight, and this earns you two weeks off. It's a nice gig if you can get it. With the right planning, you'll have the time to commit to the case if you work your ER schedule correctly. We're asking you to take the summer to investigate and see what you turn up. If you can't move the case forward by summer's end, there're no hard feelings, and you forget about your short return to the DCI."

"To compensate you for your time and expertise," Mark said, "not only will you be paid as a formal employee of the state, but we'll pay off the federal loans you took out to pay for medical school. According to our records that would be about three-quarters of your medical school debt. The private loans, unfortunately, we can't help you with."

Ethan raised his eyebrows. At forty-five years old, he was swimming in an ocean of student loan debt that, at the current rate, wouldn't be paid off for decades.

"What do you say, E?" Pete asked. "It's a good offer."

Ethan looked down at the Callie Jones file and was about to speak when his phone chimed with a text message. He knew from the ringtone that it was the hospital. He pulled his phone from the breast pocket of his scrubs, read the text, and then looked at Mark Jones.

"There's an emergency at the hospital. I've got to get back."

"Well," Pete said, "you're certainly a man in high demand."

Ethan looked at the governor again. "Can I think about your offer, sir?"

"Of course. Take the file," Mark said. "Read through it while you make your decision."

Ethan stood up and lifted the file from the table.

"I'll just get a hold of . . . ?"

"Call me," Pete said. "It's been a while, but my number hasn't changed."

PART II

Machinations

CHAPTER 10

Milwaukee, Wisconsin
Saturday, July 5, 2025

Elton John's "Goodbye Yellow Brick Road" droned from the speakers as the woman stepped out of the shower. The song was on repeat, and she'd lost track of how many times it had played that morning.

Water dripped from her body as she stared into the bathroom mirror and hummed along. Tall and toned, she had a sharp angle to her jaw that gave off a masculine vibe. Counterbalancing the severe jawline were high cheekbones that curled under her eyes and climbed her temples like dual Nike swoosh logos. Long, yellow-blond hair functioned as the perfect complement to her brilliant blue eyes. All of which was about to change.

She opened the package of jet-black hair dye, squeezing the colorant cream into the developer bottle and shaking it like she were mixing a cocktail, singing along to Elton John as she worked. She placed the nozzle to her scalp and began applying the dye to her hair, amazed at how quickly it erased the yellow blond and transformed it to black. When her hair was properly saturated, she lathered it for ten minutes.

After an additional application she climbed back into the shower. The excess dye spiraled down the drain, taking, at least temporarily, her old self with it. When she stepped from the stall and looked into the mirror this time, it was as if another woman had taken her place. For the final step of her makeover she opened a blister pack of colored contact lenses. The radiant blue iris of each eye morphed into a dark brown caramel. Her eyes became a mystical companion to the jet-black hair and completed the transformation, which was startling.

She continued to stare into the mirror, with her naked body dripping from the second shower of the day. She smiled widely to reveal perfectly straight, white teeth. When she spoke, her voice was shaky and nearly orgasmic.

"Oh, Eugenia, don't you look gorgeous!"

A tear sprouted from her newly caramel-colored eye and ran down her cheek.

"He's going to love you."

Oh, I've finally decided my future lies beyond the yellow brick road.

CHAPTER 11

Boscobel, Wisconsin
Sunday, July 6, 2025

THE WISCONSIN SECURE PROGRAM FACILITY, ONE OF WISCONSIN'S highest security prisons, was quiet as the clock ticked toward midnight. Francis Bernard lay on his bed and stared at the ceiling. His cell had no bars. Instead, there was a thick, impenetrable door with a small rectangular window and a slot through which his meals were delivered. This was life in solitary confinement at the WSPF. It was miserable. It was brutal. And for most, it was inescapable. But Francis Bernard believed he had found a way out.

Francis had been an exemplary inmate, and his good behavior earned him luxuries other prisoners could not dream of. Included in the spiffs was an old Howard Fast paperback with a ratty cover and crumbling spine. Despite the book's decrepit appearance, the words on the pages worked just fine and helped pass the time. The other extravagance was newspapers that allowed Francis to keep track of the world outside the prison. The books came as a reward for good behavior. The newspapers had to be earned.

He lay awake because he was after something specific on this night. He needed to know if the story was true. If his plan had any chance of working, it had to be. In fact, his entire life and existence depended on it. When he heard the locking mechanism on his cell door disengage, he sat up in high alert. The door opened and Mr. Monroe appeared in the doorway. Andre Monroe was the head guard at the WSPF and was a no-nonsense man who enforced the rules of the prison with brutal authority. To cross Monroe meant to bring a world of pain that no prisoner wanted and only a few could withstand.

At the sight of Monroe in the doorframe, Francis knew he was in trouble. The deal he had made was with Craig Norton, a lower-level guard. But somehow, Monroe had sniffed out the arrangement. Francis took a deep breath to prepare for the punishment—typically a stern beating from Monroe's baton.

Francis nodded. "Mr. Monroe."

"Francis," Monroe said in a careful, almost jovial voice. "How are we on this pleasant evening?"

Francis's obsessive personality wanted to point out that nearing the stroke of midnight, it was no longer "evening," but, instead, the very definition of night. And that Monroe's presence in his cell was sure to make the night very much *un*pleasant.

"Good," was all Francis said.

Monroe's hands were behind his back, as if the man were standing calmly at church service. Francis assumed he was hiding his baton so that the first strike, likely across Francis's temple, would come blindly.

"I heard some disturbing news," Monroe said. "You arranged a swap, of sorts, with Craig Norton?"

Francis swallowed but said nothing.

"Contraband of any sort is forbidden in my prison."

"Yes sir. But it wasn't contraband. It was—"

Monroe lifted his hand from behind his back. He held a manila folder from which several pieces of paper protruded.

"Yes," Monroe said. "You've never been one to partake in drugs. I've watched you closely. But just the same, offering favors to guards in exchange for information from the outside is not permitted."

Francis nodded. "Yes sir."

"However," Monroe said, walking closer to where Francis sat on his bunk. "If, in the future, you tell *me* what you need, then perhaps you and I could come to the same agreement you had with Norton."

In that moment, Francis understood that Andre Monroe was not going to beat him to within an inch of his life, as he had done to other inmates over the years. Francis's arrangement with Craig

Norton had been exposed, and now he'd have Andre Monroe as a constant visitor looking for the same thing Francis gave Norton for the occasional outside-the-prison luxury item. Francis's formulaic mind spun with what this meant, and he calculated that he'd have to find a way to accelerate his plan.

"Well?" Monroe said. "Do we have a deal?"

Francis nodded. To say no would be a death sentence.

Monroe dropped the documents onto the bed. Francis quickly paged through them and saw everything he'd asked Norton to find for him. On top of the stack was a copy of the *Milwaukee Journal Sentinel* opened to an article about Callie Jones. Francis took a moment to skim the story. It was true. With the election of Governor Jones came the rebirth of a new investigation to find his daughter, and the governor had tapped Ethan Hall—a former renegade investigator with Wisconsin's Department of Criminal Investigation, as the article described him—to lead the investigation. Francis closed his eyes. For the first time in many years, he allowed himself to believe that the walls that held him would soon fall.

When Francis opened his eyes, he noticed that Andre Monroe had inched closer and was now looming over him.

"It's everything Norton said you needed," Monroe said.

Monroe's domineering tone had softened to a more hopeful one. Nature funneled all species to the same place in the tunnel of existence. Still looking up at Monroe, Francis nodded. Reality dictated that he had no other choice.

Monroe smiled, reached for the front of his trousers, and pulled down his zipper.

CHAPTER 12

Nekoosa, Wisconsin
Monday, July 7, 2025

EUGENIA MORGAN ARRIVED HOME AND WENT STRAIGHT TO THE bathroom. She took her time under the cool water of the shower. She'd had a busy evening and an equally eventful weekend. She felt like she was dreaming. In fact, ever since his letter had arrived in her mailbox, she woke each morning worried that her mind had tricked her into believing it was really happening. But this was no fantasy.

Francis's handwritten letter arrived the week before. She had written to him many times over the years but had never received a response. Until last week. His letter was the first true piece of him she'd ever received. Everything else Eugenia had collected were trinkets and distant items of him—photos, videos, high school yearbooks, hats, and pieces of clothing others told her had once belonged to him. But the letter was the first thing produced *by* him. She'd smelled it and touched it and took in as much of him as the single page had to offer. She'd read the letter over and over again, hundreds of times until the sentences had imprinted themselves on her mind and she could recite the entire thing from memory.

In his letter, Francis had explained why he had not answered Eugenia's many correspondences over the years. The prison had allowed him to receive mail but had denied him the right to send mail. Only recently, with years of good behavior and a push by the ACLU, had Francis been granted the right to send letters through the U.S. mail. The first letter he penned was to her. And the news he delivered with his words had her positively giddy. He'd placed Eugenia on his approved visitor list and had requested her presence in Boscobel. It was a dream come true.

At the end of her shower, she twisted the faucet to cold and stood for another minute as the icy water cascaded over her body. When she stepped from the stall, she drip-dried as she ran a brush through her jet-black hair and admired her body in the mirror. She was thirty-two years old, tall, and firm. She longed for the day when she could give herself fully to him.

She dressed in silk sleeping shorts and a tank top before heading down to the kitchen where she grabbed a bottle of water from the fridge and then opened the door to the basement cellar. She clicked on the stairwell light and headed down the creaky wooden steps. When she purchased the home, the realtor had tried to avoid showing Eugenia the basement, which consisted of a large unfinished area and a small connecting bedroom. But Eugenia had immediately seen its potential.

She had spread a plush area rug over the concrete floor in the main area and hung a colorful blanket over one of the bare cinder block walls. A massive flag covered the second wall. She'd had the white flag with a single black heart in the center custom made as the perfect complement to her shrine. The third wall, however, had always been her focus when she came down to the cellar. Covering that north wall were hundreds of photos of Francis Bernard, along with news articles about the Lake Michigan Massacres from decades before. Mixed in amongst the photos of Francis were the faces of the women who had been killed. There was also a photo of Henry Hall—the police detective Francis had been convicted of killing.

Situated in front of the wall was a desk with a computer. Eugenia took a seat and shook the mouse to wake the monitor.

"Oh, hello handsome," she said when the wallpaper—a close-up image of Francis—popped onto the screen. "I can't wait to see you tomorrow."

She moved the cursor onto a file folder and opened the document to fill out the Wisconsin Department of Corrections forms that were required for visiting inmates in state penitentiaries. Now that Francis had added her to the list of approved visitors, she should have no problems. Still, she was meticulous as she filled out the forms. Prisons were notorious for denying visitation for the smallest infractions, and she was going to make sure nothing stopped her from seeing him.

When she was finished, she printed the forms and placed them in a folder on her desk. With the paperwork completed, a sense of eagerness warmed her body and converged in a swell that started near her navel and jetted downward. She stood from the desk and admired the mural she'd created of the handsome and charming Francis Bernard. Over the years she'd found photos of him from every stage of life. She had arranged the photos in chronological order, starting with Francis's childhood and progressing through his high school days. Even back then he was beautiful.

The next grouping of photos was from his time at the University of Chicago, where he played rugby and was active in the debate forum. She admired the photos of Francis on stage, standing behind a podium and wearing a suit and tie. They were juxtaposed to photos of him in short shorts and a tight rugby shirt that caused the tingling in her navel to intensify. Photos of Francis in law school and at his corporate job followed. Finally, the right side of the wall contained photos of Francis from his trial for the murder of Henry Hall, culminating with his mug shot when he was arrested. Photos of him in an orange jumpsuit at his sentencing were the final images of the mural. The man's entire life was in front of her. Her therapist called it an obsession. The medical term was hybristophilia. But Eugenia knew she suffered from neither obsession nor a medical condition. She was in love.

She sat down in front of her computer again and pulled up archived videos. The video she chose tonight was that of Francis Bernard speaking with the judge before his sentencing. She pressed play and Francis's voice echoed through the dark cellar as he pleaded his case. Even his voice was beautiful.

As Eugenia watched the video of the handsome man she loved, she touched the spot on her navel that was now on fire. She slipped her hand under the waistband of her silk shorts as the video of Francis played. A soft moan rumbled from her throat.

CHAPTER 13

Nekoosa, Wisconsin
Monday, July 7, 2025

IT WAS 10:00 P.M. WHEN THE DOORBELL RANG. EUGENIA HAD BEEN PAC-
ing the house, too anxious for her visit with Francis the following
day to watch television or read a book or do anything other than
obsess over the idea of finally seeing him. She had forced herself to
leave the basement because she knew she could spend all night
looking at photos and watching videos of him, and she needed a
good night's sleep so that she was fresh and alert in the morning.
But she feared sleep would not come. She was simply too excited.
And she dared not take a sedative for fear of oversleeping.

She had, instead, taken to cleaning the house as a way to pass
time, and was on her hands and knees scrubbing the bathroom
floor when the doorbell chimed. She stopped scrubbing and listened for a moment. The ring came again.

"Oh, for goodness' sake," Eugenia said, climbing from all fours.
Her jet-black hair was tied in a bun, and yellow rubber gloves covered her hands. Her face was flush with exertion when she walked
to the front door.

She pulled the curtain to the side and peeked through the window. Eugenia did a double take when she saw the woman standing
on her front porch. Then, she slowly opened the door. Eugenia could
have been looking at herself in the mirror, or a twin sister she did
not have.

"Can I help you?" Eugenia asked in a slow, confused voice.

The woman smiled. "Yes. Francis sent me."

CHAPTER 14

Boscobel, Wisconsin
Tuesday, July 8, 2025

SHE ARRIVED AT THE WISCONSIN SECURE PROGRAM FACILITY AT JUST past noon. Located in Boscobel, Wisconsin, roughly two and a half hours from Milwaukee, it was one of the state's highest security prisons. Her visitation time was 1:30 p.m., but she arrived early. She knew the hassles of getting through security, answering the intake questions, and dealing with the roadblocks that were intentionally set in place to discourage family, friends, and loved ones from making the trip out to the prison. But no amount of red tape could dissuade her.

She passed through the first layer of security—the questionnaire, metal detectors, and the body search, and eventually made it into the bowels of the building. It was there, in the interior of the prison, far removed from the external walls, that security cameras were strategically missing or out of service, and where the guards had free reign. In the darkened hallways they touched her inappropriately on the small of her back and even lower than that as they ushered her through doors and around corners. No laws existed in this part of the prison. If you didn't like what happened here, the only option was to stop coming. She did nothing but smile at the overly touchy and faux-polite guards who got off on touching her. When she finally arrived at the visitation area, the guard reached over her shoulder to open the door, and she heard him inhale as he sniffed her hair. It was enough to make her skin crawl, but she accepted it because she was almost there.

Finally, she sat down at the booth. A moment later, the door on the other side of the glass opened and Francis emerged. He was even more handsome in person. His blue eyes were piercing, tiny oases in otherwise dark-rimmed orbits. He kept his hair tightly cropped, different than how he'd looked before entering prison. She credited the haircut to whatever gangs Francis had been forced to join to stay safe inside. She preferred his hair longer but would never tell him that. Perhaps soon he'd be able to grow it out again. Someday, when they were together. When they could interact with one another directly rather than through a thick plate of glass. She believed that day was not only possible, but inevitable.

Francis smiled at her when he sat down and lifted the phone to his ear. She did the same and for a long moment she simply listened to him breathe.

She'd dreamt about him last night. Her cheeks flushed now as she remembered the fantasy and what she'd allowed him to do to her.

Francis placed his open palm to the glass. She did the same.

"Eugenia?" he asked.

She nodded.

"The only way this will work is if you do everything I ask, and never deviate from the plan."

"I haven't yet," she said, hypnotized by his presence.

"I haven't asked you to do the difficult things yet."

"I'll do anything for you."

CHAPTER 15

Somewhere North of Madison
Wednesday, July 9, 2025

SHE WAS STILL IN WISCONSIN, SOMEWHERE CLOSE TO MADISON. NOT far from home, but a million miles away at the same time. She knew this from watching the local news. Her room—or cell, or area of confinement, or whatever the hell she was calling the place she was being held captive—had a flat screen television hanging on the wall that allowed her to pass the time by watching any channel that came in. The best reception was the local news, which was an affiliate out of Madison. The searing heat wave that had befallen the Midwest dominated the latest news cycle. But there was something new, too. The Wisconsin authorities, under direction of the new governor, had reopened the Callie Jones disappearance case. She turned up the volume to hear the latest.

The room was equipped with a couch that converted into a bed, a coffee table, and a small refrigerator stocked with water. A bathroom with a shower was located on the other side of the room, opposite the locked door she had spent hours inspecting to identify any way of opening it, or penetrating it, or in some way getting on the other side of it where freedom waited. So far she had found no weakness in the door other than the slot through which her captor sent food every day or two. She had peeked through the hatch and saw that there was a room on the other side of the door that looked like an unfinished basement.

The news anchor had just started her report on Governor Jones reopening his daughter's case when she heard a car door slam outside. She muted the television and stood from the couch. The bag of fast food had surprised her the first time it was dropped through the slot. Since then, food had arrived like clockwork and she thought many times about an ambush. About grabbing the hand that reached through the slot to drop the food. But what she would do from that point, after she had grasped her captor's arm, was a mystery. Instead, she decided reconnaissance was her best option. She hurried to the door and lifted the hatch to peek through. She watched the landing of the basement stairs and waited for them to brighten when the upstairs door opened.

They did, and she heard footsteps bounding down the steps. What she saw next stunned her. She had always imagined a big, burly, slob of a man as her captor. Instead, she saw a woman wearing a black mask emerge from the stairwell and approach the door. She quickly lowered the hatch and moved to the side, watching as the Culver's bag was stuffed through the slot and dropped onto the floor. Just as the bag landed, she moved back to the slot and lifted it. She saw the woman walk to the landing and disappear up the stairs, leaving her alone with her fast food.

She heard keys jangle from upstairs as the front door deadbolt twisted into place.

CHAPTER 16

Milwaukee, Wisconsin
Wednesday, July 9, 2025

In the mid-1800s, stockyards were constructed in the Menomonee River Valley of Milwaukee's west side to house the thousands of cattle that came through the city by rail and eventually made it to the meatpacking district. Long ago abandoned, no one had initially been clever enough to figure out what to do with the stockyards. So, they sat empty and isolated for years. Although the valley, which stretched from American Family Field in the west to the Harley Davidson Museum in the east, had been renovated in recent decades, it still housed several abandoned warehouses from the old meatpacking district that had yet to be snatched up by builders and developers. Most of those structures sat close to the train tracks and rattled when freight lumbered past, making the transformation to condominiums nearly impossible.

As she drove through the stockyard, her heart pounded as if a rabid animal were trying to punch its way out of her chest. Francis had sent her here, and she was eager to please him by following his instructions to a tee. Lightning flashed overhead, preceding a vicious crack of thunder. Rain fell in sheets and the windshield wipers could barely keep up. She squinted into the night as her headlights guided the way. Far off in the distance she looked for the lights of American Family Field, hoping they'd provide comfort knowing that thousands of people were so close. But the retractable roof was closed and no lights were visible, adding to the foreboding and loneliness she felt.

After Francis told her the location during their visit the day before, she had repeated it to herself over and over as she made her way out of the prison. When she reached her car, she wrote everything he'd asked of her into her notebook. She had sat in the parking lot for an hour reviewing his requests, carefully replaying their conversation in her mind in order to document even the smallest detail. Most important was the number of the warehouse.

Nine. Warehouse number nine.

She crossed the train tracks and turned onto the small road that was poorly paved and in terrible condition. Rainwater filled the potholes, and her car bounced as she drove slowly through them. To her right were the train tracks. To her left was a series of abandoned warehouses. She drove until she saw it. Years of sunrises had bleached the east-facing door, melting away the paint until only a barely visible number 9 remained in splotchy white.

Miraculously, despite the decrepit nature of the building and its less than savory location, she'd found it. And with her discovery came a surge of adrenaline for what waited inside. She pulled her car close to the entrance and kept the engine running. She opened the driver's side door and stuck an umbrella into the night, depressing the button on the handle and springing it into action. Rain cascaded against the umbrella as she stood from the car. The typical drop in temperature that came with summer thunderstorms was absent tonight. Mixed with the rain was an invisible heat, as if she were standing in a steaming shower.

She walked to the warehouse door and twisted the handle, finding it unlocked as Francis told her it would be. The door creaked open, and she walked inside. The tin roof echoed from the pouring rain. She closed the umbrella and pulled out a flashlight, shining it around the interior to gain her bearings. The warehouse was empty but for random bits of garbage and paraphernalia. The place was clearly a transient spot for the homeless. Needles and syringes scattered the area, and makeshift beds were positioned near the walls.

Per Francis's instructions, she hurried to the southeast side of the warehouse, the glow of her flashlight guiding her way. When she reached the corner, she shined her flashlight upwards and found the retractable metal ladder ten feet above her. She used the hooked handle of the umbrella to grasp the lowest rung. When she pulled, the ladder clattered down until it was three feet off the floor. She dropped the umbrella, put the small flashlight between her teeth, and started up the ladder. A bolt of lightning momentarily previewed her destination—a metal-gridded gangplank and loft above.

When she reached the top, she took the flashlight from her mouth and shined it around the landing. The brown, metal footlocker was exactly where Francis promised it would be. She scrambled onto the metal loft and crawled to the footlocker. Another bolt of lightning allowed her to see through the grated metal she was kneeling on and revealed how high above the warehouse floor she was. She took a deep breath and tried to settle her nerves. When she reached the metal box, she found the large combination lock bolting the top closed. She remembered the numbers Francis had relayed to her: 21-4-36.

She spun the lock clockwise first to twenty-one, then counterclockwise to four, and finally back clockwise to thirty-six. She closed her eyes and pulled. The lock gave way, and with the disengagement came a sudden surge of heat and moisture between her legs. As she opened the top of the footlocker, a shiver ran down her pelvis and brought with it warmth between her thighs. It was then that she realized the hold Francis Bernard had on her.

Inside were dozens of old audio and videocassette tapes, as well as stacks of photos. She could only imagine what was on the cassettes, but from what the pictures showed, it wasn't hard to guess. She looked briefly at the glossy 8x10s. They were of the eight women who had perished in the summer of 1993 during the Lake Michigan murders. All the women had been found lying on the shores of Lake Michigan with their throats slashed and a black heart tattooed onto their breast.

She held one of the photos up and could hardly believe what she was looking at.

"Oh, Francis. You devil."

CHAPTER 17

Madison, Wisconsin
Thursday, July 10, 2025

Ethan walked into ER Room 6 and smiled at the young man sitting in bed. The kid was twelve and wore a dusty baseball uniform. He had an icepack pressed to the right side of his face.

"Fastball or curveball?" Ethan asked.

"Fastball," the kid said.

"I figured. Hang a curveball and they'll take it to left field. Leave a fastball in the heart of the plate and it comes back up the middle. Let me take a look."

Ethan pulled down the lamp that hung from the ceiling. The kid took the icepack from his face to reveal that his right eye was swollen shut with a significant laceration to his upper cheek.

"Nasty," Ethan said. "But the good news is that the X-rays and CT scan show no orbital fracture. So as bad as you look now, you'll be good as new in no time. No permanent damage."

"And the gash?" Mom asked.

Ethan pulled the lamp closer to get a better look. "Nice and clean. I'll sew it up using subcutaneous sutures. It'll heal without a scar. In a year you'll never know it happened. But put a little movement on your fastball. If you turn it into a cutter, they'll dribble it to short."

The kid smiled. "I'll work on it."

When Ethan was finished suturing the laceration, he said his goodbyes and allowed the discharge nurse to finish up. His shift was over and his board of patients clear. He headed to the doctor's lounge to complete his charts before going home. As he started his final chart, he heard a knock and saw Chip Carter, the CEO of the hospital, standing in the doorway of the lounge. Chip had started his career in emergency medicine before jumping ship to hospital administration. In addition to his medical degree, Chip held an MBA. Ethan suspected he made over a million dollars a year running the busiest hospital in Madison.

"Chip," Ethan said, looking at his watch. "Burning the midnight oil?"

Ethan was on days this week, working the 3:00 p.m. to 11:00 p.m. shift.

Chip smiled. "Just finished at a fundraiser and thought I'd stop by to chat."

Ethan logged out of the computer. "What's up?"

Chip produced a copy of the *Milwaukee Journal Sentinel*, which had been folded under his arm. He dropped it on the desk. The paper was opened to the article about Callie Jones.

"With the election of Governor Jones," Chip said, quoting the article verbatim, "a new investigation is being launched into his daughter's 2015 disappearance. Adding to the intrigue about the reboot of the case is that Ethan Hall—a former renegade investigator with Wisconsin's Department of Criminal Investigation turned ER doctor—has been tapped to lead the investigation."

Ethan closed his eyes. The government boys sure knew how to tighten a tourniquet. There had been soft murmurs about the Callie Jones case being reopened ever since Ethan had met with Governor Jones back in late spring. Ethan had agreed only to review the file and offer his thoughts—a task he had yet to complete. He was procrastinating and stalling and doing everything he could to avoid a formal commitment because he was weary about backtracking in life and dabbling in something that had nearly ruined him once. So, to put pressure on him and set the clock ticking, the higher-ups leaked the story to the press.

Ethan had seen the articles in the *Journal* and the *Capital Times*. Word was spreading fast, and Cherryview, the small town from where Callie Jones had disappeared, was buzzing with anticipation about a potential break in the ten-year-old cold case that had left the community dazed. One of the area's biggest missing persons cases in the last twenty years—now made even larger by the election of Mark Jones—was about to take center stage and had all the makings of a sensational summer news story. The newly elected governor, with the state's justice department at his disposal, was desperate to find answers about what happened to his daughter years earlier. Somehow, Ethan found himself in the middle of it all.

He had planned to talk to the hospital administration about the news, but Chip Carter beat him to it.

"Plus two full paragraphs about how you work at my ER and where you went to medical school and speculation about why you left your old profession. And a lot about your father, too."

"I read it," Ethan said.

"I shouldn't have to tell you this. But you're either a doctor here at my hospital, or you're an investigator with the Department of Criminal Investigation. Not both."

"I'm not investigating anything, Chip. I was asked to review the file, that's it."

"And you agreed?"

"Well, when the *governor* asks you for a favor, you typically say yes."

"I don't want it interfering with your work here, Ethan."

"It won't."

"There're liability issues that we need to consider. If you're preoccupied with a missing persons case, it could cloud your judgment in the ER. Say you send someone home and they stroke out an hour later because you missed something on their scans. The hospital would be on the hook for that."

"Probably something my malpractice insurance would cover, but I understand your point, Chip."

"Either way, it's a nightmare waiting to happen, and I've got people barking in my ear about it."

"I'm reviewing the case in my spare time. That's it, Chip. There's nothing more to it, despite the sensational headlines."

Chip thought a moment and then nodded. "Make sure it doesn't overlap with what you do here. If it does, I'll have to rethink your position with us."

"Understood."

Chip nodded before he turned and left the doctor's lounge. When he was gone, Ethan pulled the newspaper over to him.

> *Adding to the intrigue about the reboot of the case is that Ethan Hall—a former renegade investigator with Wisconsin's Department of Criminal Investigation turned ER doctor—has been tapped to lead the investigation into the disappearance of Callie Jones. Mr. Hall comes from a long line of law enforcement. His father, Henry Hall, was a detective with the Milwaukee Police Department. Detective Hall was killed in the line of duty while investigating the Lake Michigan Massacres in 1993.*

Ethan tossed the paper in the trash. Strangely, the Callie Jones case and his reluctant return to the DCI were not the main distractions in his life. That honor went to Francis Bernard—the man who had killed his father—and the idea that Ethan was about to be face-to-face with him.

CHAPTER 18

Maple Bluff, Wisconsin
Friday, July 11, 2025

Lakeside Storage was located in Maple Bluff, a small suburb of Madison on the northwest side of Lake Mendota. Early Friday morning, she walked into the doublewide trailer that acted as the storage facility's rental office and smiled at the woman behind the desk.

"Hi," she said. "I need to rent a single unit."

"What size, sweetie?" the woman asked.

"Oh, like, medium, I guess?"

"Our smallest units are ten by ten. Those are pretty tight. Then we've got two middle-sized units that are twenty by twenty and thirty by thirty. Our biggest unit is—"

"The twenty foot one should be fine."

The woman reached for paperwork and started scribbling. "What's the purpose of the storage unit?"

"Um, just clearing out my basement but not ready to part with all the junk just yet."

The woman looked up from the paperwork.

"I need a name and credit card."

"Eugenia Morgan," she said, handing over the card.

"Card gets auto charged every month. If the card gets canceled or expires, we give you ninety days to submit a new form of payment. After ninety days, we clear out the unit. Everything goes in the dumpster, no auctioning off the items like on TV."

"Understood."

She knew the credit card would eventually fall past due, but that would take a couple of months. By then, she'd be long gone and the people who Francis wanted to show the photos to would have discovered the storage unit.

"The twenty-by-twenty is eighty-nine dollars. Due on the fifteenth of each month. I need you to fill out the top with your personal information—name, address, phone number. Then sign at the bottom."

She did as she was told and scribbled a signature.

The woman tossed a small envelope onto the table. "Unit 223. The key is in the envelope and will open the side door to the unit. The bay door in the front is controlled by a keypad. Code is on the front of the envelope. It's all yours."

"Thank you," she said, scooping up the envelope and hurrying out of the office.

A few minutes later she drove the Ford Focus along the gravel path that ran in front of the storage units until she found number 223. She suspected that surveillance cameras were recording her movements, and that was just fine. She climbed from her car and walked to the large bay door. Each unit was a standalone set in a long cluster. In the background, Lake Mendota was visible between the units. She tapped the 4-digit code onto the keypad and the bay door rattled open. A wall switch ignited a bank of overhead fluorescents. She climbed back into her car, twisted the steering wheel, and reversed until the back end was just inside the unit.

It took ten minutes to unload the contents of her trunk. It was everything she had collected from the footlocker in the abandoned warehouse two nights before. Touching the items—especially the photos of the dead women from 1993—sent a shiver through her body. She arranged the photos as instructed, and knew Francis would be pleased with her work.

With the storage unit locked and secured, she pulled out of the lot and drove an hour and a half to Boscobel. It killed her to be so close to Francis without seeing him. But she was not there to visit the Wisconsin Secure Program Facility. The drive to Boscobel served a different purpose today. She found the post office, and pulled into the drive-thru lane, stopping at the mailbox. From the middle console she removed a pair of latex gloves and slipped her hands into them. Then she pulled an envelope from the glove box. It was addressed to *Maddie Jacobson*. She dropped it through the slot in the mailbox, assuring that the letter—like all the others—would have a Boscobel postmark, and pulled away.

So far, she'd accomplished every task Francis had asked of her.

CHAPTER 19

Madison, Wisconsin
Monday, July 14, 2025

ETHAN ARRIVED EARLY AND SAT IN THE FRONT ROW, LEGS CROSSED and hands folded calmly on his lap. The courtroom filled to standing room only as Ethan waited, but he never looked behind him to see who was there. Parole hearings typically took place at the prison where the incarcerated individual was being held, but due to the high-profile nature of the case, today's hearing was taking place at a courthouse in Madison.

Ethan focused his attention on the closed door at the side of the courtroom. Eventually, four parole board members shuffled in and filled the long table that waited for them, organizing their notes as they took their spots. Nameplates told the courtroom spectators who each of the members were. The side door opened, and two bailiffs entered. Ethan sat up a bit straighter and took a deep breath. The bailiffs nodded and then led Francis Bernard, dressed in an orange jumpsuit with wrists and ankles shackled, to the defense table where he sat with his attorney, a mere ten feet away.

Ethan watched as the attorney whispered into the man's ear. Francis nodded and then looked over his attorney's shoulder to take in the crowd. His gaze momentarily fell on Ethan, and Ethan liked to imagine that with the eye contact came a sense of lost hope. An icy tingle ran through Ethan's spine when the corners of Francis's lips twisted upward in a smile.

His career as a special agent at the DCI lasted ten years, during which Ethan had been responsible for putting many sick individuals behind bars. But none of those criminals had been imprisoned long enough to be considered for parole. Therefore, parole hearings were a new experience for him. Ethan had played no role in putting Francis Bernard in prison. He was, however, a key factor in keeping him there. Ethan's testimony had led to the board denying Francis's first chance at parole two years earlier. And Ethan planned to spoil things again today.

Ethan kept his gaze locked on the man's eyes, his face expressionless, until Francis finally looked away.

"Good morning," the woman sitting at the middle of the table said to get the hearing under way.

The courtroom quieted and everyone settled in.

"My name is Christine Jackson, chairperson of the Wisconsin Parole Commission. We are gathered in this courtroom on the fourteenth day of July, 2025 for the parole board hearing of Mr. Francis Bernard."

She looked down at her notes.

"Mr. Bernard, you were convicted in 1993 of second-degree homicide of Henry Hall, a detective with the Milwaukee Police Department. You were sentenced to sixty years in a state penitentiary, with the possibility of parole after thirty years. This is your second request for parole, the first having been denied in 2023. Special guests today include Whalen and Earnest Bernard, your parents, as well as your sister, Margaret. We also have special guests, Clint Dackery, retired police chief of the Milwaukee Police Department, and Ethan Hall, the victim's son."

The hearing began with Francis Bernard's attorney speaking for fifteen minutes about Wisconsin state law that required those sentenced prior to December 31, 1999 to be eligible for mandatory parole after serving two-thirds of their sentence, which for Francis meant that, despite the board's decision today, he would be a free man in eight years. The attorney then chronicled what a model inmate his client had been in the last thirty-two years. Francis had not only avoided citations while in prison, but had also entered into a religious studies program. The attorney went on about the progress Francis Bernard had made in the last several years with his faith and finding a higher power. Next up were Francis's elderly parents, who sobbed at the "loss" of their son and not being able to spend meaningful time with him for three decades. Yes, he had done a terrible thing, they admitted, but he was a different man now than he was then. He has paid his dues, his mother argued, and deserved to be with his family.

Through it all, Ethan sat stoically and waited his turn. When the parole board asked if Chief Dackery wanted to speak, he deferred to Ethan.

"No, ma'am," Dackery said. "I believe Hank's son speaks for all of us."

"Mr. Hall?"

Ethan nodded and stood.

"Thank you. My name is Ethan Hall. Henry Hall was my father. Francis Bernard killed him when I was thirteen years old. Francis Bernard not only took my father from me, he also took him from my then ten-year-old sister. When Francis Bernard killed my father, he took my mother's husband. He took my grandparents' child. He took my aunt's brother. So as I stand in this courtroom this morning, I find it amusing that Francis Bernard's attorney boasts about what a stellar inmate he's been for the last thirty years, and all the things he's accomplished during his incarceration—including, we learned this morning, that he's found Jesus. But I think it's worth noting that in those thirty years my father, too, could have done great things. He could have continued his life's passion as a detective and helped many more families during his career. He could have raised his two children. He could have walked his daughter down the aisle at her wedding. He could have witnessed the birth of his grandson. He could have cared for his wife when she fell ill with cancer. He could have been there to bury his parents when they passed. So in the thirty years that Mr. Bernard has supposedly been working to become a better person, those are the same thirty years he took from my father who never had the chance to become more than he was the day he knocked on Francis Bernard's front door."

Ethan paused. The courtroom was eerily silent.

"And, this morning, I think it's important for the parole board to understand *why* my father knocked on Francis Bernard's door that day. My father, as a detective with the Milwaukee Police Department, went to Mr. Bernard's home to question him about a series of murders that had taken place in the Milwaukee area that summer. My father was the lead detective in the Lake Michigan Massacres, as they were called back then. You see," Ethan said, looking at the members of the parole board, "someone was killing women and dumping their bodies on the shores of Lake Michigan during the summer of 1993. Slicing their throats and tattooing black hearts on their chests."

"Ms. Jackson," Francis's attorney said as he stood. "I regret the interruption, but it's crucial to note that my client was charged and convicted of a *single* crime, which he has admitted to and has professed his deep regret about. Francis Bernard was never, and I repeat, *never* charged or linked to the crimes Mr. Hall just mentioned."

"Francis Bernard was never charged, but he was a suspect in those murders," Ethan said. "And that's why my father went to Mr. Bernard's home that day. To question him about the Lake Michigan murders. It's important to note, in the context of potentially granting this man his freedom, that he was a suspect in the deaths of eight women that summer. And when my father arrived at his home to question him about those murders, Mr. Bernard shot him in the face. And what did Francis do after he shot a Milwaukee PD detective? Did he flee? No. Did he call an ambulance? No. He walked back into his home and burned it to the ground. He started a fire in his basement that ravaged the entire area. The fire department was called only when the flames and smoke grew heavy enough for neighbors to notice. When they arrived, they found my father dead in the front foyer and everything in the basement destroyed. So as the board considers Mr. Bernard's pleas for release, I ask you this: Why do you think he killed my father? And why do you think the first thing he did afterward was set his basement on fire?"

More ghostly silence as Ethan paused again.

"Francis did those things to hide evidence that would identify him as the Lake Michigan Killer."

"Again," Francis's attorney said, still standing. "I urge the board to disregard Mr. Hall's conjecture that my client was in any way associated with any crimes other than the one he was convicted of."

"Yeah," Ethan said. "I urge you to do the same thing. Disregard my conjecture, by all means. But I also urge you to ask Francis Bernard, not if he is remorseful about killing my father, but *why* he killed my father. Please ask him why he killed a detective who entered his home for the sole purpose of asking him about eight women who had been murdered that summer. And then ask him why he burned his home to the ground moments later. And then, if he can figure out answers to those questions, please ask him one more."

A final pause brought back the deafening silence as Ethan turned his gaze from the parole board members to Francis Bernard.

"Ask him why, after he was arrested for killing my father, dead women stopped showing up on the shores of Lake Michigan."

Ethan sat down and folded his hands again on his lap. The hearing lasted another thirty minutes and ended with the board unanimously denying Francis Bernard's request for parole.

CHAPTER 20

Milwaukee, Wisconsin
Monday, July 14, 2025

Detective Maddie Jacobson sat behind her desk at the Milwaukee Police Department. She tried to work but was getting nothing accomplished that morning. Her time with Ethan at the cabin up north felt like a lifetime ago, and any peace those quiet days had offered was long gone.

"Jacobson," another detective said as he walked past her cubicle. "Isn't the parole hearing today?"

Maddie nodded. "Yeah." She checked her watch. "Going on right now."

"How come you're not there?"

Maddie pushed a smile onto her face. "I went last time." She patted her chest. "Didn't think I could stomach looking at him again."

"Hang in there. There's no way the son of a bitch is getting out."

She lifted her chin and smiled as her colleague hurried off.

Maddie Jacobson had been sixteen years old when she narrowly escaped becoming the Lake Michigan Killer's next victim. For thirty-two years Maddie had carried the burden of being the sole survivor and only woman to keep her life after being abducted from the Milwaukee area during the summer of 1993. Now forty-eight, Maddie still bore the wounds from that long-gone summer. A scar traced her abdomen, from her navel to her sternum, where he had inserted the knife. The internal bleeding and blood loss had temporarily stolen the sight from her left eye, now restored to the minimum level of visual acuity needed to enter the police academy. In the mirror and in photos, the remnants of Bell's palsy were still visible—a paralyzed facial nerve that faintly drooped the left side of her face. And a red, blotchy scar decorated her left breast from where he had tattooed a black heart into her skin. Even the skills of a plastic surgeon had not been able to fully erase it.

The physical reminders, however, paled in comparison to the psychological damage that was done. Mercifully, the years had erased much of her memory about her time in captivity, so that today, only with great effort and concentration, could Maddie recall how she had managed to escape from the shores of Lake Michigan after he brought her there to kill her and pose her body like the eight other women he'd claimed that summer. Those memories included a makeshift knife she'd crafted from the edge of a picture frame and a piece of driftwood she found in the sand. Maddie had used both to win her freedom.

Days after her escape, Francis Bernard had been arrested for the murder of Detective Henry Hall, and dead women stopped showing up on the shores of Lake Michigan. Maddie was certain, beyond any reasonable doubt, that Francis was the man who abducted her. But no hard evidence had ever linked him to her, and any proof that might have existed was incinerated when Francis set his home ablaze.

It was thirty years later, at Francis's first parole hearing in 2023, that she first met Ethan Hall. They were both there to speak out against Francis being released. The man had affected each of their lives in ways unimaginable—nearly killing Maddie and setting loose a lifetime of nightmares every time she slept; and leaving Ethan fatherless when he was just thirteen years old. Their pain had brought them together, and a shared commitment to keep Francis behind bars strengthened their union. Now, two years later, she and Ethan were more than lovers. They were soulmates, initially united by grim circumstances, but forever tied to one another by a mutual determination to prevent the evils of one man from dictating their lives or happiness.

Despite the fact that Francis had been behind bars for more than three decades, Maddie could not rest easy. A decade earlier, after Francis Bernard had been in prison for twenty-two years, the first letter arrived. It came a week after the ACLU won a legal battle demanding better living conditions in the prison where Francis was held. One of the stipulations granted inmates in solitary confinement access to the U.S. postal service, allowing them to receive and send letters through the mail. And like clockwork, a new letter had found its way to Maddie's mailbox every year since.

"Hey." She heard Ethan's tender voice behind her and slowly spun around in her chair to face him.

"Well?"

"Denied," Ethan said.

Maddie let out a deep breath. "Thank God."

CHAPTER 21

Milwaukee, Wisconsin
Monday, July 14, 2025

MADDIE PULLED A PLASTIC EVIDENCE BAG FROM HER DESK DRAWER and handed it to Ethan. It held the latest letter, the tenth one Maddie had received. Like all the others, she would run this one through the crime lab at the Milwaukee PD. But they both knew it would be clean. The previous letters had been microscopically analyzed by forensic technicians, but to no avail. No prints, no DNA, and nothing to trace the letter back to Francis Bernard—other than the Boscobel postmark. It was naive to think Francis would make a mistake on his tenth letter.

Ethan read through the plastic.

> *My Dearest Maddie,*
> *Oh, how time flies. Eight years left, unless the parole board makes an early decision. I can't wait to see you again. The next time we visit Lake Michigan, I'll be the only one who leaves the shore alive. As always, it's a promise.*

The letter was dated the previous week, before today's parole hearing. It was signed, as each of the previous ones had been, with a single heart colored in with black ink.

"I'll never understand how he's sending them," Maddie said.

Ethan continued to stare at the letter. "The ACLU forced changes to the Wisconsin Secure Program Facility to allow inmates access to the USPS. That's how."

"But prison authorities said they'd monitor his mail."

"To the extent that they're allowed," Ethan said. "The ACLU is powerful, and they fight hard. The warden doesn't want funding denied to his prison, so although he might promise to intercept Francis's outgoing mail, there's no guarantee that it's ever actually happened."

"But how could he do it without leaving a trace of DNA? Or a single fingerprint? There's no way he has access to gloves in his prison cell."

Ethan shook his head. "I don't know."

They'd been through it before. The paper and the ink had been analyzed, as well as the penmanship. It was clear that Francis was receiving help from someone. Perhaps one of the guards.

Maddie took a deep breath. "So I'll just endure his threats every year until the son of a bitch is finally released."

"I'm working on that," Ethan said.

Maddie shook her head. "It's the law. It doesn't matter how much you work on it, Ethan. Francis will be up for mandatory parole after serving two-thirds of his initial sixty-year sentence. He was grandfathered into the system. That's forty years, which is eight years from now. So no matter how hard we try or how many parole hearings you speak at, there's a hard stop coming in a few years."

"Unless something happens in prison. Mandatory parole is based on inmates staying out of trouble and not committing other crimes while incarcerated. Sending threatening letters through the mail is a crime."

"We've tried, Ethan. However he's getting these letters to me, he's too smart to allow himself to get caught."

Ethan dropped the evidence bag containing Francis's letter onto the desk and lifted Maddie's chin with his hand. He kissed her on the lips. She forced a smile, the Bell's preventing the left side of her lips from quite matching the right.

"You know I'm never going to let anything happen to you, don't you?" Ethan said.

"You know I'm going to put a bullet through his head if he ever gets out of prison and steps foot on my property?"

Now Ethan smiled. "I'm counting on it."

CHAPTER 22

Boscobel, Wisconsin
Tuesday, July 15, 2025

THE FOLLOWING DAY ETHAN DROVE ONE HOUR AND FORTY-FIVE MIN-utes west of Cherryview to the town of Boscobel, Wisconsin and pulled through the gates of the Wisconsin Secure Program Facility. The maximum-security state prison sat on one hundred sixty acres of desolate land west of Madison and housed some of Wisconsin's most dangerous criminals, including Francis Bernard.

Ethan flashed his temporary DCI badge to the guard at the security booth, who confirmed that Ethan was on the list of scheduled visitors for the day and waved him through. Ethan pulled past the three levels of fencing that surrounded the prison—an innermost motion detection fence, a non-lethal but immobilizing electrified fence in the middle, and a tall outer fence draped with four layers of razor wire—before parking in the main lot. The prison building was bone white. The only contrasting colors were the black bars that secured the windows. Gray AstroTurf took the place of grass—another indication that the place was void of the basic joys of life, even color.

It was never easy to visit Francis Bernard—neither logistically (it required an hour of red tape to finally sit in the chair opposite the man), nor mentally (it took everything Ethan had to stare his father's killer in the eye)—but it was necessary. Both for himself and to honor the memory of his father. So he did it. And he'd continue to do it.

Ethan cooperated with the guards at each stage of the process. Some knew him from back in the day, most did not. The DCI badge helped facilitate the process and, finally, he arrived at the visitation booth. At the WSPF, prisoners were never allowed direct contact with visitors. Instead, thick glass separated inmates from those who came to see them, and communication came through a constantly monitored phone system. But it was not just visitors from whom inmates were prevented from having direct contact. It was everyone. The incarcerated at WSPF were housed in single unit cells where they spent nearly every waking hour. There was no mess hall, which forced prisoners to eat in the solitude of their cells. There was no prison yard where outdoor activities could be enjoyed with fellow inmates. There was no weight room or library or community center. Prisoners at the WSPF were alone. The only interactions they had were with the guards and, through six inches of tempered glass, those who came to see them.

The ACLU had filed lawsuits against the state of Wisconsin claiming that the prison was less a correctional institute than a practice in the art of sensory deprivation. And it was because of these fierce restrictions, Ethan believed, that Francis Bernard had never once declined a visitation request from him. The man was desperate for human interaction, even if it came from the son of the man he was convicted of killing.

Ethan's face was expressionless when Francis sat down on the other side of the glass. Francis Bernard had been thirty-two years old when he killed Ethan's father. He was sixty-four today. Despite the fact that he'd spent exactly half his life behind bars, the man looked improbably healthy, other than his ghost-white skin from lack of sun exposure. His hair had hardly grayed, and he was a bundle of muscle. To pass time, Ethan imagined, Francis spent his days in a repetitive loop of pushups and sit-ups and squats in his cell. The alternative was to wither away in madness.

It was Francis who lifted the phone first.

"Hello, Ethan," Francis said when Ethan placed the phone to his ear.

"Every time your parole comes up, I'll be there at the hearing," Ethan said.

"I know."

"As long as I'm alive, I'll never allow you to get out of here."

Francis nodded. "My attorney believes that mandatory parole will come in just over eight years. I was grandfathered into the parole system since I was sentenced before it was revised in 1999. I'll be out in due time. So, although I appreciate your vigor, your presence at my parole hearings doesn't really matter. But I'm sure it fulfills some need for you to make your father proud."

Ethan had never taken the bait. He knew Francis wanted to see him lose his cool. He never did. He never gave Francis anything to work with. And Ethan had been very careful to never mention his relationship with Maddie Jacobson, or the fact that he knew about the letters Francis was sending her.

"But eight years is a long time," Francis said. "You know they force me to eat in my cell, and that every second day they grant me one hour outside. And even then I'm by myself."

"When you kill a cop and eight women, do you think you should be treated differently?"

"I was convicted of a single homicide, Special Agent Hall."

Ethan had never corrected Francis's misnomer of his title.

"The state of Wisconsin didn't treat Jeffrey Dahmer the way they're treating me."

"Forgive me if I don't shed a tear because you're lonely."

"Forgive you?" Francis said. "Of course I will. The real question is will you forgive *me*?"

This caused Ethan to pause.

"It's eating you alive," Francis continued. "The hatred."

Another pause.

"And the guilt."

Francis smiled and waited. Sixty seconds passed as he stared at Ethan, who did his best to look calm and comfortable under the man's icy gaze.

"The guilt of no longer being a special agent with the department of criminal investigation."

Ethan's eyes flicked to his left. The first indication that Francis had gotten to him.

"Oh, yes," Francis said with a smile. "You never told me, but I've learned that you are no longer in law enforcement."

Francis's smile dissipated. When he spoke again his tone was vile.

"You *quit*. You quit because you couldn't live up to your father's expectations. You quit because you couldn't handle the things you saw. You quit, Ethan, to play doctor and save people. Do you really think daddy is proud of you now?"

Ethan's Adam's apple rose and fell as he swallowed.

"How do I know all of this? I'm stuck in a cell twenty-four hours a day with no access to the outside world. But you see, the guards here offer certain information in exchange for . . . *favors*. Sometimes those favors leave a bad taste in my mouth, but this last time was worth it. I heard all about Henry Hall's son, who ran away from the DCI with his hands over his ears to pursue medicine. But Doctor Hall has been rehired by the DCI to look into a cold case, recruited by the governor himself. So it seems you're in such high demand that you hardly have time to come all the way out to Boscobel to let me know that you'll be at my next parole hearing in two years. Really, Ethan, don't you have more pressing work to do?"

Ethan forced a smile. "Time's up, Francis. But don't worry, I'll be back in six months. Plenty of time for you to service the guards simply to learn that I went to medical school. Now *that* seems like time well spent."

Ethan hung up the phone and stood. Francis stayed seated and kept the phone to his ear. He stared at Ethan and continued to talk. Ethan should have walked away. He should have turned his back on Francis Bernard and returned in six months, but there was something in Francis's eyes that prevented him from doing so. Francis pointed to the phone and nodded. Reluctantly, Ethan lifted the phone again.

"It won't be six months, Ethan. You'll come back to talk sooner than that."

"I doubt it."

Ethan was about to hang the phone on the wall again when he heard Francis utter a name. Ethan's eyes shrunk to slivers, and he put the phone back to his ear.

"What did you say?"

"Callie Jones." Francis grinned. "The governor has asked you to work his daughter's case. You'll want to talk with me about Callie much sooner than six months, Ethan. I've got lots to tell you about what happened to her and where she is."

PART III

Best Friends

CHAPTER 23

Milwaukee, Wisconsin
Wednesday, July 16, 2025

D R. LINDSAY LARKIN WALKED INTO THE OFFICE BUILDING IN DOWNtown Milwaukee that acted as the Midwest hub for her booming online therapy and counseling business. She had started her company out of Milwaukee, but *The Anonymous Client* had expanded nationwide and was growing nearly faster than Lindsay could keep up with demand. She managed by putting the right people in charge of business growth and development while she concentrated on the clinical side. She was making a name for herself by seamlessly combining psychology and business. So much so that she'd made the *Forbes* 30 Under 30 list.

The Anonymous Client occupied two full floors of the 100 East Wisconsin Building in downtown Milwaukee. Lindsay stepped off the elevator and pushed through the glass doors, where her assistant, Beth, met her with a cup of coffee and the day's calendar.

"Morning, Dr. Larkin."

"Good morning. What's the day look like?"

"You have a very busy Wednesday."

Beth handed over the day's schedule as they walked the hallway toward Lindsay's office. "Gayle Kirk from *The New York Times* is here for the interview at nine. I blocked your whole morning. Then you have a meeting with Dr. Ramón. She's the potential new hire. And then a full afternoon of client sessions."

Lindsay looked through the printed schedule as she walked into her office and sat behind her desk.

"Gayle Kirk?"

"It's been scheduled for weeks. The *Times* has wanted to run an exposé for a while. We agreed on this morning."

Lindsay said nothing as she stared at the schedule.

"I mentioned it the other day before you left," Beth said.

"No, no. I'm sure you did. It just slipped my mind. Where are we doing it?"

"The interview? In the conference room."

"Give me five minutes."

CHAPTER 24

Milwaukee, Wisconsin
Wednesday, July 16, 2025

T HE MAHOGANY TABLE WAS IMMACULATE AND DOMINATED THE CON-
ference room. When the space served its true purpose, those who
ran *The Anonymous Client* occupied the sixteen places around the
table. They included the chief financial officer, the head of clinical,
the practice manager, board members, and Dr. Lindsay Larkin,
who always sat at the head of the table as the founder, owner, and
CEO of the booming online company. Today, though, the room
and the table were empty, and Lindsay decided on a less regal location in the center.

She stood when the reporter from *The New York Times* walked
into the conference room.

"Dr. Larkin? Gayle Kirk."

Lindsay smiled. "Hi Gayle. Welcome. And, please, call me Lindsay."

"Thank you. This place is amazing," Gayle said with wide eyes.
"Your assistant gave me a tour."

"Thank you."

The floor-to-ceiling windows of the conference room looked out
over Lake Michigan, where sailboats drifted under the sweltering
summer sun.

"And thanks, by the way, for coming all the way to Milwaukee to
do this."

"It's my absolute pleasure," Gayle said. "I've been trying to get
this interview for nearly a year, so I should be thanking you. I know
how busy you are, so I'll try not to take too much of your time."

"The morning is yours," Lindsay said.

Gayle took a seat and pulled notes from her bag.

"My intention is to introduce our readers to you and your unique company, delve into your background, and then take a deep dive into your philosophy on mental health and how you have single-handedly revolutionized the psychology industry with your brand of online counseling."

"Sounds expansive," Lindsay said. "I'm ready when you are."

"Great. Tell me about your background."

"I was born and raised in Cherryview, Wisconsin. It's a small lake community just outside Madison. I attended UW Madison, where I studied psychology. When I graduated, I wanted to avoid the medical industrial complex and forge a new way forward to help those looking to improve their lives."

"Let's take a detour there. How do you define the 'medical industrial complex'?"

Lindsay smiled. "Simple. It's our current healthcare system. Although, a more accurate term is 'sick care' because the whole system is designed to produce chronic disease, and then perpetually treat those afflicted by the diseases the system creates with an endless stream of pharmaceutical products."

Lindsay smiled again.

"Trust me. I know many consider my position on this topic extreme, but I have yet to meet anyone who can disprove it."

"Disprove that the U.S. healthcare system creates, rather than cures, disease?"

"Let me give you an example," Lindsay said. "The sugar and grain industries are massive contributors to and influencers of the U.S. government. This is not speculation, just look up the numbers. The sugar and grain industries spend millions on lobbying efforts each year in order to get their agendas passed. The result of this decades-long campaign is that the FDA has placed grains and carbohydrates as main components to a healthy diet. The result? Over the last five decades, America has become fatter and sicker. Forty percent of Americans are obese. About seventy-five percent are chronically overweight. This has led to, among other things, a diabetes epidemic. And who profits most from this overweight, diabetic population? The pharmaceutical companies that produce medicine to treat this chronic disease. A disease, by the way, that affected a much smaller portion of the population in the '60s, before sugar and carbs were pushed as part of a healthy diet. About one point five percent of the population suffered from diabetes in the 1960s. Today, it's over eleven percent.

"So, doctors are busy treating their overweight, diabetic patients, while pharmaceutical companies turn giant profits churning out new medication to treat a condition that is mostly self-inflicted. That, in a nutshell, is the medical industrial complex. And diabetes is just a single example. My approach to mental health is to keep every client who comes to us for help out of the vicious cycle of that convoluted system."

"And how do you achieve this?"

"First, we don't employ members of the medical industrial complex. That includes psychiatrists who push drugs on their clients. Nor do we refer clients to psychiatrists."

"You treat all your patients in-house, in other words."

"First, we don't have *patients*. We have clients. The word 'patient' suggests someone suffering from disease, and suggests that medicine is the ultimate solution. Our clients are simply individuals who need our help to become healthier. And we don't *treat* clients, we help them achieve their goals."

"Well, your philosophy is certainly catching on. You're headquartered here in Milwaukee, but you have offices throughout the country. Isn't that right?"

"Yes. *The Anonymous Client* has offices in all fifty states. But the offices are more for administrative purposes than for places to help clients. Most of our work with clients is done online."

"Yes," Gayle said. "That's what I want to discuss next. You've revolutionized the psychology industry by bringing it online. Can you tell me how you've managed to take up so much market share of the online counseling space so quickly?"

"As you know, bringing counseling online wasn't revolutionary. Many tried to do it before me. But our philosophy is what's unique. All the other online counseling platforms are based around the concept of treating sick patients. It's a terrible model, as you can tell by how many online counseling companies are failing since we've come into the space. As I mentioned, we help healthy clients become healthier. That's one of the reasons we've grown so quickly. The other is that our clients are given the option of staying anonymous, and that's been the real game changer."

"Tell me how that works."

"A client seeking our services is able to approach us through our online portal, choose a psychologist, and then undergo sessions not only from the comfort of their own home, but also anonymously. Many clients, thanks again to the intentional negative connotation the medical industrial complex has attached to mental health and therapy, still feel stigmatized by speaking with a therapist. Clients who feel marginalized have the option of speaking with one of our therapists anonymously. We've found that this has allowed many who might otherwise not have sought counseling to come forward."

"How does a client stay anonymous?"

"Our online platform is state-of-the-art. I majored in psychology at UW Madison, but I minored in computer engineering. Since I was young, I've always had a knack for computers and coding. And I applied that background to the first generation encryption prototype we now use across the country. For those clients wishing to stay anonymous, they utilize an online filter that hides both their face and their voice. Our therapists will sometimes ask specifics about the client, such as gender and age, but it's entirely up to the client how much they wish to share. The encrypted, anonymous filters are managed by a third party to ensure our clients' privacy. And many people who might not have sought face-to-face counseling have come on board through the anonymous online portal."

"Amazing," Gayle said. "So it sounds like you were, perhaps, initially interested in computer programming as a career?"

"I was. And that was the plan. I was going to get my degree in computer engineering and move to Silicon Valley. But those plans got derailed and I made a shift to psychology."

"What changed your trajectory that inspired you to go into psychology?"

"Well," Lindsay said, puckering her lower lip, "*inspired* is probably not the right word. But there was an instigating factor."

Lindsay shifted in her chair.

"When I was in high school, my best friend went missing."

"Callie Jones," the reporter said.

"Yes. Callie disappeared without a trace from our little town of Cherryview. It left many people, including myself, reeling with grief. Callie's mother, sadly, was never able to overcome that grief and took her own life. I was heartbroken and had so many questions. I needed badly to speak to someone about how I was feeling, and to find a way past my grief. But my parents didn't believe in psychology or therapy. They had fallen victim to the idea that mental health was something to hide. Something to deal with privately and on your own. Time heals all wounds, and all that nonsense from back in the day. My freshman year of college, I took an intro to psych course and learned that there were ways to deal with grief, and your feelings in general. I decided then that no one should go through what I was going through. At least not alone and without guidance. I wanted to help people overcome their grief, no matter what was causing it. It was then that I realized I would dedicate my life to that cause."

"And so, from a terrible tragedy—the loss of your best friend—you've managed to find meaning in life while simultaneously helping so many others. Your story is very moving."

Lindsay blinked several times to prevent tears from spilling down her cheeks. She maintained her powerful CEO persona as she smiled.

"Thank you."

CHAPTER 25

Milwaukee, Wisconsin
Wednesday, July 16, 2025

LINDSAY LOGGED OFF HER COMPUTER AFTER FINISHING HER FINAL counseling session. Each hour-long session was taxing, and Lindsay was relieved she was finished for the day. *The New York Times* interview from that morning felt like a week ago. As she rubbed her eyes, she heard a knock on the door.

"Sorry to bother you," Beth said. "But there's someone here to see you. I told him he needed an appointment but . . . he's a detective, I think, and said he needed to speak with you."

Lindsay sat up straight in her chair. Whatever fatigue she had been feeling evaporated.

"A detective?"

"He said he needed to speak with you about Callie Jones."

Lindsay lifted her chin slightly. She'd read the articles over the last few weeks about Callie's dad reopening the case. She figured it was only a matter of time before someone tracked her down.

"Show him in."

A moment later, a good-looking gentleman walked into her office. He was tall and fit. Only his graying temples betrayed middle age.

"Dr. Larkin?" he said. "I'm Ethan Hall with the Department of Criminal Investigation."

The man showed Lindsay a badge.

"Did Callie's dad send you?"

She saw the man pause with indecision.

"He might be the governor today, but I still remember him as the guy who used to throw Callie and me off the dock and into Lake Okoboji when we were little. Everyone calls him *Governor* Jones now, which still blows me away. Don't get me wrong. I voted for him, but he'll always be *Mr.* Jones in my mind. Callie's dad."

"Makes sense. I read that you and Callie were best friends."

"Back in the day, yes."

"To your original question: Governor Jones *is* the reason I'm here, but he didn't send me directly. I'm reinvestigating Callie's disappearance."

"So I've read. Cherryview is vibrating with anticipation. My folks still live in town, and they said that since word broke, everyone is hoping Ethan Hall—the renegade detective turned doctor—will be able to solve the unsolvable case of Callie's disappearance. Maybe if you do, Cherryview can go back to being known for its cherry trees and not a missing girl."

"I'm just reviewing the case at the moment. I might find nothing at all."

"I'm curious why Mr. Jones thinks this many years later that you'll be able to find answers about what happened to Callie when no one could figure it out right in the aftermath. We all waited for answers back then, but got none."

Ethan shrugged. "I'm not sure why the governor believes I can shed light on what happened to his daughter. But he obviously has newly acquired clout and power, and he's using it as a last ditch effort to find some closure. The bottom line is that he asked for my help, and I agreed to look into the case."

"And he specifically chose *you?*"

"He did."

"Why?"

"My old partner worked the case."

"Pete Kramer?"

Lindsay had spoken at length with the man during the original investigation.

"Yeah. Pete and the governor are close, and Pete suggested me."

"You were a special agent with the Division of Criminal Investigation, and then you quit to go to med school?"

"Retired, not quit. But yes."

"Why did you retire?"

"Who's questioning who here?"

Lindsay smiled. "You came to my place of work. I think I have the right to ask a few questions."

"That's fair. Let's see. I was exposed to a lot of things while I was a special agent. And some of those things I still see when I close my eyes. I knew if I kept it up for another ten years, it wouldn't have been good for my health—mental or physical. So I decided I could better help people by going into healthcare."

Lindsay laughed.

"Is something the matter?"

"I'm not a fan of medicine. If I break my arm, you'll be the first person I see. But for my overall health and mental well-being, I will stay far, far away from the U.S. healthcare system. But your story only explains why you left law enforcement, not why our newly elected governor pulled a physician out of the ER to help him figure out what happened to his daughter a decade ago."

"I had a one-hundred-percent solve rate when I worked for the DCI. I guess the governor is hoping I can keep that streak alive as I look into his daughter's case."

Lindsay raised her eyebrows and nodded. "Okay. How can I help?"

CHAPTER 26

Milwaukee, Wisconsin
Wednesday, July 16, 2025

"I'M HOPING YOU CAN TELL ME ABOUT THE SUMMER CALLIE WENT missing," Ethan said. "Callie's mom has passed. And her father, although desperate and willing to help in any way he can, hasn't provided much useful information in the couple of times we've spoken. Also, I learned during my years investigating crimes against teens and young adults that parents have a skewed view of their kids. When it comes to teenaged victims of crime, it's much more likely that their friends can offer useful information than the victims' parents."

Lindsay nodded. "I spoke with the police and detectives, including Pete Kramer, after Callie disappeared. But I'll tell you everything I know about her and about that summer. Ten years later, my memory is likely not as good as when this all happened."

"I have access to the case file and transcripts of all the interviews that were conducted. I've just started digging into them. Don't worry if your memory isn't perfect. Let's start with you and Callie."

Lindsay nodded. "Sure. Callie and I met in kindergarten and became inseparable. We had other friends throughout grade school and high school, but we were always best friends. And when we got to high school, we both tried out for and made the volleyball team. Callie and I were the only freshmen on the varsity squad, so we had to stick together. Volleyball made us closer."

"And from what I've read in the case file, the girls' volleyball team was a big deal in Cherryview."

Lindsay smiled. "Yeah, we were. As far as Cherryview, Wisconsin was concerned anyway. Callie and I started as freshmen and helped lead the team to the state championship game that year. We lost, but just barely." Lindsay playfully smacked her fist into her palm. "We were so, so close. Callie and I found this quote we used to throw around after that game—'the tragedy of life is not that man loses, but that he almost wins.'" Lindsay smiled. "We were so close that year, and it hurt so bad. We promised to never get that close again and lose. And we didn't. As sophomores, Callie and I took over the team and won state that year. And again our junior year. In little Cherryview, Wisconsin, Callie and I were superstars."

Lindsay laughed. Another attempt to hold back tears.

"Callie and I made girls' volleyball popular. The stands were packed with fans for every home game—students and parents, but also just people from town who wanted to watch us play. For those three years, we drew bigger crowds than the football team. And if you know anything about small towns in Wisconsin, you know Friday night football dominates. But we gave football a run for its money those years."

Lindsay forced a smile.

"Then, after junior year, Callie . . . she went through a lot of stuff that summer. Stuff I probably should've been a better friend about."

"Like what?"

"Her parents split, and her mom remarried right away. There were rumors about an affair, and that was hard for her to deal with. And Callie hated her stepdad. He was really creepy. She was stuck living with her mom because Mr. Jones was MIA with all the political engagements and keeping up his image. Callie was always worried about getting in any sort of trouble for fear that it would reflect badly on her father. As if any little thing Callie did that wasn't perfect could ruin his political career. So she was always walking on eggshells. It felt like only during an actual volleyball match could she forget about all the pressures of her life and just be herself."

Lindsay shrugged.

"Anyway, with all that was going on, Callie became really distant and our friendship sort of became strained."

"Strained how?" Ethan asked.

Lindsay shrugged. "There was a time when we would tell each other everything. But that summer she sort of folded in on herself and . . . I don't know, stopped sharing things with me. I mean, look, in retrospect we were high school best friends. We had our ups and downs, and lots of girl drama. It's just taken me a lot of years to get over the idea that she disappeared during one of our downswings. I knew something was bothering her that summer, and I didn't take the time to figure out what it was. And then . . ."

"She disappeared," Ethan said.

Summer 2015

Cherryview, Wisconsin

*T*HE START OF THE SCHOOL YEAR WAS STILL ANOTHER MONTH AWAY, BUT summer practices were in full swing, and today's ran late. Callie was in charge that day, and she always made a point of extending practice later than the scheduled stop time. It was Callie's way of showing her new coach that she and the team were a serious bunch ready to win another state championship. And when she encouraged her teammates to push on despite wanting to quit, it displayed her leadership. Lindsay did the same when she was running practice, but she was more obvious about it, not as genuine, and the team knew Lindsay was just trying to impress Coach Cordis. Callie was shrewder.

This afternoon, she started the last quarter of practice, which was designated for conditioning, ten minutes later than normal. And, based on a consensus she took from her teammates, decided to extend the two-mile-end-of-practice run to three miles. With the late start and additional mile, even the fastest, strongest, and best-conditioned team members would finish practice late.

Callie ran from the street and onto the track that encircled the high school's football field, crossing the finish line in a dead sprint fifty yards in front of her closest contender. Then, she waited a few minutes to allow the rest of the faster runners to pour across the finish line. When the track was sufficiently crowded so that her absence would not be missed, she wandered off and ran back up the street. She was shifty about it, not wanting her other teammates to notice her doubling back for fear that they would join her.

It took just a minute to run into her first teammate.

"Let's go, Molly! You've got this!" Callie cheered as she ran past. A few yards farther and she came across two more teammates.

"Let's do this! Almost there!"

And so it continued until she came to the last girl, who was struggling with the added mile. When Callie reached her, she turned and ran alongside her.

"How you doing?"

"Not good," the girl said. "I might puke."

"Who cares?" Callie said. "So you puke. It won't kill you. And if you puke and work through it, Coach will notice."

"I think I'm last."

"You are. But you're still going to finish. And you're going to finish strong. Ready?"

"For what?"

"We're going to sprint this last leg, all the way into the track."

"Not sure I can."

"I am."

"You are what?"

"Sure you can do it. Let's go!"

Callie took off in a sprint, and her teammate followed close behind. Soon they were running side by side. As they grew closer to the track, Callie put her hand on the girl's back, ushering her the last of the way and, finally, across the finish line. She high-fived the girl, and then glanced out of the side of her eye to make sure Coach Cordis had noticed her efforts.

Ten minutes later, the track was clear as the volleyball squad headed into the locker room. Callie stayed behind. As the day's team leader, she was in charge of packing up the outdoor practice courts. Callie hauled a mesh bag filled with volleyballs over to the giant bin next to one of the practice courts.

"Hey," Coach Cordis said as he walked over. "Nice job today."

Callie smiled. "Thanks."

"Gracie has a hard time with conditioning. Great job helping her across the finish line."

"She would have made it without me. I was just encouraging her."

"You were pushing her. Probably harder than she would have pushed herself. You're a great captain, Callie. And we're going to have a really good season if you keep it up and get the rest of the team to work as hard as you do."

"I'll try."

Blake Cordis was a first-year coach. He graduated from UW Madison in May and was about to start his first year teaching history. He landed the *head-coaching job by chance when the long-running girls' volleyball coach retired unexpectedly due to health issues. Blake was a last-minute replacement, but the girls warmed to him quickly. He had been in college at this time last year, and Callie knew he was not too far removed from where she was now—a high school senior struggling with all the things students deal with. She continued to remind herself of this every time she and Coach Cordis were alone together, which seemed to happen more and more lately.*

He placed his hand on the small of her back, above the band of her shorts and below the bottom of her sports top. The skin-to-skin contact sent a quiver through her chest as he leaned in and whispered in her ear.

"I'm counting on you this year, Callie. It's my first year here, and I need you to make me look good, so they hire me back next year."

Callie laughed awkwardly. Her cheeks flushed and her stomach buzzed with something—excitement, maybe, or was it still the adrenaline from the run?

Blake Cordis stood up straight, but his hand remained on her back. She didn't mind. If he were a boy from her school, she'd think about kissing him. But he wasn't a classmate. He was her coach.

Still, it didn't stop her from thinking about it.

The letter waited on the desk in her bedroom, the seal of the University of Cincinnati stenciled across the front. Despite the fact that it was addressed to her, Callie saw that the envelope had already been opened. Her mother, having seen the seal, knew that the letter inside either declared Callie's acceptance to the ultracompetitive, eight-year, direct-to-medical school program, or carried a regretful denial, and could not help herself.

Callie unfolded the letter and read the first line:

Congratulations! We are happy to inform you that you've been accepted into the DIRECT program at the University of Cincinnati.

Materializing like a ghost from the ether, her mother was in the doorway of her bedroom.

"Well?" she asked, as if Callie was supposed to have missed that the envelope had already been opened. As if her mother hadn't already read the letter and had the next eight years of Callie's life plotted out like a melodramatic romance novel.

Callie went along with the charade because it was simply her mother's way. Callie was expected to ignore certain truths—like that her mother cheated on her father and was remarried to a man whose ick factor was off the charts; or that her mother was using Callie to fill whatever void existed from her younger years; or that her mother had opened her acceptance letter and read every word while Callie was at school—all so that the perfect little existence that was being created could remain a blemish-free fairy tale. Callie had learned long ago not to challenge this anomaly. To do so set her mother off on an overly theatrical response that included feeling betrayed and depressed for days.

The theater was too much to deal with so, instead, Callie smiled and held up the acceptance letter as if she were about to deliver breaking news.

"I got in!"

"Oh, sweetheart! That's fabulous!"

Her mother rushed into her bedroom and embraced her in a tight hug.

"Damien," her mother yelled. "Damien, come up here. Callie has some wonderful news."

This, too, was a dare Callie knew not to challenge. She'd much prefer telling her dad the "good" news before sharing it with her stepfather, but to verbalize that wish—or mention her father at all—would throw the household dynamic into a weeklong frenzy of arguments, silence, and faux hurt feelings.

Her stepfather walked into her bedroom—something Callie allowed only because her mother was present. Damien more than creeped Callie out with the way he looked at her and her friends. She started locking her bedroom door at night ever since he'd moved in that summer.

"Callie was accepted into the DIRECT program," her mother said.

"Well that's just fantastic," Damien said, continuing the charade.

"You'll have to let them know this week," her mother said. "That you accept."

Callie raised her eyebrows, scanned to the bottom of the letter where this fact was stated, and then smiled at the ridiculousness of it all.

"I'm going to call Dad to let him know."

Like icing running down the side of a too-warm muffin, the smile melted from her mother's face. Callie wanted them both out of her bedroom and knew mentioning her father was the best way to do it.

"Go right ahead," her mother said before turning and walking out of the room.

When her mother was gone, it was just Callie and Damien. Callie on her bed, Damien a few feet away.

"Why do you have to do that?" Damien asked.

"Do what?"

"Throw your father in her face?"

"I just got accepted to college and medical school at the same time. I think it's pretty normal to want to tell my dad about it. I mean, he's going to take care of the tuition anyway. It's not like you're able to pay for it, are you Damien?"

"Your mom just wanted a moment to celebrate with you. She's proud of you."

"You're not allowed in my room. That's the one rule my dad still gets a say in, even though my mother ruined her marriage by having an affair with you."

"Callie, we didn't have an affair. That's just another lie your father told you. And if you think your dad is so great, why don't you go live with him?"

Damien took a step closer to her.

"Because he doesn't have time for you, that's why. He's too busy with his business and his budding political career. Every other weekend is enough for him, because all he really wants is to run for governor and tend to his ego. And if he ever becomes the chosen one and actually gains the backing he needs to run for governor, you'll likely see him less than you do now. So you should really start treating your mother better. She's the one who's looking out for you."

Damien turned and left her room. When he was gone, Callie jumped from bed and slammed the door, still holding her acceptance letter in her shaking hands.

Callie sat on her bed. It was just past 10:00 p.m. She hadn't left her room since she'd opened her acceptance letter. She hadn't called her father, either. As much as she resented her mother's hovering, her dad was no better. The details of the divorce had never been made known to Callie or her sister, but there were rumors and insinuations that it was not her mother who had cheated first. And her father was happy to settle the whole thing quietly and without spectacle and move on. His political career was too new and delicate to survive a nasty divorce that included skeletons dancing from closets.

As much as Callie despised Damien, he was right about her father. Mark Jones was a man on a mission. If he wasn't at work, he was attending a fundraiser and rubbing elbows with the Who's Who of Wisconsin politics. Even if she called him now, he wouldn't answer. And whatever message Callie left, it would be two or three days before he got back to her. She felt alone and isolated in what was supposed to be a joyous moment in her life.

She thought briefly of calling Lindsay. Instead, though, she picked up her phone and scrolled through her contacts until she found the number. She was nervous to dial it, but he had told Callie to call at any time and for any reason. They were a team, he had told them all, and he would be there for any of them if they needed him. Before she could change her mind, she typed a text message:

Coach Cordis, I'm having some issues at home. Could you come pick me up?

The reply was instant.

Of course. At your house?

Callie's insides swirled with anxiety and anticipation.

No. At the park down the street.

Drop me a pin. Ten minutes?

OK.

Callie slipped her cell phone into the back pocket of her jeans and quietly twisted the handle on her bedroom door. Her mother's door was closed, and she saw the blue light of the television seeping from underneath it. Her mother and Damien were watching television in bed—their nightly ritual.

She closed her door and snuck down the stairs. She tried to make it past the family room without her sister noticing, but didn't make it. Her younger sister was an up-and-coming volleyball star. Jaycee Jones was about to join the Cherryview girls' volleyball team as a freshman, and her skills were rumored to rival Callie's. There had always been a fair amount of jealousy, disguised as competitiveness, between the two sisters, and their relationship was hit or miss.

"Where are you going?" Jaycee asked.

"Out."

"Out where?"

"Just out. I need to get out of the house for a little while."

"Mom said you got accepted to the DIRECT program."

"Yeah. My acceptance letter came today."

"Nice!"

"Thanks," Callie said.

Today, their sister rivalry took a backseat, and Jaycee's excitement was the first bit of genuine emotion Callie had felt about the news.

"If mom wakes up or comes down, don't tell her I left. Okay?"

Jaycee waved. "If you get caught, leave me out of it."

Callie said nothing more before slipping out the back door. She hurried through the night, her insides ready to explode. When she reached the park at the end of her street, she saw a car in the lot with its headlights on. She walked over and climbed into the passenger seat.

"Thanks for doing this, Coach."

Blake Cordis smiled. "When one of my players needs me, I'm always there for them. Especially you, Callie."

They drove the quiet streets of Cherryview for thirty minutes and then up to the bluff that rose above the south end of Lake Okoboji, where Callie's house sat on the shoreline. Blake pulled his car into a secluded spot but kept the engine running so that the air conditioning could fight against the muggy summer night. A nearly full moon laid a silvery glow onto the surface of the water below. The Crest, an island in the middle of the lake that held a popular restaurant for boaters and two sand volleyball courts where Callie and Lindsay often played, was visible in the distance.

"I heard from University of Cincinnati," Callie finally said.

"You did? And?"

She forced a smile. "I got in."

"To the dual program?"

Callie nodded.

"Congratulations. That's a big deal!"

"Yeah, I guess."

"Tell me what it is again. It's a direct-to-medical school program, right?"

Another nod. "So I would basically do my normal four years of undergrad. But they would be heavily focused on science courses. You know, bio and chem and physiology. I wouldn't take any of the elective courses. Then, after four years I go straight into the medical school at Cinci. The next eight years of my life, all planned out and wrapped up like a pretty little present placed under the Christmas tree."

"Wow, Callie. That's amazing."

"Yeah, it's . . . you know. It is what it is."

Blake cocked his head. "You don't seem as excited as I would expect."

"I know it's a big deal and it's ultracompetitive and there are only a few spots in the whole country and I should be super excited, but . . ."

"But what?"

"But the whole thing was my mom's idea. I mean, I swear I think she

wants this more than I do. And she wants it, not for me, but so that she can, I don't know, brag to her friends about what a successful daughter she has."

"You don't want it?"

"I want to be a doctor. I want to go to medical school. I just want to do it the normal way. I want to have a normal college experience, not this limited, hyper-focused thing my mother signed me up for. I'll be the only person at school in this accelerated program. Does that sound like a recipe for fun? Does that sound like the best way to make new friends?"

"Have you talked to your parents about taking the more traditional route? Just doing your normal four years of undergrad and then applying to medical school?"

Callie laughed. "My mother would need to be rational for me to have that conversation with her. She is not."

"How about your dad?"

"He just does what my mom says. They're divorced. He pays the bills but that's about it. I see him twice a month. But he's deep into politics and he's made it very clear that I am a direct reflection on him, and that any trouble I get into in high school would ruin his political career. I'm not a trouble-maker, lucky for him. But he also wants me to shine so that he looks good. He's the up-and-coming political powerhouse with the all-American daughter who's on her way to saving the world as a doctor. No one is excited for me, only for what my potential success can do for them."

Blake leaned closer to her. Callie could smell his aftershave. The butter-flies fluttered inside of her.

"This is a big deal, Callie. It's a huge opportunity, but you have to make sure it's right for you."

She turned toward him, and it was as if the car had shrunk in half. They were face-to-face, looking at each other in a way they had never done before. The glow of the moon illuminated half his face, and he seemed at once more mature than any of the boys in her grade, yet not much older than she was.

Without thinking more about it, she leaned closer to him. After a moment of hesitation, he cut the distance and their lips came together. They kissed softly at first, and then more aggressively before Blake pulled away.

"Whoa," he said, sitting back in the driver's seat. "Hold on."

"What's wrong?"

"Uh, well, let's see. You're one of my soon-to-be students, so there's that.

You're also one of my players and I'm your coach, and I'm pretty sure you're underage."

"I'll be eighteen in a few weeks. And you literally just graduated college. You're, like, twenty-two."

Blake shook his head, still catching his breath. "Twenty-one. I'll be twenty-two in September."

"So," Callie went on, "we're not even four years apart. If you were twenty-five and I was twenty-one, would this be a big deal?"

"I'm not twenty-five, and you're definitely not twenty-one. And the law is the law."

"I don't care about the law," Callie said, unbuckling her seatbelt so that she could cross over the middle console.

She kissed him again and felt him resist for a moment. But she was persistent and before long she felt his hands grab her thighs and slide up her jean shorts as he pulled her across the console and onto his lap.

Callie rode in the passenger seat. It was close to 10:00 p.m. and she had snuck out to be with Blake again. They had been spending more and more time together lately, and Blake had warned that they needed to be careful.

"How about after I turn eighteen," Callie said. "Are we still going to sneak around then?"

"Yes," Blake said. "Maybe after you're in college and no longer one of my student athletes we can be less careful."

"I'll be a legal adult in August."

"In the eyes of the law, yes. But it's still a bad look. And the school for sure can't know anything about this."

Blake pulled into the gas station and parked far from the pumps, outside of the range of the security cameras.

"If we're still together when I'm, like, twenty? Are we still going to sneak around?"

"Not like this. But we'd have to sit down and talk to your parents at that point."

"Ha!" Callie said. "You think I'd ever ask my parents for permission to see you?"

"Not now, no. But when we're both a little older and you're out of the house and away at school, a lot can change between you and your parents. That's all I'm saying. But for now, during your senior year and while I

start teaching in the fall, we have to keep things quiet. Really, really quiet. Got it?"

Callie looked at him through the darkness. "Yeah, I get it."

"You haven't told any of your friends, have you?"

"About us? God no. They'd freak out. And for sure none of them would stay quiet about it."

"Not even Lindsay, right?"

"Why are you asking about Lindsay?"

"Because you guys are best friends."

"I haven't told her a thing, and don't plan to."

Blake nodded.

"So explain it to me again. What are we doing at this gas station?" Callie asked.

"I need a prepaid cell phone."

"What's the matter with your phone?"

"You can't call my phone anymore. Or text. We need a prepaid phone so we can talk. No one's able to trace it."

"Trace it?"

"Like if your parents ever look at your phone."

"My parents never look at my phone."

"But just in case they ever do. My number should not be in your call list, Callie. The school has a strict policy against students texting teachers directly. If we buy a prepaid phone, we can text back and forth without worrying someone will find out. Just keep using that app to erase our text threads."

"You're being paranoid."

Blake handed her money.

"The phones will be up by the register. Grab a Samsung. They have the most minutes on them. And pay cash."

Callie took the money and stared at him.

"Trust me," Blake said. "This is the safest way for now."

"I hate all this sneaking around."

"It won't be forever. But for now, this is how we have to do it."

Blake leaned over and kissed her before Callie exited the car and walked across the dark parking lot of the gas station.

PART IV

All In

CHAPTER 27

Boscobel, Wisconsin
Wednesday, July 23, 2025

S INCE FRANCIS BERNARD HAD UTTERED CALLIE JONES'S NAME, Ethan was all in on the investigation. He'd nearly killed himself at the ER the week before by working six straight days of twelve-hour shifts. But it had earned him two weeks off, which he combined with two weeks of vacation time. He now had a month free from his responsibilities at the ER, and he planned to spend every moment on the Callie Jones case.

During the past week, after his long and grueling shifts at the hospital, Ethan spent his free time poring over every detail of the Callie Jones file. He met with Mark Jones and had a long discussion with the man, allowing Callie's father to paint the picture of the dysfunctional Jones family from the summer of 2015. He met with Callie's best friend, Lindsay Larkin, who filled in details about Callie's troubles during the summer she went missing. He'd met with Damien Laramie, Callie's stepdad, who was still angry and bitter that Callie's "selfishness that summer," as the man put it, had led to his wife's taking of her own life. There was a lot to unpack.

Ethan poured a cup of coffee and sat at the kitchen table. In front of him was the Callie Jones file. Two inches thick with pages that were dog-eared and tattered, it was obvious that someone—likely Pete Kramer—had been through the file a number of times. Ethan opened the front cover to a photo of Callie. Auburn hair, honey-brown eyes, and an olive complexion. Her teeth were white and straight, and the girl offered an intoxicating smile—the kind,

Ethan could tell, that made everyone feel welcome. She looked impossibly young and innocent. Staring at the picture of the missing girl raised long-buried feelings of despair and hopelessness that had driven Ethan from this profession years ago. He turned the page and read a short bio.

Callie Jones was seventeen years old and about to start her senior year in high school but had already received an early acceptance to the University of Cincinnati and a partial athletic scholarship. She was set to play volleyball for the Bearcats while embarking on the challenging eight-year, direct-to-medical school program. Only a handful of such spots were available nationwide, and one of them had been awarded to Callie Jones. There was even talk of Callie capturing a spot on the women's Olympic volleyball team if she continued to excel in college.

Pretty, athletic, and smart, Ethan thought. *Was about to conquer the world, until she disappeared.*

Ethan turned the page. Callie was last seen by her teammates on Saturday, July 18, 2015, out at The Crest—an island in the middle of Lake Okoboji known for late night parties and general debauchery.

As he read through the file, Ethan ignored the whispers that told him he was too far removed from this type of work to offer anything meaningful to the case. The thoughts were his mind's way of protecting him, of discouraging him from steering his life off a cliff—which was exactly what would happen if he became involved with the DCI again. But deep inside, Ethan knew he had no choice. Pete Kramer's dying plea had gotten the conversation started. The governor's promise to erase two hundred thousand dollars of student loan had kept his interest. But the final push had come from the least likely of sources. How on earth Francis Bernard knew anything about Callie's case, and why the man was dangling it in front of Ethan, was something he could not begin to comprehend. But he sure as hell was going to find out.

Ethan closed the file and pulled out the timeline he had created of Callie's known interactions in the week before she disappeared, which culminated in Callie driving her parents' boat out to The Crest the night she disappeared. Ethan had arranged a second meeting with Lindsay Larkin for the upcoming weekend to visit the island and retrace Callie's footsteps that night.

Up to this point, his early investigation told him that Callie Jones had the weight of the world on her shoulders that summer. An overbearing mother, a new stepdad, an MIA father, and the news about acceptance into a direct-to-medical school program had all combined to form a perfect storm of anxiety, frustration, and duress. A thought crossed Ethan's mind as he pieced together the details of the girl's life. *Had Callie Jones run away?*

The whispers from the dark corners of his mind grew louder and told him that in order to answer that question, and the hundreds of others that were forming, he was going to need help. Inexplicably, that help resided in the person he least wanted to ask.

He packed up the file and headed for the door.

"Take a seat," the guard said.

Four hours later, with help from the DCI and a push from the governor's office, Ethan had managed an impromptu visit to the Wisconsin Secure Program Facility in Boscobel. He sat at the visitation booth and a minute later the door on the other side of the glass opened. Francis Bernard appeared—hands cuffed in front of him. The shackles on his ankles forced him to move with a controlled shuffle. Francis looked toward booth #4, and a shrewd smile came across his face. Nothing flagrant. Just a delicate twist to the corners of his lips. Still, it was impossible to miss the man's joy that Ethan had returned so soon.

Ethan's visits over the years had served a single purpose—to remind Francis that his appeals were futile, and that he would never see another day of freedom in his life. Despite the fact that Ethan had been victorious on this front for the last several years, the man always offered a pompous expression of joy. As if Francis knew something Ethan did not.

Francis sat opposite him and raised his cuffed hands to the phone, lifted the receiver from the hook, and placed it to his ear just as Ethan did the same on his side of the glass. Francis's smile grew larger.

"That was fast."

"You said you knew something about Callie Jones. What is it?"

The elated expression fell from Francis's face, replaced by faux disappointment. "Is that what this is about? We're not going to talk about your father?"

"What do you know about Callie Jones?"

"Oh," Francis said, his forehead wrinkling as if confused. "I know plenty."

"Bullshit."

Francis smiled again. "Are we going to play games, Ethan?"

Ethan remained silent.

"If you thought I knew nothing, you wouldn't be here. You believe . . . no, in fact, you are *certain* that I know *something.* And since the big boys recruited you out of retirement, you're under pressure to deliver. So you're sniffing for information wherever you think you might find it. Even embarrassing yourself by coming all the way out to Boscobel to ask *me* about Callie Jones. It's sad, really. You're so lost that you have to ask your father's killer for directions."

Francis looked up to the ceiling, as if he were on camera.

"*Alleged* killer, to anyone who's listening."

"Yeah," Ethan said, nodding his head. "That's what I thought. You don't know shit. You're just so lonely that you'll say anything to get someone to come and see you. Even me, the guy who promises to keep you here forever. *That's* sad."

"You've heard the Tolkien quote: 'Not all those who wander are lost,' haven't you?" Francis said, picking up as if Ethan hadn't said a word. "But the unspoken part of that quote, the natural assumption and the real truth, is that all those who are lost certainly wander. And you are as lost as a puppy in the night, Ethan. So I'm going to help you. I'm going to help you stop wandering in the darkness. I'll give you some direction. Do you want direction in your life, Ethan?"

Ethan said nothing as the seconds dragged past.

"I won't make you beg. That's beneath me. Are you ready?"

Ethan stared unblinkingly through the glass.

"Go to Menomonee Valley in Milwaukee, to the old, abandoned stockyards. Find a decrepit looking warehouse. Number nine, Ethan. Are you paying attention? Warehouse number nine in Menomonee Valley. High up on one of the walls is an envelope with something for you. Go, Ethan. Find what's there. Do your thing, Mr. One Hundred Percent. And then, come back and we'll talk some more."

Francis smiled, hung up the phone, and left the visitation booth.

CHAPTER 28

Milwaukee, Wisconsin
Wednesday, July 23, 2025

As SOON AS ETHAN EXITED THE PRISON HE JOGGED ACROSS THE parking lot to his Jeep Wrangler. He shuffled through the console until he found a pen and paper, onto which he scribbled *Warehouse 9, Menomonee Valley*. He headed east toward Milwaukee. For two and a half hours Francis Bernard's voice rang in his ears.

Not all those who wander are lost, but all those who are lost certainly wander.

He blinked his eyes and tried to quiet Francis's voice, but still it echoed through his head.

So I'm going to help you out, Ethan. I'm going to help you stop wandering in the darkness. I'll give you a bit of direction. Do you want direction in your life, Ethan?

How, Ethan wondered, could Francis Bernard know *anything* about Callie Jones? The man had been in prison for years before Callie disappeared in 2015. Ethan considered that Francis could be sending him on a wild goose chase meant to show Ethan that he had some control over him, even from the confines of a maximum-security prison.

There's an envelope there, Ethan. Do your thing, Mr. One Hundred Percent.

Ethan made it to the outskirts of Milwaukee, and then found his way into the city. Menomonee Valley was located in the heart of Milwaukee and consisted of old stockyards that used to house cattle for the meatpacking district. Long abandoned, they had fallen into disrepair over the course of decades. The valley, now mostly reno-vated, still had tough spots that were no-go zones for most folks.

The sun was setting, and long shadows crept across the roads. Ethan crossed a set of freight tracks and turned right onto a dilapi-dated road riddled with potholes. Fog seeped from manhole covers before disappearing into the heat of the evening. When he came to the warehouses, he slowed. Each building consisted of a large bay door that retracted upwards. Next to each bay was a door painted with a number. Most of the numbers were faded and illegible, but Ethan could clearly make out the number 3 on one of the doors. He drove past several warehouses until he came to number 9.

Off in the distance he saw the lights of American Family Field. The Brewers were at home and fending off both the heat and the Pittsburgh Pirates. The livelihood of the ballpark felt like a galaxy away from the eerie bank of abandoned warehouses Francis Ber-nard had sent him to. He pulled next to warehouse number 9 and looked around at the forsaken valley. Before exiting the Wrangler, he opened the glove box and retrieved his Beretta 92FS pistol. The DCI had not formally armed him, but Ethan was a legal gun owner and rarely ventured far from home unarmed. Old habits die hard.

He walked to the warehouse door and peeked through the glass. The building was as abandoned as the valley it stood in. He checked the Beretta to make sure a round was chambered, then twisted the door handle and pushed it open. It squeaked into the evening and a waft of heat came from the building. Even as the sun was setting, it was close to ninety-five degrees outside. With a long summer day of the sun beating down on the metal roof of the ware-house, Ethan guessed the temperature was closer to 120 degrees in-side the building.

He raised his gun and walked through the doorway. A thin coat of perspiration covered his face, and the stench of rotting garbage assaulted his nostrils. The setting sun offered a soft brilliance through the dingy windows positioned at the top of each wall of the ware-house. He took a quick look around to make sure the place was empty, and then turned on the flashlight of his cell phone and walked the perimeter of the warehouse. Along the northeast corner he looked up and saw something in the shadows, a form protruding from the wall. He used the flashlight to get a better look. Ten feet up, a manila envelope had been secured by duct tape.

"Son of a bitch," Ethan whispered, allowing his mind to contemplate only for a moment how Francis Bernard could have known about this envelope, or how long it had been there.

He looked around until he found an old crate that he pulled over. He stepped onto it and gained his balance before reaching up and grabbing the envelope, which he ripped free from the tape that held it. He shined his flashlight on the rest of the wall and, seeing nothing else, jumped down from the crate and hurried outside.

He was drenched in sweat from the sweltering warehouse. The ninety-five degree external temperature did little to cool him off. He climbed into the Wrangler and cranked the AC before he tore the envelope open. He turned the package upside down. There was a single item inside and it spilled onto the passenger seat.

It was a '90s-style, prepaid Samsung cell phone.

CHAPTER 29

Cherryview, Wisconsin
Thursday, July 24, 2025

Ethan sat at the desk in the small office of his home. The surface was cluttered with the Callie Jones case. Since his visit to warehouse #9 in Menomonee Valley, Ethan had zeroed in on Callie's cell phone records from the original investigation, which consisted of pages and pages of calls the girl had made the summer she disappeared.

Callie's phone had been recovered from North Point Pier on Lake Okoboji, where her boat had been found secured to the dock. Callie had taken her parents' boat out to The Crest to attend a party the night she disappeared. No one had seen her after she left the island. The boat had been discovered Sunday morning at North Point Pier, along with Callie's phone and the girl's blood at the end of the dock.

Pete Kramer and his team had dug deeply through Callie's phone, doing the grunt work years before and painstakingly identifying nearly every incoming and outgoing call and text message. There was only one number from that summer that had gone unidentified and could not be registered to a user. That number had been linked back to a prepaid, disposable phone that had never been found.

Pete Kramer and his team had gone to the effort of tracking down the serial number of that phone, and then found the barcode to determine the make and model—a Samsung disposable phone that had been purchased at a gas station in Cherryview. Pete had used the Wisconsin Department of Justice databank and DCI forensic techs to determine the date the phone had been purchased, and then pulled security footage from the gas station on the day of the purchase. The grainy video showed Callie Jones walking to the register and paying cash for the phone. What Callie had done with the phone, and who she had given it to, was a glaring hole in Pete Kramer's original investigation. But now, ten years later, Ethan sat in his home staring at the Samsung phone Callie had purchased, confirmed by the serial number. And Francis Bernard had led him to it.

As Ethan thumbed through the pages chronicling the calls made from Callie's phone, he saw that nearly every one had pinged a tower in Cherryview. On a hunch, he decided to log every call or text Callie had made that pinged a tower outside a twenty-mile radius of Cherryview, Wisconsin. During the year that started January 1, 2015, and ended July 18, 2015—the last day anyone saw Callie Jones—Ethan found thirty pings outside the Cherryview radius. He pulled a clean sheet of paper in front of him and listed the cities where the cell towers were located. All were in Wisconsin, with many located between Madison and Milwaukee. A cluster was in northern Minnesota, which was explained by a fishing trip Callie had taken with her sister and father in early July. Only one, Ethan noted as he reviewed the list, had originated in Chicago. It was made on Thursday, July 16, 2015 at 10:00 a.m. Two days before she disappeared. The number Callie had called was the prepaid Samsung.

Ethan dialed Pete Kramer's number. He picked up on the first ring.

"Hey, I'm reviewing Callie Jones's phone records, and I think I came across something. What can you tell me about the unidentified number that showed up in Callie's caller log?"

"We looked pretty hard at the phone," Pete said. "Our tech guys were able to identify that calls and texts were made between the two numbers—Callie's and the burner phone."

"I don't see any transcripts of the text messages."

"That's because we were never able to recover them. My guys believe Callie used an encrypted texting app that automatically deleted the text threads after she sent them. They found footprints of text threads but nothing more. It was a dead end. Why? You find something?"

"Maybe. I see a single call from Callie's phone to the burner number that pinged a Chicago cell tower on July 16."

"Yeah, we saw that, too," Pete said, reciting the case from memory. "The call was made from Callie's phone to the burner phone, but it never led anywhere. The burner was a bust, we never found it."

Ethan wasn't ready to mention that the prepaid phone the DCI had been unable to locate ten years ago was now resting on his desk. Mostly because he wasn't prepared to explain to his old partner how he'd stumbled across it. But Ethan was curious what Callie Jones was doing in Chicago two days before she went missing.

"The girl's phone," Ethan said. "Is it still in evidence?"

"I'm sure it is."

"Any chance I can get my hands on it?"

"E, you got something?"

"I'm not sure, but I need the girl's phone to find out."

CHAPTER 30

Cherryview, Wisconsin
Friday, July 25, 2025

THE FOLLOWING DAY, ETHAN PULLED UP TO THE BIG HOUSE ON LAKE Okoboji and parked in the driveway. He hadn't called ahead. With his backpack strapped over a shoulder, he walked to the front entrance—a gargantuan set of wooden French doors—and rang the bell. When no one answered, he rang again. Another minute passed before he heard an unidentifiable noise emanating from some place off in the distance. He backed away from the front porch and listened. It was a steady back-and-forth clanking that was unexplainably irritating. He followed a stone-lined walkway around the house. The clinking grew louder with each step as he progressed toward the back.

As he emerged through a canopy of jasmine bushes, Lake Okoboji came into view. The source of the racket also became apparent. Christian Malone and three others were playing pickleball on what looked like a newly poured court that overlooked the lake. The four players stood mesmerizingly close to one another and banged a yellow wiffle ball back and forth across the net. The noise from the paddles hitting the ball was loud and obnoxious, and Ethan wondered if the neighbors complained. But enough acreage surrounded Christian Malone's mansion for the nails-on-the-chalkboard clatter to dissipate before reaching adjacent homes.

Ethan approached the court as Christian served the ball, waited for the return, and then began a new rally that consisted of a flurry of back-and-forth smashes until Christian ended it with an over-head volley that sent the ball into the hydrangeas and ended the game. The players tapped paddles across the net before Christian turned and smiled when he saw Ethan.

"My favorite doctor is making a house call!"

Christian raised his hands as if under arrest.

"Don't worry, Doc. I'm drinking water, I promise."

He ran to the side of the court and lifted a Yeti tumbler to his lips to take a long swallow.

Ethan laughed.

"I didn't come to check on your water intake. I need some help from my favorite retired tech guru."

Christian looked at his pickleball friends, all of whom appeared to be in their seventies or beyond, and pointed at Ethan. "This is the doctor who helped with my kidney stone a few weeks ago. Saved me from surgery."

"I didn't even do that. Actually, he passed it before I could do much for him."

"Ah," Christian said, "the sign of a good doctor is humility. Can't even accept my gratitude for helping me narrowly escape the oper-ating room." Christian turned to his friends. "Same time tomorrow?"

Everyone agreed and headed to the driveway and their cars. When his friends were gone, Christian turned to Ethan.

"Sorry to play up the kidney stone thing. I told them I was an eyelash away from needing surgery. Pickleball with those guys is cutthroat. I need any advantage I can get. If they think I'm recov-ering from some ailment, they'll go easy on me."

"Those guys looked like they were all in their seventies and twice your age."

"Age makes no difference in pickleball. They'll butcher me up and serve me raw if given the chance. I've played the sick card for a couple of weeks, but I guess the jig is up now."

"Sorry to out you."

Christian finished his water and waved his hand. "No worries. The kidney stone angle helped me win a few games. It's all good. So what brings you by?"

"I need some help with something I'm working on."

"Come on in."

Ethan followed Christian inside and slipped his backpack off his shoulder, setting it on the kitchen stool. He unzipped the top and removed a plastic evidence bag. Inside was Callie Jones's cell phone that Pete Kramer had retrieved from evidence. No one had laid hands on it for ten years.

"What do we have here?" Christian said, inching closer to get a better look. "Is that an evidence bag?"

"It is."

Christian raised his right eyebrow.

"It's a long story."

"Try me."

Ethan nodded, knowing he'd have to come clean if he wanted Christian's help.

"You and I have a lot in common."

"Oh yeah? You have recurrent kidney stones and like pickle-ball?"

"No. You left your previous life behind for something different. I did the same."

"I left Silicon Valley because it was going to kill me if I stayed."

Ethan nodded. "I used to be a detective, and I left that world for the same reason."

Ethan saw Christian lift his chin slightly, understanding but wanting more.

"I was a special agent with Wisconsin's Division of Criminal Investigation."

Christian angled his head as he worked through it all.

"You left law enforcement . . . to be a doctor?"

"I did. Because if I stayed it would have killed me. I used to investigate kid crimes, and I saw too much violence against young people. Things I was never able to stop. The best I could do was hunt down the people who committed the crimes and bring them to justice. After a while, it stopped being terribly satisfying because in the wake of that tiny victory was still a dead kid. So I retired, went to medical school, and now I try to help people *before* they die."

Christian pouted his lips. "So what are you doing with a phone sealed in a plastic evidence bag?"

"I'm doing an old friend a favor. Ten years ago, my previous partner worked a missing persons case that went cold. As sort of a last
ditch effort to find answers, he and the governor have asked me to
take a look at the case and see if I find anything."

"And did you?"

"I'm hoping you can tell me." Ethan pointed at the evidence
bag. "Back in 2015, a girl named Callie Jones disappeared from
right here in Cherryview, Wisconsin. Last time she was seen was
leaving The Crest." Ethan pointed to the lake through the floor-to-
ceiling windows. "Investigators found her cell phone and her boat,
along with drops of her blood, at North Point Pier the next morning. This is the girl's phone."

Christian placed the tips of his fingers together and flexed them,
clearly anticipating that his computer skills were about to be called
upon.

"What do you need?"

"Agents with the DCI did a search on the phone, found some incoming and outgoing calls registered to a prepaid cell phone. That
lead never went anywhere, other than to suggest that Callie Jones
was in contact with someone who wanted to stay anonymous."

"Sounds suspicious."

"It is. And I need your help with a couple of things. First, Callie
made a bunch of calls and sent a string of text messages to this prepaid number. The tech guys at the DCI can see the footprints of
the text threads to know that they existed, but were never able to
recover the actual texts. They think she used an app that automatically erased the texts after a set period of time. I need to know if
you can find them."

"The texts?"

"Yeah."

"Maybe. If I get into the guts of the phone. What's the second
issue?"

"Last night I did some digging and looked into the location of
where calls originated from in the six months leading up to her disappearance. Nothing stood out except one call that pinged a cell
tower in Chicago. She made the call two days before she went missing, and I want to know if there's any way to figure out where, exactly, she was in Chicago when she made that call."

Christian squinted his eyes and took a moment to process the question. The man was clearly in his element.

"I'd have to get my hands on the SIM card."

"We can do that. You just have to wear gloves."

Christian pointed at the phone. "Bring that with you and come into my office."

Ethan grabbed the evidence bag that contained Callie Jones's cell phone and followed Christian through the first floor until they came to the end of a long hallway. Christian opened the door to reveal a large room filled with several computer monitors, a standing desk, and an eighty-five inch television mounted on the wall. As soon as Christian entered the room, each monitor simultaneously blinked to life.

Christian shrugged and tucked a long strand of sandy blond hair behind his ear. "You can take the kid out of Silicon Valley, but you can't take Silicon Valley out of the kid." He raised his eyebrows and widened his eyes. "Let's take a look at that phone."

CHAPTER 31

Chicago, Illinois
Saturday, July 26, 2025

THE DAY AFTER ETHAN VISITED CHRISTIAN MALONE HE MADE THE DRIVE
from Cherryview to Chicago. Using GPS tracking software and
identifying the cell towers the phone signal pinged, Christian had
triangulated Callie Jones's likely location when she made the call
from her cell phone on Thursday, July16, 2015. Christian offered a
disclaimer that he couldn't be sure, but also gave Ethan the im-
pression that he had little doubt that the call had originated near
the corner of West Division Street and North Milwaukee Avenue
in Chicago's Wicker Park neighborhood. And, specifically, from
1152 North Milwaukee Avenue.

Ethan pulled to the intersection now and stopped at the red
light, taking in the establishments on each of the corners. There
was a Polish deli on the southwest corner, a dry cleaners across the
street, and veterinary clinic next door. The light turned green, and
Ethan pulled through the intersection. As he headed down Milwaukee Avenue, he came to the address Christian had provided
and saw a Planned Parenthood clinic on his right.

A block down he found a parking spot on a side street and
pulled his Wrangler to the curb. He doubled back to the clinic and
walked inside. The woman behind the reception desk offered a
confused expression when he walked in.

"Can I help you?" she asked.

Ethan removed his DCI badge and showed it to the woman.

"My name's Ethan Hall. I'm an agent with the Wisconsin Division of Criminal Investigation. I need to ask a few questions about a missing persons case from a few years back to see if there's any way to confirm that the victim visited this clinic."

The woman seemed unequipped to handle Ethan's inquiry.

"You probably need to speak with my supervisor."

"That would be great."

A moment later a woman emerged from the back.

"Hi. I'm Cheryl Stowe."

Ethan made the same introduction.

"I'd love to help you," Cheryl said. "But patients who visit the clinic are protected by HIPAA regulations, so I wouldn't be able to tell you if the person you're looking for visited the clinic or not."

Ethan nodded. "Understood. The girl I'm interested in is named Callie Jones. She went missing from a small town up near Madison in 2015. I've got good forensic cell phone evidence that places the girl at this location at 10:00 a.m. on Thursday, July 16, 2015, two days before she disappeared. The only reason I can think that a seventeen-year-old girl who lived in Wisconsin was standing outside this building in Chicago was to visit this clinic. Maybe because she was pregnant and looking to have an abortion. The forensic evidence placing her here was strong enough for a judge to issue a warrant that allows me to take a look at your records."

Ethan produced the search warrant but didn't mention that the judge, who issued it at 8:00 p.m. the previous night, was a close personal friend to Governor Mark Jones.

The supervisor swallowed hard and nodded her head. "Of course. I can show you anything you need. I just need to make a call and run it past my boss."

"Of course."

Thirty minutes later Ethan was sitting in Cheryl Stowe's office as she typed on her computer.

"I run the clinic now as the supervisor," Cheryl said, "but back in 2015 I was a nurse. Our digital records go back to 2008, so we should be able to access what you're looking for from July of 2015 through the electronic medical records system. If this girl came to the clinic, I'll know in a minute. You said her name was Callie Jones?" Cheryl asked as she typed. "You have a date of birth?"

"August 7, 1997."

Cheryl finished typing and shook her head.

"No record of a Callie Jones visiting us. Is Callie the full name?"

"Yeah," Ethan said, disappointment heavy in his voice.

"This girl went missing?"

Ethan nodded "Two days after she made a call outside of this clinic, she disappeared."

"And you know for sure she visited our clinic?"

"No. But I *do* know that a seventeen-year-old girl from a small Wisconsin town one hundred fifty miles from here made a call when she was standing on the corner outside of this building. Two days later she disappeared. My hunch is that she was pregnant and traveled to Chicago to have an abortion. And her pregnancy may be directly related to her disappearance."

"Lots of patients who come to our clinic don't use their real names. Many women, especially teens, are scared their parents will find out. So they use aliases. This girl you're looking for might've done that."

"So Callie could have traveled to Chicago, used an alias, and had an abortion without her parents being involved?"

"Yes," Cheryl said. "Parental consent is not required by law to have an abortion in Illinois. However, if this girl was a minor, defined as under the age of eighteen, she would have needed parental consent to undergo an abortion in Wisconsin back then."

"But not here?"

Cheryl shook her head. "Not here in Illinois, no."

The early pieces of the puzzle Ethan was constructing began to align. Callie Jones was pregnant and had come to this clinic, where her parents wouldn't be notified, to have an abortion. She came all the way to Chicago so that her politician father and overbearing mother would not find out. Then, she made a call, possibly from this very building, to the prepaid cell phone she had purchased with cash. The phone that now sat in Ethan's home. The phone Francis Bernard had somehow led him to.

"You said you worked as a nurse in 2015?"

"Yes sir. I've been here nearly twenty years. I was the head nurse back in 2015."

"As head nurse, your role was?"

"Head nurse is also called Mamma Bear. Most women who come in here are struggling with their decision because of how stigmatized our society has made abortion. I helped the women, especially the younger ones, through the process."

Ethan pulled his backpack off his shoulder and unzipped the top. He pulled a file folder from inside and opened it, then slid a photo of Callie across the desk.

"I know it was a long time ago, but have you ever seen this girl before?"

Cheryl pulled the photo closer and slowly placed her hand to her chest.

"Oh my God. That's her."

CHAPTER 32

Chicago, Illinois
Saturday, July 26, 2025

"**I** KNOW THIS GIRL," CHERYL SAID, HOLDING UP THE PHOTO OF CALlie. "She came to our clinic. It was years ago, but I remember her."

"How?" Ethan asked.

"Because . . ." Cheryl choked back tears. "She came back to thank me."

"Thank you for what?"

Cheryl took a deep breath and stared at the photo. "This girl came in and was clearly in turmoil. She told me she didn't want her parents to know she was pregnant, or that she was going to have an abortion. I could tell she was scared and unsure about her decision."

"Her decision to have an abortion?"

"Yes. She told me she was a star athlete of some sort."

"Volleyball."

Cheryl nodded. "Yes, that's it. And she had just been accepted to college. Or it was college *and* medical school. An elite, eight-year program. And because of it all, she was carrying a heavy burden on her shoulders."

"Listen, Cheryl, I believe everything you're saying because that matches Callie Jones's situation. But how can you remember all of this so clearly ten years later?"

"Because of something she said to me. It was a quote, and I've never forgotten it. She said, 'The tragedy of life is not that man loses, but that he almost wins.'"

Ethan remembered his conversation with Lindsay Larkin. She had mentioned the same quote, and that she and Callie had used it for motivation after losing the state championship freshman year.

"It stuck with me," Cheryl said. "I've never forgotten it. And I misinterpreted what she was trying to tell me. I thought she was suggesting that her pregnancy was going to cause her to lose all the things she had worked so hard for—her acceptance to college, the chance at going to medical school, her status with her parents, her friends, all of it. But that's not what she meant. She meant that the baby she was carrying was her chance at winning what she really wanted out of life. And that she was so close to obtaining it, but was about to lose it."

"About to lose it because she was going to have an abortion?"

"Yes. After she explained that to me, I told her to wait. People think all we do here is encourage abortions, but that's not true. We help women in need. And this girl was in desperate need of help. I told her to wait on the abortion and to think about it. To talk with the father about it."

"And she did?"

"Yes. She decided to wait on the abortion and left. But she came back the next day. When I saw her again, I thought she had decided to go through with it. But that wasn't why she'd come back. She came back to thank me for helping her figure things out. She said she was going to have the baby, and I could tell, just from her demeanor, that she was a different person than when I had met her the day before. Happier. More content. She gave me a big hug, told me I'd changed her life forever, and that was it. She left and I never saw her again. Until now," Cheryl said, looking at the photo of Callie Jones. "But I never forgot this girl. In some way, she changed my life as much as she said I changed hers."

Ethan ran a hand through his hair at the revelation. "You'll agree to give a formal statement explaining everything you just told me?"

Cheryl looked up from the photo. "Is she okay?"

Ethan shook his head.

"She's been missing for ten years. But what you just told me may help me figure out what happened to her."

"I'll help any way I can."

Ethan took Cheryl Stowe's contact information and headed out of the clinic. He'd just made the first break in a ten-year-old cold case. And it had originated with Francis Bernard.

CHAPTER 33

Somewhere North of Madison
Saturday, July 26, 2025

SHE HEARD THE CAR DOOR SLAM. IT HAD BEEN TWO DAYS SINCE THE masked woman had come to slip food through the door slot. She hurried to the other side of the room and lifted the slot to peek through. She heard the front door upstairs open, and then footsteps as they pounded down the basement stairs. When the woman emerged from the staircase, a black balaclava covered her face. Seeing that the woman was on a beeline toward the door, she let go of the flap and it clattered shut.

A moment later, the slot opened, and a pair of handcuffs rattled through and fell to the floor.

"Take the cuffs and go to the other side of the room," the woman said.

The woman's words were short and curt. Did she have an accent?

"Now!" the woman said, filling her with a jolt of fear and a sense of dread that something terrible was about to happen.

She took the silver handcuffs from the floor and hurried to the other side of the room. The woman lifted the slot and spoke through the opening.

"Close the bathroom door."

She did as instructed.

"Now cuff yourself to the doorknob."

She looked down at the cuffs and then back to the door slot.

"Cuff yourself to the door or this will get really ugly really fast!" The woman's voice rose an octave with each of the last few words.

She forced her mind to work, to think through her options. There were only two: do as she was told and suffer the consequences of willfully giving up her ability to fight should this woman enter the room or, refuse and see what comes of it.

The woman spoke through the slot again, this time her voice was slow and calm.

"Cuff yourself to the door or I will spray chemicals into the room that will cause you to pass out. That's the hard way to get this done, but I'm willing to do it."

She saw a hose of some sort poke through the door slot. Tears welled in her eyes until they streamed down her cheeks.

"Okay," she yelled, taking the cuffs and securing one end around her left wrist and the other around the bathroom doorknob.

The hose disappeared and the woman peered through the slot.

"Show me," the woman said. "Pull your arm away."

She pulled against the cuffs to prove that she was securely fastened to the door.

The slot closed and a key rattled in the lock. Then, for the first time since she'd been there, the door opened. The woman walked into the room. She was tall and lanky.

"Please. Don't hurt me."

The woman threw something at her, and she reactively closed her eyes and flinched. When she heard a flop, she opened her eyes and saw a newspaper on the floor in front of her. It was a copy of the *Milwaukee Journal Sentinel.* She examined the front page and saw that it held today's date.

"Hold the paper in front of you," the woman said.

Since entering the room, large sunglasses hid the woman's eyes, while the black head covering concealed her face.

"Hold it up," the woman said.

She reached down and grabbed the newspaper.

"In front of your chest," the woman said. "Just under your chin."

She held up the paper and saw the woman raise her phone. The flash bleached her retinas, and she barely saw the woman throw something else in her direction before turning and walking out of the room. The door slammed shut and the lock rattled again. A moment later she heard footsteps climb the stairs, and the deadbolt of the main entrance slide into place.

When the purple afterimage faded and her vision returned, she looked down at her feet to see what the woman had thrown at her. It was the key to the handcuffs.

CHAPTER 34

Cherryview, Wisconsin
Saturday, July 26, 2025

Ethan poured two cups of coffee and sat with Maddie at his kitchen table. He ran his hands through his hair.

"She was pregnant?" Maddie asked.

"According to the nurse at Planned Parenthood, yes. She went to Chicago to have an abortion but decided against it."

"So you have a seventeen-year-old pregnant girl who decided to keep the baby. If I were the lead on this case, my list of people who disliked that idea would be long."

Ethan had taken Maddie through the last week of his investigation.

"It would include the father of the child. Maybe he was a classmate who didn't want a kid as a teenager. It would include Callie's mother, although that sounds awful. She wanted this perfect little life for her daughter, who was supposed to go on to become a world-renowned surgeon. Having a kid as a teenager doesn't fit into that plan. It would include her father, too. Governor today but a state senator back then and an up-and-coming politician star. A *missing* teen daughter would draw more sympathy from potential voters than a *pregnant* teen daughter. And I'd take a serious look at the girl's stepfather. Make sure nothing sinister was going on between them."

Ethan raised his eyebrows. "Those are some rough accusations, Detective Jacobson."

"I'm just telling you how I would approach this if I were handling the case."

"They're all logical angles. If Callie's mother had something to do with her disappearance, we'll never know. She killed herself the year after Callie went missing."

"Maybe the guilt got to her."

Ethan squinted as he considered this. "It's possible."

"And her dad?"

"The argument of saving his political career is valid, but that's assuming he knew Callie was pregnant. Everything I've uncovered suggested he did not. Also, why would he reopen the case ten years later if he got away scot-free?"

"Yeah," Maddie agreed. "Pretty risky, especially when no one was putting pressure on him to reexamine the case."

"The stepfather is a pretty ugly thought. I'll have to put some thought into how to approach that topic."

"So that leaves the father of Callie's baby," Maddie said. "Any idea who that was?"

"Nope. But I have to believe he was communicating with Callie through the prepaid Samsung."

"Are you running forensics on the phone?"

Ethan shook his head. "Not formally, but I've got a friend working on it."

"You haven't told Pete about the phone? Or Governor Jones?"

"Not yet."

"They asked for your help, Ethan. You've found something no one else found back then—she was pregnant. And you found the prepaid phone Callie was calling and texting, which likely belonged to the father of her unborn child. They'd want to know all that."

"Yeah. They'd also want to know how Francis Bernard led me to the prepaid phone in the first place. I don't know how to explain that yet."

"Then go back and ask him."

Ethan nodded and closed his eyes momentarily at the thought of speaking with Francis again.

"I'm meeting with Lindsay Larkin today to retrace Callie's footsteps from the night she disappeared."

"And Francis?"

"I'm on the visitor's log to see him tomorrow."

Ethan knew he had no choice but to return to Boscobel. He had to find out what Francis wanted from him, and what else the man knew about Callie Jones.

CHAPTER 35

Cherryview, Wisconsin
Saturday, July 26, 2025

Ethan climbed onboard the Metal Shark 32 Defiant, which was part of a fleet of patrol vessels owned by the DCI and housed with the Madison Police Department. He turned and offered his hand to Lindsay Larkin, who stepped from the dock and onto the boat. He reached to help Pete Kramer, but Pete swatted his hand away.

"I'm not some damn invalid," Pete said.

Ethan didn't protest or mention that Pete was, in fact, the very definition of an invalid. Instead, he stepped back as Pete tossed the cane he had recently started using into the boat and managed to step down into the cabin unassisted, landing hard and unceremoniously onto the seat. An officer with the Madison PD fired up the engine and pulled away from North Point Pier.

The humidity was thick, and the afternoon temperature hovered around 100 degrees. Ethan was dressed in slacks and a short-sleeved shirt. Lindsay was in a silk tank top and jeans. Pete had mercifully removed his sport coat once he was seated on the boat. As the Defiant took off, they all welcomed the breeze.

"There's an island in the middle of the lake," Pete said over the hum of the engine. "They call it The Crest. There used to be a bar and grill out there, but it shut down in 2017. Callie was there the night she disappeared. To the best of my knowledge, it's the last place anyone saw her alive."

"You were there?" Ethan asked Lindsay. "That night at The Crest?"

"Yes, all of us were. All our friends and most of the volleyball team."

"And you saw Callie?"

Lindsay nodded. "Yeah, we drove out to The Crest in her parents' boat. I was with her all night, until she left."

The Defiant banked to the left as it cut across Lake Okoboji. A light mist came from the bow and sprayed Ethan's face, offering a reprieve from the heat. They glided across the lake for fifteen minutes until the engines revved down and The Crest came into view. It was a small piece of land just a few hundred yards wide that peeked from below the surface of Lake Okoboji. A long pier that had seen better days reached out from the land like an arthritic finger. The driver guided the Defiant alongside the pier and Ethan tied off the bow.

"Back in the day," Pete said, "this used to be a popular restaurant and bar. The only one on the lake."

Ethan looked across the lake. In every direction, the shoreline was dotted with homes. An unpaved access road twisted from the mainland and ran to the backside of the small island.

"And Callie lived on the lake?"

"Yes," Lindsay said. "She had a big house in Harmony Bay." Lindsay pointed off to where Callie used to live.

Ethan remembered that Harmony Bay was also where Christian Malone's mansion was located. He wondered if the tech guru had made any progress on pulling the deleted text threads from Callie's SIM card. Francis Bernard and their upcoming visit, which was scheduled for Sunday morning, also intruded on his thoughts, but Ethan blinked away the distractions. He reminded himself of his old mantra when he used to do this for a living. *One thing at a time, Ethan.*

They all stepped off the boat and headed toward a neglected building that stood a few yards from the dock.

"I'd think this place would be a goldmine," Ethan said. "The only restaurant on a lake crowded with homes."

"It was," Lindsay said. "Back in high school it was very popular, but people stopped coming after Callie disappeared. Bad vibes and rumors about what happened to her kept residents away."

"What were you guys doing that night?" Ethan asked.

"Playing volleyball out on the sand courts. Come on, I'll show you."

They walked around the old restaurant until the volleyball courts came into view, now just rectangles overgrown with weeds and bare poles between which the nets used to hang.

"These volleyball courts were a big attraction back in the day," Lindsay said. "They were always full. And when people saw that Callie and I were playing . . . you know, a lot of people liked to watch us."

Ethan imagined the pretty, blond, seventeen-year-old who drew a huge crowd of fans that watched her compete on the volleyball court and also followed her out to The Crest to watch her play pickup games in the sand. He imagined middle-aged men watching Callie Jones from the stands, and the bad intentions that might have been born from secret admiration.

"Did you two have . . . I guess I'd call them *fans*? Was that a thing?"

Lindsay shrugged. "Maybe, but none that we knew of. Cherryview, in general, was our fan base."

Ethan pulled out a notepad from his pocket. It was new. He jotted down a note.

"So you guys played volleyball that night?"

"Yes. And we were getting ready to play two guys from the football team who had challenged us. It was a thing that happened all the time. The guys always wanted to play us because they could never beat us in a two-on-two game. Word had spread that we were going to play, so people started coming out of the restaurant and gathering around the court to watch. We were waiting for the game in front of us to finish up. But we never ended up playing that night."

"Why?"

Lindsay shrugged. "Callie got a text and had to leave."

"Who texted her?"

"Her mom. Callie said she needed her to come home."

"What time was this?"

"Nine o'clock. She left and that was the last time I saw her."

"It was the last time anyone saw her," Pete said. "And the text wasn't from her mother. Phone records show the text came from the pre-paid Samsung."

Ethan walked onto the weed-infested volleyball courts, his feet sinking into what little sand remained on them. He looked around, imagining Callie Jones standing in that exact spot ten years earlier.

Summer 2015

Cherryview, Wisconsin

Saturday, July 18, 2015

CALLIE STOOD AT THE EDGE OF THE SAND VOLLEYBALL COURT AND TRIED *to watch the game unfold. Patrons of the restaurant cheered when one of the players spiked the ball into the sand to win a point. Callie knew they were cheering, not for the point itself, but because it brought the game closer to its conclusion. And once the current game was over, Callie and Lindsay would take the court to challenge two football players who were talking trash. Callie and Lindsay were undefeated in sand volleyball out on The Crest, and every football player wanted to be the one to end their streak.*

The crowd was growing by the minute, but Callie's thoughts were elsewhere. She had gone to The Crest only to placate her friends, who had given her a world of shit when she had mentioned that she didn't want to go out on Saturday night. She wanted to be somewhere else tonight. She stared at her phone and waited for a text back from Blake. She'd been trying to reach him since practice that morning, but all her texts and calls had gone unreturned that day. Finally, her phone buzzed with a text message.

What's wrong?
Callie quickly typed back.
I need to see you.
Where are you?
The Crest.
You okay?
I need to talk to you about the baby.

There was a pause with no return text. Callie felt an urgency to tell him. She wanted to call him rather than text, but it was too noisy on The Crest and she feared someone would overhear. She looked around to make sure no one was paying attention to her.

I'm keeping it.

The reply this time was instant.

You didn't go through with it?

No. I want this baby WITH YOU. I want to start a life with you. I need to see you tonight.

Do you have your parents' boat?

Yes.

Meet me at North Point Pier. I'll be waiting on the dock.

I love you, Blake.

I love you, too.

Callie stared at her phone a moment longer. Her life was about to change, and she felt the weight of the last year lift from her shoulders. She was ready for every bit of what was coming. She took a deep breath and wiped a tear from her cheek as a smile came to her face. She slid her finger across the text to delete the thread from her phone. The encrypted texting app she and Blake used promised that deleted text threads were gone forever. The app was Blake's idea. He'd always warned her about leaving traces of their communication on her phone.

She turned from the sand courts, ready to run to her boat.

"Who was that?"

Callie looked up from her phone. Lindsay was standing behind her.

"Oh, um, my mom," Callie said. "She wants me home."

Lindsay squinted her eyes and made a sour face. "It's nine o'clock on a Saturday."

"The regular crowd shuffles in," Callie sung, trying to divert Lindsay's attention from the urgency she was emitting. She forced a smile. "There's an old man sitting next to me . . ." She crinkled her nose. "No?"

"We're playing next."

"I can't, Linds. My mom's all over me about something."

"Why is your mom such a buzzkill?"

"You think anything my mom does makes sense?" She shook her head. "She's probably having a breakdown about something. I'm going to take the

boat home. Be back in an hour. Then we'll play those guys. Kick their butts."

"You sure you're okay?"

Callie felt another tear run down her cheek. She quickly wiped it away. "Yeah. All good. I'll see you later."

Callie hurried off to her boat.

CHAPTER 36

Cherryview, Wisconsin
Saturday, July 26, 2025

THEY CLIMBED BACK INTO THE 32 DEFIANT AND PULLED AWAY FROM The Crest. Ethan continued to write in his notepad, adding to the timeline he'd created of Callie's movements the night she disappeared.

"You said it was nine o'clock when Callie left The Crest?" Ethan asked Lindsay over the hum of the boat's engines.

"Yeah. I remember the time because she made a 'Piano Man' joke when I mentioned that she was leaving at nine o'clock on a Saturday."

"The regular crowd shuffles in?" Pete said.

"Yeah." Lindsay nodded. "Like that."

"And Callie's younger sister said she stopped home around nine fifteen," Pete added. "She grabbed a sweatshirt before heading back out in the boat."

Ethan had read in the case file that Jaycee Jones mentioned covering for Callie a few times that summer, when Callie snuck out late at night. Jaycee didn't know who Callie had been meeting up with, only that Callie had asked Jaycee to cover for her if her mother ever asked where she was.

"There it is," Lindsay said, pointing off to the right. "That's Callie's old house."

The Madison PD officer banked the Defiant and headed toward

the shore. He cut the engines as they approached the dock. Ethan checked his watch.

"It adds up if she left The Crest at nine and headed home. It took us fifteen minutes to get here. Callie's sister said she stopped home just to grab a sweatshirt and then headed right back out. Five minute turnaround, let's say?"

Lindsay and Pete agreed, and Ethan jotted a note on his pad. He pointed at the driver. "Take us back to North Point Pier."

The Defiant's bow rose as the engines dug into the water. It took six minutes to make it back to the pier.

"Callie's boat was found tied to the dock Sunday morning," Pete said.

"If she left her house at nine twenty and drove straight here, that puts her at this spot before nine thirty. Where were her phone and blood found?"

They all climbed from the boat and walked to the end of the dock where the gravel path that led to the parking lot ended.

"Right here," Pete said. "Her phone was on the ground, and blood spatter was found right about here." Pete pointed down at the gravel.

Ethan remembered the crime scene photos from the file.

"So Callie was on The Crest at nine o'clock getting ready to play a game of beach volleyball when she received a text. She tells her best friend the message was from her mother. But we know it was actually from the prepaid Samsung."

Ethan looked around North Point Pier.

"She makes a brief stop home and then leaves again in the boat. The next time the boat is seen is by a fisherman Sunday morning who can't launch their Whaler because Callie's boat is tied to the dock and blocking the boat launch."

"Correct," Pete said. "Cops showed up to tow the boat. They ran the tags and gave the Jones's a courtesy call. That's when Callie's mom said she noticed Callie had never come home from the night before. And that leaves one, big, fat question," Pete said. "The one I've been trying to answer for ten years."

Ethan cocked his head. "Who texted her out on The Crest?"

"Bingo," Pete said.

Ethan had yet to tell Pete he'd discovered that Callie Jones was pregnant when she disappeared. Or that she had decided, just the day before, to keep the baby rather than go through with an abortion. Ethan had a strong suspicion that the text message Callie had received when she was out on The Crest had come from the baby's father.

He looked across the lake. Christian Malone's mansion was barely visible in the distance. He hoped the tech guru was making progress on recovering the text threads.

CHAPTER 37

Boscobel, Wisconsin
Sunday, July 27, 2025

ETHAN MADE IT THROUGH SECURITY AND STARED THROUGH THE GLASS at the empty seat in front of him. He worked to hide his frustration that he was in the position of needing information from his father's killer. A loud beep sounded. The light on the wall above the entrance blinked, followed by a long buzzing noise as the lock disengaged. The door opened and Francis shuffled into the visitation area with his hands cuffed in front of him and his ankles shackled. The man's ice-blue eyes seemed out of place against his impossibly pale skin.

Ethan lifted the phone and placed it to his ear when Francis sat down. Francis did the same.

"You need a tan, Francis. You're looking deathly pale."

"That's because they leave me in my cell for days at a time, despite the fact that state law dictates that inmates spend two hours each day out of confinement."

Ethan crinkled his brow in confusion. "You're not expecting me to get choked up, are you?"

"No. I'm just laying the groundwork."

"For what?"

"Did you find my package?"

"Yeah, and I want to know how you knew the phone was there."

"So I can assume that Special Agent One Hundred Percent did some research on that phone?"

Ethan nodded.

"So you know it is the prepaid burner phone your DCI friends could not locate in 2015 during their original investigation. And you know that little Callie Jones called its owner many times."

Ethan had done the math and worked the angles in his mind. Francis had been in prison for thirty-two years, since 1993. Callie Jones went missing in 2015. There was no earthly way for the man to have been directly involved in her abduction.

"Francis, how do you know anything about Callie Jones?"

"We've already covered that."

"How did you know where that phone was located?"

"Oh, Ethan," Francis said with a curl of his lips. "I know much more than the location of the phone the girl was calling. I know who the owner of the phone was, and where the girl is today."

Ethan forced himself to stay calm.

"How? You were in prison for more than twenty years when Callie went missing."

"How I know is immaterial. *What* I know is crucial. And most importantly, what I want in exchange for that information."

Now Ethan smiled. "You're not so stupid to think I'd actually negotiate with you, are you?"

Ethan leaned toward the glass, close enough to see the folds of Francis's translucent irises. He anticipated that Francis would try to leverage whatever he knew about Callie's disappearance for some favor he believed Ethan could help him with. But in just a short period of time Ethan had turned up enough new information about the Callie Jones case to feel confident that with more time and continued determination, he'd figure the rest out on his own. Who the father of Callie's baby was, and whether that person had anything to do with her disappearance. Francis had overplayed his hand, and he could go to hell with whatever request he was about to make.

"You can keep whatever information you've gathered," Ethan said, "from whatever demeaning ways you've gathered it, to yourself, Francis. I'll never give you a thing, other than the promise of a lifetime in that little, lonely cell of yours."

"Go back to the warehouse, Ethan."

Francis held Ethan's gaze without blinking.

"High in the rafters is a footlocker," Francis said, a restrained urgency to his tone. "Go there, Special Agent Hall, and see what's waiting. Then come back here and see if you can keep the promise you just made."

Francis hung up the phone and stood from the chair, keeping his unblinking stare on Ethan until the guard took his arm and led him away.

CHAPTER 38

Milwaukee, Wisconsin
Sunday, July 27, 2025

ETHAN DROVE INTO THE ABANDONED SECTION OF THE MENOMONEE River Valley in the heart of Milwaukee, crossed the freight tracks like he had last time, and sped down the decrepit road, his Jeep Wrangler bouncing through the potholes until he found Warehouse #9. He grabbed a flashlight from the middle console and retrieved his Beretta from the glove compartment, which he tucked into his waistband as he approached the warehouse door. He turned the knob and pushed it open. The squeaky hinges echoed into the empty space as the warehouse breathed hot air through the doorway that put an immediate glaze of sweat on Ethan's face and neck.

He walked into the dark space, shined his flashlight around to make sure it was empty, and then turned his attention to the southeast corner where he saw a loft high in the rafters. He hurried over, looking up at the landing twenty feet above him. A ladder hung down from a metal grate, the bottom rung at Ethan's eye level. He pulled on the ladder to test its strength, and when he was convinced that the old, rickety thing would support his two-hundred-pound frame, he pulled himself up and climbed the rungs to the loft above.

When he made it up to the landing of the loft, he shined his flashlight around to see a metal footlocker set in the corner. He climbed the rest of the way onto the jetty and crawled to the box.

He examined it for signs of a booby-trap or any other indication that opening the top would bring him bodily harm—something he'd never put past Francis Bernard. Finally, Ethan lifted the lid and shined his light inside. He saw two items resting at the bottom of the footlocker.

The first was an 8x10 photo. Ethan squinted in the darkness. The photo was of a young woman standing in a room and hand-cuffed to a door. She was holding a copy of the *Milwaukee Journal Sentinel*, the front page of which held yesterday's date.

Ethan examined the photo for another moment before retrieving the second item from the footlocker. It was a copy of the *Milwaukee Journal Sentinel*, opened to an article covering the details of a local Milwaukee woman who had gone missing weeks earlier in June. Her name was Portia Vail. Ethan looked back at the 8×10 and knew he was looking at the missing woman. And that somehow, from the confines of solitary confinement at a maximum-security prison, Francis Bernard was responsible for her abduction.

When Ethan lifted the article to read the details, an index card fell from the pages of the newspaper. It slipped through the metal grating and floated to the warehouse floor below. With the photo of the missing woman in hand, Ethan scampered down the ladder, jumped the final few feet, and landed hard. He found the index card and shined his light onto it to read the message written in steady block lettering.

Hurry, Special Agent Hall. Callie Jones is dead and buried, but the clock is tic tic ticking on this one . . .

PART V

The Other Girl

CHAPTER 39

Cherryview, Wisconsin
Sunday, July 27, 2025

ETHAN ORGANIZED HIMSELF AT HIS KITCHEN TABLE. HE HAD PLACED both the photo of the girl and the newspaper into Ziploc bags to preserve whatever evidence might remain on them. He opened his laptop and typed the name *Portia Vail* into the search engine. The first result was the *Milwaukee Journal Sentinel* article, the same one that was now sealed in a makeshift evidence bag on his counter. He opened the link and read.

> *Milwaukee, WI, July 26, 2025*
>
> *Portia Vail was reported missing by her fiancé on Friday, July 4. She had been absent from her job at the University of Wisconsin–Milwaukee, where she works as a research assistant, for the week. The twenty-seven-year-old was last seen Saturday, June 28. A cell phone belonging to the victim was found at her apartment, along with her purse and other personal items, suggesting that her disappearance was not linked to a robbery. According to sources, the victim's apartment showed no signs of forced entry.*
>
> *The Missing Persons Division of the Milwaukee Police Department is handling the case, but has not returned the Sentinel's calls for comment.*
>
> *This is an active investigation. If anyone has information about Portia Vail they are asked to call the hotline number below.*

Ethan shifted his gaze from the computer to the photo of Portia Vail handcuffed to a bathroom door. He grabbed the Ziplocs containing the newspaper article and the photo and hurried out the door. He climbed into his Wrangler and headed east toward Milwaukee. He called Maddie on the way.

CHAPTER 40

Milwaukee, Wisconsin
Sunday, July 27, 2025

Ethan PULLED INTO THE PARKING LOT OF THE DISTRICT 2 HEADquarters of the Milwaukee Police Department. Maddie met him at the front entrance of the white stone building. She walked him through the office until they arrived at her desk, which was located in a cubicle set amongst the other detectives' workspaces.

"Portia Vail," Ethan said. "You know anything about her?"

Maddie nodded. "Yeah. She's missing. We've got two detectives on her case now. Four weeks gone, no breaks. Why?"

"I went to see Francis again. He offered more information on Callie Jones in exchange for my help with something."

"With what?"

"We didn't get that far. I told him to piss off. That's when he sent me back to the warehouse in Menomonee Valley, which is where I found these."

Ethan dropped the Ziploc bags onto Maddie's desk. Maddie lifted the one that held the 8×10 photo.

"What the hell is this?"

"Somehow, the son of a bitch knows where Portia Vail is being held."

Maddie examined the photo of the woman handcuffed to a door and holding a newspaper to display the date. "How is that possible?"

"Someone has to be helping him. I called Pete Kramer and told him everything. He put the warehouse under surveillance. If that's Francis's drop site and someone is working with him, we'll know about it soon enough. But right now, I need everything the Milwaukee PD has on Portia Vail."

"Let me make some calls."

"Maddie, I don't want to put you in a bind, but we need to keep this quiet until we know how Francis fits into it all."

Maddie nodded. "Got it."

CHAPTER 41

Milwaukee, Wisconsin
Sunday, July 27, 2025

MADDIE DID SOME SLEUTHING AT THE STATION AND FOUND THE name of Portia's fiancé, who had initially reported her missing. She and Ethan decided to start there. It was late afternoon when they found the address on Clement Avenue in the Bay View neighborhood and walked up the steps to the apartment. This was Maddie's jurisdiction, and since she was sticking her neck out by going behind the back of the detectives who had the case, she took the lead on their stealth operation.

Maddie knocked on the door and a man answered. He looked to be about thirty.

"Nicholas Brann?" Maddie asked.

"Yes?"

"Maddie Jacobson with the Milwaukee PD."

The Bell's palsy that drooped the left side of her face came out in full force when she was under duress or involved in stressful situations. And sneaking around a case that was not hers qualified as such. Smiling made the paralyzed facial muscles more obvious, but offering a stoic face void of expression was not conducive to obtaining information. She pressed her lips together and settled on a soft grin.

She held out her badge. "This is my partner, Ethan Hall."

Ethan held up his DCI badge.

"Did you find her?"

"Not yet," Maddie said. "We need to ask you a few questions. Can we come inside?"

"Yeah, sure."

Around the kitchen island a moment later, Maddie asked, "You're the one who reported your fiancée missing, correct?"

"Well, no. I mean, yes I reported Portia missing, but she's not my fiancée. Portia and I used to be engaged. We broke it off a few months ago but had decided to give it another go. So technically, she's not really my fiancée. That's what I meant."

"Start from the beginning."

"I already spoke to the police and gave a statement to another detective about all of this."

"We know. But there's been a new development in the case, and we need you to start from the beginning again and tell us everything."

"Have you found . . . something?"

Maddie glanced at Ethan. "Maybe, but we need to understand the situation better. So help us out. When was the last time you spoke to Portia?"

"Saturday morning. June twenty-eighth. She spent Friday night here at my place."

"Was that unusual?"

"Not back in the day. But it was the first time we'd . . . you know, the first time she'd stayed over since we decided to get back together."

"How long had you guys been engaged before you broke it off?"

"A couple of months. But we'd dated for three years before that."

"Why did the engagement end?"

Nicholas shook his head. "Stupid stuff. Her family lives down in Florida and she wanted to have the wedding down there, but my family lives here so that was an issue. Just silly things that we couldn't agree on and that got blown out of proportion. Then we thought maybe we were rushing things, so we decided to take a break."

"When was that?"

"Three months ago."

"So you guys were broken up for the past three months and had just gotten back together. She stayed over Friday, June twenty-seventh. And you saw her Saturday morning?"

"Yeah, briefly. She left early. Said goodbye and that was it. I was still in bed. I waited for her to call me because, you know, it's that stupid thing you do. See who's going to call first. But when I didn't hear from her after a couple of days, I called her. I couldn't reach her, and she never returned any of my texts. Sometimes we connect through social media, but when I saw that she hadn't posted anything all week, I called her parents and then we called 9-1-1."

Maddie changed angles.

"Back to the breakup. Was there another woman involved?"

"No, it was nothing like that. Like I said, it was just stupid stuff."

"Was she maybe seeing another guy?"

Nicholas took a deep breath and exhaled it. "Not while we were together."

"But after you broke up?"

"Yeah. Portia told me that she had a brief thing with a guy. We were on a break, so I let it go."

Maddie squinted her eyes. "You know this guy's name?"

"That she was seeing?"

Maddie nodded.

"Yeah. I told the other detective about him. Guy's name was Blake Cordis."

CHAPTER 42

Beaver Dam, Wisconsin
Monday, July 28, 2025

ETHAN DROVE HIS JEEP WRANGLER WHILE MADDIE SHUFFLED THROUGH papers in the passenger seat. Because she was not formally assigned to the Portia Vail case, they avoided taking her unmarked squad car out to Prescott Estates, where Blake Cordis worked. The previous day, after they had spoken to Portia Vail's fiancé, Maddie went back to the station and pulled everything she could find on the Portia Vail case. She and Ethan spent Sunday night at her house combing through the files.

Over Chinese carryout and light beer, Ethan had brought Maddie up to date on the nebulous connection between Portia Vail, Blake Cordis, and Callie Jones. Blake Cordis had been Callie's high school volleyball coach, but beyond that Ethan was stumped at how the man fit into the puzzle Francis Bernard was crafting. When midnight came, they returned the files to the box Maddie had taken from the station and decided their best chance at answers was to pay Blake Cordis a visit. They made love into the small hours of night, attempting to distract their thoughts away from Francis Bernard, the man who had altered each of their lives so tragically as to imprint himself forever onto their existence.

As they drove now, Maddie read through the stack of papers she'd pulled from the Portia Vail file that listed every incoming and outgoing call and text from the girl's phone over the previous year. In the last three months, starting in April, Blake Cordis's number was either called or texted one hundred twenty-seven times—far greater than any other number. When they examined Portia's contact list, it was noted that Blake's number had been added as a new contact on April 2, 2025—just after Nicholas Brann mentioned he and Portia had split up.

"A hundred twenty-seven calls or texts in ninety days," Maddie said as they drove the long, lonely roads of central Wisconsin on the way out to Beaver Dam. "That's some hot and heavy stuff."

"Sounds like it."

Maddie turned a page. "Okay, so listen to this. About a week before Portia went missing, the calls between her and Blake Cordis stopped. Mostly. She stopped calling him, but he kept calling her. Lots of incoming calls from him. And several texts. But no return calls from Portia."

"So Portia and Nicholas take a break," Ethan said. "She hooks up with Blake Cordis as a rebound guy, and after three months decides she wants to get back together with Nicholas. She stops responding to Blake Cordis's calls and texts, and stays at Nicholas's apartment on Friday, June 27—the first time she's stayed at his place since the breakup. She wakes up Saturday and leaves. No one's seen her since."

"Except you, in the picture Francis Bernard somehow led you to."

As he drove, Ethan tried again to piece it all together—the governor appointing him to his daughter's cold case, Blake Cordis who had been Callie's new volleyball coach, and now Portia Vail, who was involved in some sort of relationship with Cordis. And intertwined within it, like an overgrown and uncontrollable weed, was Francis Bernard.

"Portia's been gone for a month," Maddie said. "We have to assume she's running out of time."

"I have a feeling that's what Francis is counting on."

Hurry, Special Agent Hall. Callie Jones may be dead and buried but the clock is tic tic ticking on this one . . .

CHAPTER 43

Beaver Dam, Wisconsin
Monday, July 28, 2025

THE PRESCOTT FAMILY MADE THEIR FORTUNE IN LUMBER. THE FAMILY had been clearing forests and shipping timber across the country since just after the Civil War. Although Prescott Lumber still held a significant spot in the family's portfolio, it was no longer the largest entity. That distinction went to Prescott Park, the horseracing facility just north of Milwaukee. The Thoroughbred racetrack was home to some of the country's largest horseracing events and had even managed to snag the coveted Breeder's Cup in the early 2000s. Jacques Prescott, the current patriarch of the family, also owned the largest breeding farm in Wisconsin, and over the years had entered three of his horses into the Kentucky Derby.

Three generations of financial success brought with it a large real estate portfolio. Jacques Prescott and his family lived on ten thousand acres of land near Beaver Dam that included a fifteen-thousand-square-foot main home, several guest cottages, and stables that housed thirty-two horses. Blake Cordis, one time teacher and head volleyball coach for the Cherryview High School girls' volleyball team, was now the head groundskeeper and the man in charge of just about everything that happened on the Prescott property. Ethan and Maddie pulled up to the large cast-iron gate where a security guard sat in an air-conditioned booth. Ethan rolled down his window.

"Can I help you, sir?" the security guard asked.

"Yes." Ethan showed the man his DCI badge. "Ethan Hall with the Wisconsin Department of Criminal Investigation. This is Maddie Jacobson, a detective from Milwaukee."

Maddie offered her badge.

"We're looking for Blake Cordis."

The security guard studied the badges before he slowly nodded. "He's probably out by the stables. I'll have to call him on the radio."

"Please do that, thanks," Ethan said.

Ten minutes later the cast-iron gates glided open as a green John Deere Work Series Gator UTA sped down a gravel path, stirring up a cloud of dust into the summer heat behind it. Ethan saw that Blake Cordis, dressed in jeans and a T-shirt, was solidly built with thick forearms and bulging biceps.

The guard exited the booth and had a word with Mr. Cordis before Blake walked over to Ethan's Wrangler.

"Blake Cordis. Something I can help you with?"

Ethan and Maddie raised their badges again.

"Ethan Hall, Wisconsin DCI. Is there someplace we can talk?"

Blake took a step back and surveyed Ethan's Jeep. "You off duty, Officer?"

"Special Agent. And this is Detective Jacobson."

"What's this about?"

Ethan glanced at the security guard and then back to Blake. "I think you're going to want to have this conversation in private."

Blake slowly nodded.

"Follow me. We can talk in the stables. My office is air-conditioned. We can get out of this heat."

Blake hopped back into the Gator and pulled a U-turn. Ethan followed. They drove along the gravel path for half a mile until the horse stables came into view over the crest of a rolling hill. So expansive was the Prescott property that Ethan saw nothing but open fields and white picket fencing in the distance. As they approached the stables, Blake slowed to a stop, and Ethan parked next to the Gator. He and Maddie climbed from the Wrangler.

"Blake Cordis," Blake said, extending his hand as he walked back toward Ethan.

Ethan shook it. "Ethan Hall. This is Maddie Jacobson."

Maddie shook his hand, and they all headed into the stables. Horses stood in individual stalls fanning their tails against the heat. The animals paid little attention to the three as they walked past. At the far end of the building Blake opened the door to a glass-walled office. Ethan and Maddie followed him inside.

"This heat is oppressive," Blake said.

Each of their faces was covered in perspiration from the short walk.

"Coffee or water?" Blake asked.

"No thanks," Ethan said.

Maddie shook her head.

"Take a seat." Blake pointed to the couch. He sat on an end chair and reached for the pack of Saratoga cigarettes on the coffee table. "Mind if I smoke?"

"It's your office," Maddie said.

Blake pulled the long, thin cigarette from the pack and held it up.

"Saratoga 120s. Terrible habit I started in high school and haven't been able to break. They don't even make these anymore," he said as he lit the cigarette and took a deep drag. "I have to order them off the Internet, and they cost a fortune."

"You're not a Marlboro man?" Maddie asked.

Blake lifted the hand that held the cigarette. "These are the only ones that taste decent to me. Probably just be easier to quit, but that ship has sailed. What can I help you with?"

"You know someone named Nicholas Brann?" Maddie asked.

Blake exhaled a stream of smoke from the corner of his mouth. "No. Who is he?"

"A gentleman who lives down in Milwaukee. He reported his fiancée missing a couple weeks ago. You know who his fiancée is?" Maddie asked.

Blake's eyebrows raised. "How would I know that if I don't know who the guy is?"

"Portia Vail," Ethan said, studying the man carefully when he revealed the name.

Blake Cordis paused as he was about to take another drag.

"Yeah, I know Portia."

"We know you do," Maddie said. "You met her back in April."

"Yeah," Blake said with a shrug. "We were dating." He took another pull from the cigarette. "But I didn't know she was engaged."

"She wasn't," Maddie said. "She and Nicholas were on a break. Until recently, when they decided to give it another go. You know anything about that?"

Blake squinted his eyes. "Asked and answered, detective. I didn't know she had a fiancé, which means I didn't know she'd gotten back together with him."

"When was the last time you saw Portia?"

"I, uh . . . it was, I guess a month ago. Beginning of summer, anyway. She broke things off and told me she needed some time."

"Time for what?" Maddie asked.

Blake shrugged. "It was just her way of telling me that she wasn't into me anymore. We were pretty casual."

"From what we know, you two were anything but casual."

"Look, for the first few weeks after we met, everything was great. Pretty normal stuff at the beginning, right after you meet someone and start hooking up. But then things cooled off and we were trying to figure out if we wanted a real relationship."

"As opposed to what?"

"Just hooking up. But when I told her I wanted a little more than that, she sort of put on the brakes."

"Did that upset you?"

Blake looked briefly at Ethan before returning his gaze to Maddie.

"Yeah. I was disappointed because I was into her."

Ethan chimed in. "But then she told you she was getting back together with her fiancé."

Blake calmly shook his head. "I can keep saying it as many times as you need to hear it. Portia never told me she had been engaged. And she never gave me a reason for wanting to break things off. She just stopped returning my calls. After a week or two, I got the point."

Ethan looked at Maddie. This made sense from what they'd seen in Portia's phone records.

"When was the last time you were in Milwaukee?" Maddie asked.

"About a month ago. Portia and I went out to dinner. It was the last time we were together. If you want the exact date, I'd have to check my credit card."

"What happened that night?"

"We had steaks at Mo's in the city, and I stayed at her place."

There was a short pause.

"What's going on?" Blake asked. "Something happen to Portia?"

"No one's seen her since Saturday morning, June twenty-eighth," Maddie said. "Didn't show up to work all week. Her fiancé called to report her missing on Friday, July fourth."

Blake Cordis slowly closed his eyes.

"And you saw my number in her phone and think I had something to do with it."

"It's a reasonable suspicion," Ethan said.

"This is the first I'm hearing about Portia being missing."

"You don't seem particularly concerned," Maddie said.

"I hope she's okay, but I didn't know her all that well. We dated for a few weeks and slept together a few times. That's the extent of it."

"You're just over thirty years old," Ethan said, "and in that short lifetime, you've now been, at the very least, acquaintances with two women who have gone missing. You've either got a terrible track record with women, or it's really dangerous to know you."

"Okay," Blake said, exhaling a cloud of smoke and nodding his head. "I get it. You guys did some poking around on me."

Ethan stood up. "Sure did, pal. Blake Cordis was a first-year history teacher and the head coach for Cherryview High School's girls' volleyball team in 2015 when another girl went missing."

"I'm not doing this again," Blake said.

"The DCI has reopened the Callie Jones case and put me in charge of the investigation."

Blake stubbed out his cigarette and also stood. "Am I being arrested for anything?"

"Not yet," Ethan said.

"Then I'm going to ask you both to leave."

"You don't want to answer any more questions about Portia?" Maddie asked.

"Not unless you're arresting me, and then not without my attorney being present." Blake smiled. "Are we good?"

"Don't plan on traveling anywhere," Maddie said. "Just in case we need to talk some more."

A few minutes later, Ethan and Maddie pulled through the cast-iron gate and sped away from Prescott Estates.

"What do you think?" Ethan asked.

"I don't know," Maddie said. "He seemed surprised to hear she was missing."

"Agreed. Or he's a really good actor."

Maddie looked at Ethan as they turned onto the lonely country road. "One thing is for sure. We're not going to get any information from Blake Cordis, which means you have to ask Francis what he wants. And you have to do it soon."

CHAPTER 44

Boscobel, Wisconsin
Monday, July 28, 2025

FOR THE FOURTH TIME IN TWO WEEKS, ETHAN SAT IN THE VISITATION booth at the Wisconsin Secure Program Facility. Less than twenty-four hours had passed since he was last face-to-face with his father's killer. He sat at a middle window in a long line of booths separated by wooden planks bolted into the cinderblock wall. It was taking longer than normal for Francis to arrive. Ethan worried that when he needed most to speak with the man, Francis would refuse his visitation request for the first time.

Finally, the light on the wall began to flash. A moment later the door buzzed and then opened. His father's killer shuffled to the booth and sat across from him. But Francis Bernard had morphed in the last few days into something other than the man who had killed his father. He had become, puzzlingly, a source of information that Ethan was dependent on. And the man seemed to know it.

Both men lifted their phones.

"You're going to tell me where Portia Vail is being held," Ethan said. "And after we make sure she's safe, you're going to tell me everything you know about Callie Jones."

"Of course I will," Francis said, as if insulted. "What do you think I am, an animal?"

"Talk."

"Talk?" Francis smiled. "The information I have is not free."

Ethan leaned closer to the glass. "You either tell me where this girl is being held, or your shitty life in this place will get much, much worse."

"Oh, Ethan. Let's agree to a couple of ground rules as we start negotiations. First, you stop making empty threats. You have no idea what my life is like in here, which is why you naively believe you can make it worse. You cannot, which is why I am in such a position of power. They've already stripped me of everything that they can legally get away with, and a few extras when they can. The petty things I'm allowed come only because the ACLU has forced the prison's hand, and the warden has no choice but to agree to those accommodations or lose funding. So I've hit what you call rock bottom, and there is no earthly way you can make things worse for me."

"Francis," Ethan said, matching the man's even tone. "Tell me where Portia Vail is being held."

"Second ground rule," Francis said. "I'm calling this a negotiation only in the sense that I'm going to give you something in exchange for you giving me something. But this is not a negotiation in the sense that we will haggle back and forth. I will tell you where Portia Vail is being kept. I will tell you where Callie Jones's body is located. In exchange, you will give me what I want."

Ethan stayed silent for a moment and thought through his options. He could hang up the phone, leave the prison, and work like mad to figure out the connection between Francis Bernard and Portia Vail. If he was lucky and caught the right breaks, he might find the girl alive. But the truth was that Francis had painted him into a corner, and they both knew it.

Francis's smile grew larger.

"You've figured it out, haven't you, Ethan. You've figured out that, from the confines of my isolated cell, I've trapped you. It's just occurred to you that you have no choice but to agree to my terms. Callie Jones has been dead a long time. Worms are slithering through that girl's bones. I knew there would be no sense of urgency to meet my demands just for what I can tell you about her case. But Portia Vail is another story. She's still alive. How long that remains the case is up to you, Ethan."

"What do you want?"

Francis's response came without hesitation.

"To be transferred out of this inhumane facility to Columbia Correctional Institution in Portage, Wisconsin. If Columbia was good enough for Jeffrey Dahmer, it's certainly good enough for Francis Bernard."

"A transfer?"

"Yes."

"How do you think I'm going to be able to get you transferred?"

"I want to be part of the general population, Ethan. I want to have a cell with bars, not the windowless room that's been my home for the last many years. I want to eat in a mess hall with other human beings, not in the confines of my cell. I want to walk outside in a prison yard and see the sun again. I want access to books and magazines. None of these demands are negotiable, and you have exactly one week to meet them."

"I'll ask you again, Francis. How do you think I'm going to be able to do what you're asking? And in that timeframe?"

"Because you have the ear of the governor, and he will be interested to know where his daughter's remains are located. With her remains is evidence that will reveal her killer. And I'm certain the governor doesn't want Portia Vail's blood on his hands. He has the power to get me transferred immediately. Today is Monday. I want to be transferred out of this hellhole in one week from today. If I'm not on my way to Columbia Correctional next Monday, the girl dies. Don't test me on this. The time you thought you had to figure out what happened to Callie Jones is gone. Poor little Portia Vail's life is now in your hands."

Francis lowered his voice.

"No time to think, Ethan. Only time to act."

Francis hung up the phone and stood. A guard was by his side a moment later leading him away from the visitation booth and back to his isolated cell with the windowless door from which Ethan knew he was about to be liberated.

CHAPTER 45

Madison, Wisconsin
Tuesday, July 29, 2025

THE MEETING TOOK PLACE THE FOLLOWING DAY AT THE EDGEWATER Hotel in Madison. It was their second meeting at the hotel. Ethan and Pete arrived first and were run through a security check before entering the suite. So much had happened since Saturday afternoon when Ethan and Pete had toured The Crest with Lindsay Larkin. And now, the clock was ticking. Pete stood at the window and looked down at Lake Mendota.

"They're here," Pete said.

Ethan joined him at the window to look down at the circular drive on the side of the hotel. Three black SUVs drove in and parked. Ethan watched as members of the Wisconsin Dignitary Protection Unit poured out of the first and third vehicles and cleared the path to the front entrance. Finally, Governor Jones climbed from the middle SUV and walked into the hotel. A few minutes later, Pete opened the door to the suite and the governor entered, while a member of the security detail waited in the hallway.

"Governor," Pete said, shaking hands.

"Sir," Ethan said, taking his hand.

"What have you learned?" Mark Jones asked, urgency in his voice. Even ten years after his daughter went missing, the man sounded desperate for answers.

"I'm not sure I've *actually* learned anything, but I definitely have some updates," Ethan said, pointing at the conference table where they all sat.

"I'm going to jump right in," Ethan said, "because we're under a time crunch due to developing circumstances."

Mark Jones nodded.

"As I'm sure you know, my father was a detective with the Milwaukee Police Department," Ethan started.

"I'm familiar with your history, yes."

"My father was killed in the line of duty in 1993. Francis Bernard is the name of the man who shot my father."

The governor nodded. "Bernard is currently at the Wisconsin Secure Program Facility in Boscobel."

"Correct. He's been there thirty-two years, and was up for parole just recently, which was denied. I went to see him afterward. He and I have had a bit of a fiery relationship."

"Understandable." Mark Jones pursed his lips. "But with all due respect, Ethan, what's Francis Bernard got to do with my daughter's case?"

"That's what I'm trying to figure out. I went to see Francis after the parole hearing. He knew that I had been assigned to reopen Callie's case."

"How the hell would someone who is basically in a legal version of solitary confinement know that we reopened my daughter's case?"

"Good question," Ethan said. "I suspect the information, which made it into the local papers, was leaked to him by a prison guard. That's my best bet."

"Okay. But why is this important?"

"Francis told me that he had information about your daughter's case."

Governor Jones placed his elbows on the conference table and slowly clasped his fingers together, squinting his eyes at the same time. "What kind of information?"

"He led me to an abandoned warehouse in Menomonee Valley. There, taped high on one of the walls, was an envelope that contained an old '90s-style flip phone. Pete and I did some forensics on the phone and discovered it was the prepaid phone that appeared in the list of calls made from Callie's phone."

The governor stood and began pacing the room.

"Please explain to me how a man who would be on death row in any state other than Wisconsin knows the location of the prepaid cell phone my daughter had been calling in the weeks before she disappeared. A phone everyone believes belonged to her abductor, but no one could find during the original investigation."

"I'm working on that, sir. Francis was already in prison in 2015 when Callie went missing, so we know that he was not directly involved with her disappearance. The information about the phone has to have come from the outside."

"How? Who?"

"A few options there," Ethan said. "First are the guards. They are Francis's only real source of information, and it's possible one of them knows something about your daughter's case. One or more of the guards could be feeding Francis information. Following that lead would require the establishment of a task force to look into each guard, their extended family, and acquaintances, to see if we can find a link back to your daughter. The second possibility we considered was that an old cellmate of Francis's provided him with information about your daughter, but to the best of our knowledge Francis has not had a cellmate in the last ten years since Callie went missing. And his interaction with other prisoners has been extremely limited. Francis has been in solitary confinement and with only short breaks from his living conditions."

"So you have no idea?" the governor asked.

"We have an idea," Pete said. "Actually, we think we've figured it out." Pete nodded at Ethan.

"We think the information Francis has is coming from someone who has visited him recently. Pete did some legwork through the DCI and obtained a visitor's log of everyone who has visited Francis Bernard in the last several years. The list is short. It includes me and a woman named Eugenia Morgan. Pete is taking the lead and putting her under surveillance."

"Who is she?"

"We don't know much yet, other than that she lives up in Nekoosa. We're working to figure out who she is and what her connection to Francis Bernard is."

"Where's the phone now?" Mark asked.

"I've got the forensics team at DCI looking at it," Pete said. "As soon as anything comes back, I'll let you know."

Ethan refrained from mentioning that he had Christian Malone working on recovering the deleted text messages from Callie's phone. Christian, he knew, had come to Cherryview to get away from stress and drama. Mentioning him to the governor was ill-advised.

"I want to see the son of a bitch," Mark said. "I want to see Francis Bernard."

"That's not a good idea," Ethan said.

"The bastard is dangling information about my daughter in front of us like a carrot. I want to speak with him."

"Hear Ethan out, Mark."

The governor stared at Pete a moment and then looked at Ethan and nodded.

"Francis has managed to put himself into a powerful position," Ethan said. "In addition to the cell phone, Francis led me to a photo of a woman named Portia Vail. She went missing from Milwaukee about a month ago. Francis knows that if his demands are tied to another girl who has recently gone missing, then we'll have to act quickly."

"Act quickly to do what?" Mark asked.

"Comply with his demand for a transfer to Columbia Correctional Institute, where security is lighter and where he will not be kept in solitary confinement."

The governor continued to pace.

"Francis also promises," Ethan said, pausing at what he needed to say. "To provide the location of your daughter's body in exchange for the transfer. And supposedly, with your daughter's remains are clues about who killed her."

The governor ran his hands through his hair. Ethan knew that even a decade later, Mark Jones had hoped his daughter might be found alive.

"Sorry to be so blunt about this, sir. But Francis knows you have the power to make the transfer happen, and he's giving you one week to get it done. He wants to be transferred next Monday."

"Or what?"

"Or Portia Vail dies."

CHAPTER 46

Nekoosa, Wisconsin
Tuesday, July 29, 2025

ELTON JOHN'S "GOODBYE YELLOW BRICK ROAD" ECHOED THROUGH the bathroom as she stepped from the shower and examined her body in the mirror. The tattoo of a python twisted around her calf and climbed up her thigh, slithering around her hip until the head of the snake crept to her navel, mouth open and fangs exposed. She turned sideways and raised her arm, pulling her right breast to the side to examine the newest tattoo etched into the side of her ribcage—a black heart.

As she dried her hair and applied makeup—dark eyeliner and thick mascara—she replayed her journey to the rail yard and the abandoned warehouse from two weeks before, and her success in securing the storage unit where she placed the contents of the footlocker. She wanted so badly to tell Francis how well she had done setting up all the photos just like he'd asked her, and that she had followed his every command to a tee. But she'd have to wait until the next time she saw him, which, if things went according to plan, wouldn't be long now. Soon she'd be able to see Francis as much as she wanted. They'd finally be together. But only if she followed the plan, and followed it perfectly.

She finished her makeup and then dressed. She checked her watch. Five minutes until the required therapy session began. She hurried to the kitchen table, opened her laptop, and followed the login prompts.

CHAPTER 47

Milwaukee, Wisconsin
Tuesday, July 29, 2025

Dr. Lindsay Larkin finished her morning meetings, skipped lunch, and took the cup of coffee her assistant handed her.

"What's my afternoon look like?" Lindsay asked.

"Busy," Beth said. "You've got six clients scheduled from noon until six o'clock. Then the evening board meeting until seven. Then the fundraiser at The Box."

"That's tonight?"

"Yes. Should I cancel?"

"No. I have to make an appearance."

Lindsay walked into her office and sat behind her desk. She lifted her cup. "Keep the coffee coming this afternoon. I'm exhausted."

"Will do. Let me know if you need anything else."

After Beth closed the door, Lindsay logged onto her computer and opened the case file for her first session of the afternoon. She scrolled and clicked through the encrypted screens until she was granted access to the virtual meeting room, where she waited for her client to arrive. Eventually, the link connected, and her client's face popped onto the screen. Lindsay turned on her microphone.

"Eugenia, good to see you."

Lindsay watched Eugenia Morgan smile into the camera and knew immediately something was off. Eugenia was an assigned client Lindsay had taken pro bono for the work she did for the state of Wisconsin Department of Corrections. *The Anonymous Client* had a long history of working with inmates to improve their mental health. Occasionally, a case like Eugenia's got passed to her, and Lindsay took it.

Eugenia Morgan suffered from hybristophilia, which was defined as the phenomenon of an individual being sexually aroused by and attracted to a criminal offender. Years before, Eugenia had fallen under the spell of a man convicted of kidnapping and raping a teenage girl. Eugenia had started a relationship with the man in prison, writing him letters and visiting him frequently. She had even agreed to marry him. When the convict sent Eugenia a letter instructing her to kidnap a girl and share photos with him, Eugenia had broken out of the spell long enough to go to the authorities. The convicted man was charged and tried for conspiracy to commit abduction and sex trafficking, found guilty, and sentenced to another two decades in prison.

In exchange for her cooperation, Eugenia was granted immunity but required to complete one hundred twenty hours of court-supervised therapy to deal with her hybristophilia. She'd been seeing Lindsay for months.

As Lindsay observed her client, she had a sense that Eugenia had regressed.

"How have you been, Eugenia? Since we last talked?"

"I don't know. Good, I guess."

"You don't sound convincing. Tell me about it."

Eugenia took a deep breath and looked away from the camera. "I don't want to get in trouble."

"Eugenia, anything we discuss during a session is protected by doctor-client privilege. Nothing you tell me will get you in any trouble."

"Yeah, but the judge who is making me meet with you, won't he find out what we talk about?"

"Absolutely not. I have no contact with that judge other than filling out the paperwork to show that you are completing the required therapy."

"You don't ever talk to him?"

"Never. And I wouldn't even if he contacted me. By law, I'm not allowed to divulge anything you and I discuss during our sessions."

There was a long pause. Lindsay was careful not to break the silence. It was important to allow Eugenia to initiate the discussion.

"I went to see him."

Lindsay slowly nodded. "Francis Bernard?"

Eugenia nodded. "Yeah. I visited him."

"When?"

"A few weeks ago. Just after the Fourth of July."

Lindsay was careful not to react to this. Instead, she nodded and kept an even tone to her voice. "Relapses happen. We should never feel ashamed about them. I could tell when you logged on that something was bothering you."

Lindsay paused.

"How do you feel about going to see him?"

Another long pause

"I wouldn't have gone if I didn't get a thrill from it."

"Getting a thrill from visiting Francis Bernard is one thing," Lindsay said. "Visiting a criminal in prison is not a crime, Eugenia. What got you in trouble last time was how far you allowed your relationship to go. You nearly became an accomplice in a crime."

Eugenia nodded. "I know. But I didn't. I went to the cops."

"What happened when you visited Francis?"

"We just talked. You can't, you know, touch each other or anything where he's at. He's behind glass the whole time."

"Did he ask any favors of you? Did he ask you to do anything for him that would put you in jeopardy of breaking the law?"

There was a long pause, longer than the others that had taken place during the session.

"No."

Lindsay knew she was lying.

CHAPTER 48

Nekoosa, Wisconsin
Tuesday, July 29, 2025

S HE CLOSED THE LAPTOP AFTER HER SESSION AND HURRIED OUT THE door. She had so much to do and so little time to do it. She drove two and a half hours into Milwaukee and found the Walker's Point neighborhood, where the gun shop was located on West Washington Street. Inside, the smell of metal and Rem oil greeted her. The suppressed pops from the shooting range out back subtly echoed into the display area. She walked to the counter and perused the guns for a moment until a kindly, middle-aged man with a white goatee and an enormous gut stood from the stool and came over to offer his assistance.

"Looking for anything in particular?" he asked in his polite, Midwest accent.

"Yes," she said. "I'm looking to add a handgun to my collection."

"Anything specific?"

The type of gun came from memory.

"A Sig Sauer P365 Rose."

The man nodded. "Excellent choice. We have several Sig Sauers on display."

"Would I be able to fire one?"

"Of course. We have a full range out back. I would just need a photo ID to run a background check to get things started."

She nodded and smiled, reached into her purse and produced a driver's license that she handed over to the portly man. She also produced a CCW permit, which she pushed across the counter. The man took the permit and the ID.

"Eugenia Morgan," he said as he typed her name into the computer. "Pretty name."

"Thank you."

"I'll run this quickly and pull the Sig from the back."

When the man returned, she filled out the necessary paperwork and was on the range twenty minutes later. She ran through a full magazine enjoying how the P365 felt in her hand. She was able to handle the mild kickback without a problem, and knew the gun would serve its purpose perfectly.

She would have to use it in the very near future and wanted to make sure that when she did, she hit the person she was aiming for.

CHAPTER 49

Milwaukee, Wisconsin
Tuesday, July 29, 2025

FOR HER SECOND PURCHASE, SHE CHOSE TACTICAL ZONE IN MILWAUkee. She walked into the store and found a sales rep.

"I'm looking for a Kevlar vest."

The man nodded. "We have several brands. Anything in particular?"

"I'll take your suggestion if you're able to show me a few."

"Sure. Follow me."

She followed the man to the northeast side of the store, where the combat paraphernalia and tactical equipment were located. Knives of all shapes and sizes decorated the wall, along with compasses, watches, canteens, and other essentials needed on the battlefield. There was even a corner display of beer cozies. It took twenty minutes for the man to showcase the Kevlar accessories, and she ended up choosing the Citizen Armor SHTF Tactical Vest, after the sales rep promised that if a round were shot into her chest, the vest would stop the bullet cold.

The purpose of the vest, she told the sales rep as she handed over her credit card, was a sport-shooting range program she was participating in that required all its participants to wear Kevlar. She gave no explanation for why she was also purchasing a Victorinox Swiss Army Knife with a drop point blade, but flirted just enough so that the man would remember the tall lady with jet-black hair and mesmerizing caramel eyes when authorities came to ask questions, which they surely would in the coming days.

"Good luck," the sales rep said, handing her the box with the Kevlar vest inside.

"With what?"

"The shooting-range program."

"Oh, right. Thank you."

She smiled and took the vest. She hoped a bullet never found her chest, but just in case something went wrong, she would be protected. Hope for the best, prepare for the worst.

She had just a few more tasks to complete before next Monday. She climbed into her car and adjusted the rearview mirror so that the unmarked police car came into view. She had learned the man behind the wheel—an older gentleman with a limp—was Pete Kramer, a special agent with the Department of Criminal Investigation.

She'd always known Francis was smart. But she was starting to suspect that he was a genius, and the long game he was playing was masterful.

CHAPTER 50

Beaver Dam, Wisconsin
Tuesday, July 29, 2025

THE WINDOW OF BLAKE CORDIS'S HOME OPENED WITHOUT PROTEST. There was no reason to lock the house. The chance that a random intruder would find their way to his cottage, which was situated in the middle of Prescott Estates, was a statistical improbability since there had never been a reported burglary on the grounds. Still, out of habit, Blake usually locked the front door. So, she had made sure to unlock this window the last time she was at the cottage to see him. She climbed through the window, carrying with her a Callaway 9-iron golf club, and headed straight for his office.

Sitting behind the desk, she logged onto Blake's computer. It took just a minute to access the internal links and get to the guts of the device. Ten minutes more and she had what she needed, and after another ten she had the computer set and organized. She skipped a dramatic exit out the window, choosing instead to leave through the front door. But before she did, she opened the closet in the front foyer and placed the 9-iron in the back corner. She grabbed a package of Saratoga 120 cigarettes off the coffee table on the way out, caring little if Blake Cordis questioned why his front door was unlocked when he returned home from work.

CHAPTER 51

Boscobel, Wisconsin
Wednesday, July 30, 2025

GOVERNOR MARK JONES WAS ESCORTED INTO WARDEN ARI CUT-lass's office at the Wisconsin Secure Program Facility on Wednesday morning. It had been less than twenty-four hours since his meeting with Ethan Hall, during which he had learned that Francis Bernard had set in motion a proverbial ticking time bomb that not only threatened a girl's life, but Mark's political career if he mismanaged things. He'd also learned, in the most definitive manner in a decade, that his daughter was dead.

"Governor," the warden said when he walked in. "To what do I owe the pleasure of an unannounced visit?"

"Hey, Ari. Sorry to drop in unannounced."

"Not at all. Something big must have come up to pull you out to crappy, little Boscobel from your cushy mansion in Madison. Something important?"

"I'm afraid so, yes. It has to do with one of your inmates. Francis Bernard."

"Bernard? He's a lifer." Ari looked up in contemplation. "Actually, he's not. He was grandfathered in and probably has mandatory parole coming at some point. But he's been here thirty years."

"Thirty-two," Mark said. "And I need a favor."

"Oh yeah?"

"We need to transfer him to Columbia."

"Why?"

"Grab a cup of coffee and take a seat. I'll tell you all about it."

After he listened to the governor's story, Ari Cutlass cocked his head. "That's quite a situation you're in. How long has this girl been missing?"

"A month. And my guys are worried she doesn't have much time left."

"Damn, Mark."

"Tell me about it. But there's even more to the story. Somehow the son of a bitch claims to have information about my daughter's case. And he's willing to hand over what he knows only after he's transferred. I'd consider this a personal favor, Ari, if we can make this happen quickly."

"Quick isn't the issue, Mark. I can send him up to Columbia today. The problem is the liability. If I approve the transfer and Bernard gets dumped into general population at Columbia and then kills someone, I'm on the hook."

"I'll make sure you've got immunity from any liability."

"That's a nice promise, but your signature will be on the transfer order below mine. So if something breaks bad up at Columbia, you'll be in as much shit as me."

"I'm calling in a favor, Ari. Not only for this missing girl, but for my daughter as well. What will it take to make this transfer happen on Monday?"

The warden looked up at the ceiling as he thought. "I'd at least need Bernard to undergo a psych eval and have the doc confirm that he's mentally fit to associate with other inmates. If we can get that, there'd be a layer of protection in place just in case something goes wrong up in Columbia. We can blame it on the shrink."

"How quickly can you facilitate a psych eval?"

"I'll make some calls. But scheduling the eval is not the problem. The sociopath passing it will be."

CHAPTER 52

Milwaukee, Wisconsin
Wednesday, July 30, 2025

Ethan was out to dinner with Maddie and doing his best to keep his mind occupied until he heard back from Mark Jones about the governor's progress with pulling strings to make the transfer happen on Monday.

"Do you think he'll be able to get it done in a week?" Maddie asked.

"If he believes Francis and his threats," Ethan said, "he doesn't have a choice but to get it done."

"Has Francis given you a reason not to believe him yet?"

Ethan shook his head. "Unfortunately, no."

His phone rang and he pulled it from his pocket.

"Ethan Hall."

"Hi. It's Lindsay Larkin."

"Yes?"

"Something's come up, and I need you to come to my office right away."

"What's the matter?"

"I need you to see something. And it can't wait."

Ethan looked at Maddie, who squinted her eyes to ask who was calling. Ethan held up a finger.

"It has to do with the case?" he asked.

"It does," Lindsay said.

"How pressing is it?"

"I need you to see this now. Tonight."

Ethan looked at his watch. "I'm in the city. I'll be there in thirty minutes."

CHAPTER 53

Milwaukee, Wisconsin
Wednesday, July 30, 2025

ETHAN DROPPED MADDIE AT HER HOUSE AND ARRIVED AT THE Anonymous Client headquarters at close to 8:00 p.m. He rode the elevator to the thirtieth floor and found Lindsay Larkin waiting for him when the elevator doors opened.

"Thank God," she said.

"What's wrong?"

"Follow me. I need to show you something."

Ethan followed Lindsay through the empty hallways. The employees had left for the night. He walked into Lindsay's office, and she pulled a chair behind her desk so that it rested next to hers.

"I need you to watch this," Lindsay said, pointing at her computer monitor.

"What is it?"

"Just sit."

They both sat and Lindsay worked the mouse until her computer monitor went momentarily black before blinking back online.

"What's this?" Ethan asked.

It looked like a pending conference call.

"I record my therapy sessions," Lindsay said. "With all my clients. It allows those clients who wish to review their sessions an opportunity to do so. It also allows me to refine my approach to certain clients."

"You record your online sessions?" Ethan asked. "Is that legal?"

"All our clients sign consent forms. So, yes, it's legal. I just finished a session with a new client this evening and I need you to see it."

Ethan looked at Lindsay.

"No," she said before Ethan could ask. "That is *not* legal. I could lose my license for what I'm about to show you, but I don't know what else to do."

Ethan looked from Lindsay to her monitor and back again. "What's going on?"

She clicked the mouse, and a recording of the therapy session began to play. In the upper right corner Ethan saw Lindsay's face appear in the window as she waited for her client to log on. Then, the larger window in the center of the monitor blinked to life, showing a blurred image of a person in a hoody, their features unrecognizable.

"What am I looking at?"

Lindsay paused the video. "The client used our encrypted filter to hide their image and disguise their voice. It's how clients who wish to stay anonymous, stay anonymous."

Lindsay clicked the mouse again and the video played.

"Good afternoon. I'm Dr. Larkin."

Ethan watched the screen as the anonymous client spoke for the first time. The person's voice crackled with an artificial intelligence filter that automated the human voice into what sounded like a customer service prompt.

"I need your help."

"Of course," Lindsay said. *"That's why I'm here."*

"I know you, Lindsay. And you know me. It's why I've come to you for help."

Ethan watched the monitor. On screen he saw Lindsay pause and look briefly into the camera, her eyes betraying her confusion, before continuing.

"Okay. What can I help you with?"

"I've done a terrible thing."

Another pause.

"Do you feel comfortable telling me about it?"

"I made a girl disappear."

Ethan continued to watch Lindsay Larkin on the computer screen, recognizing again the hesitation in her eyes. The image of the anonymous client was blurred and distorted and gave nothing away.

"Does, uh . . . this girl have a name?"

"Yes. You know her."

This time the pause was long enough for Ethan to turn from the computer screen and look at Lindsay. He saw fear in her eyes. Ethan swallowed audibly as he returned his gaze to the monitor. Finally, the anonymous client spoke.

"Her name is Callie Jones, and I need you to help me forgive myself for what I did to her."

CHAPTER 54

Milwaukee, Wisconsin
Wednesday, July 30, 2025

"**I** NEED THE NAME OF THE CLIENT," ETHAN SAID.

"I can't give that to you."

"I'll get a warrant."

"I don't think you understand. I can't give you the name of this client because I don't have it to give. I don't know the client's name, or anything about him. Or *her.* They used the encrypted anonymous filter."

"Give me a break. This whole thing is a gimmick. A very lucrative one, for sure. But I don't believe for a second that there's no way to find out who this guy is. How did he pay for the session? Judging by the looks of this place, you're not giving out free therapy."

"Our anonymous portal is handled by third party vendors, payments included. I can't get this person's name, even if I decided to break my ethical pledge in order to do so."

"The DCI has IT guys. They'll get through the encryption."

"I don't think so. When I created this company I did so with something like this in mind. And I started college as a computer engineering major before pivoting to psychology. I hired the best people to set up the anonymous features of the business because the entire company is based on the promise that the privacy and security I've put in place will protect my clients' identities. So, no, I don't think government-employed tech guys making sixty grand a year will be able to get through my encryption, even if I agreed to let them try."

"And you're telling me you won't?"

"No, I'm not going to allow the DCI to hack into my system publicly and expose my client. My livelihood is based on my company's reputation of keeping our clients anonymous. I've built this company quickly in just the last few years. Its explosive growth has happened exactly because I won't compromise my ethical obligations for *any* reason."

"Even to find Callie's killer?"

Lindsay took a deep breath. "Look, if I attempt to go behind the scenes to learn the identity of this client by pulling aside the security curtain I've put in place, and word gets out that I did so, my business would crumble. No one would trust my platform any longer."

"So why show this to me?"

"Because Callie was my best friend. And someone just admitted to killing her."

Ethan walked around to the other side of the desk.

"So if you won't allow me to hack your encryption, then what's your plan?"

"I want to keep meeting with the client. I think if I do, I'll get them to tell me who they are. It might take a while. Maybe a few sessions, but I'll be able to do it."

"I don't doubt it. From everything I've read about you, you're a very skilled psychologist. The problem with that plan is that we don't have that kind of time."

"What do you mean?"

"There's been a development with my investigation, and I've found myself up against the clock. I need to know who this client is, and I don't have time for you to pull it out of them over the course of several therapy sessions."

"What have you found?"

Ethan nearly told her about Portia Vail and that the girl's life was in his hands. He nearly told her about Francis Bernard and the man's impending transfer, which Mark Jones was racing to arrange for Monday. A transfer that Ethan might be able to stop if he could learn the identity of this anonymous client.

"Is it something about Callie?" Lindsay asked.

"It's related to her case. That's all I can tell you for now. But the bottom line is that we don't have time for you to meet with this client to learn their identity. That could take several sessions, and we can't do it. You'll just have to take my word for it."

Lindsay stood up and they faced each other across the desk.

"I'll let you look," she said. "I'll give you what I have on my end and see if your guys can get through the encryption. But I need you to promise me you'll do it quietly."

"I'll do better than to keep it quiet. I'll keep it off the grid."

"How do you plan to do that?"

"I know a guy who can help."

"At the DCI?"

"No. Just a friend."

CHAPTER 55

Cherryview, Wisconsin
Wednesday, July 30, 2025

IT WAS CLOSE TO 10:00 P.M. WHEN ETHAN PULLED UP TO THE MANSION that sat on the shores of Lake Okoboji. He rang the doorbell, which Ethan knew sent a soft tone through each room of the house. A moment later, Christian Malone answered the door.

"Sorry to call so late. But I'm in a bind and need some help."

"I'm still on Cali time. Ten o'clock is not late. What's going on?"

"I've got something else that's come up that I could use your help with."

"Come on in."

Ethan followed Christian through the enormous house and into the kitchen, where they sat at the island. Christian opened two New Glarus Spotted Cows and handed one to Ethan.

"Thanks," Ethan said.

"I'm still working on recovering the text threads from the girl's SIM card. I found the footprints, but the actual texts are still garbled with an old, first-generation type encryption. Looks like she used a text encrypting application to send and receive texts from the prepaid Samsung, and then deleted the texts afterward. The app used a time stamp that permanently erased the threads after seven days, so the likelihood that I'll recover all the texts are slim. The best I can do is try to pull the last few text threads that were sent before the phone's battery powered down, which would have stopped the time stamp. Should be a few days' worth if I can navigate through the encryption."

"Appreciate your efforts, Christian. I'm looking for a text thread from the Saturday she disappeared. That was July 18, 2015."

"The only way that will happen is if the phone's battery died down without being charged. If that happened within, let's say twenty-four hours of the girl going missing, then the encryption app wouldn't have been able to erase the last few texts she sent. I'll keep working on it. Something else came up, too?"

Ethan nodded. "Ever heard of *The Anonymous Client*?"

Christian shook his head as he took a sip of beer. "No."

"It's an online counseling platform based out of Milwaukee that offers psych consults and sessions from the comfort of your home."

"So you talk to your shrink over a Zoom call?"

"Sort of."

"You want me to talk to someone about my PTSD from passing my kidney stone?"

Ethan smiled. "One of the features of the platform, and what's made it so popular, is that patients can choose to speak to their doctor anonymously. The concept has eliminated the stigma that prevents most people from seeing a shrink."

"How does one go about staying anonymous?"

"Through an encrypted filter that hides their face and disguises their voice. I spoke with the founder of the company, and she told me that everything is handled through a third party. Payments, registration, everything. So if someone wants to stay anonymous, she claims they're able to."

"Interesting concept. Why are you telling me about it?"

"It has to do with the case I'm working on. The founder of *The Anonymous Client* was a friend of the victim back in high school. Her name is Lindsay Larkin and I've been working with her on the Callie Jones case. Earlier today, a new patient registered and logged into Dr. Larkin's online portal for a session with her using the encrypted filter."

"Okay?"

"During the session, this client confessed to killing Callie Jones."

Christian raised his eyebrows.

"There are some pretty strong laws pertaining to doctor-patient confidentiality. But if a patient confesses to a crime, those are thrown out the window. I could go through the proper channels and get a warrant. And then have the DCI tech guys try to get through the encryption."

"But?"

"But Lindsay Larkin is worried about her business, which prides itself on securing the privacy of those who login anonymously. If word got out that the DCI hacked into her counseling portal to find this client's identity, her business model would crumble."

"And? I highly doubt your main concern is some shrink's business model."

"No, my main concern is that I'm up against the clock. I've got a hard deadline on Monday, and, quite frankly, I'm not sure the guys at the DCI can get it done that quickly. But I thought if you took a look, maybe you could get through the encryption before then to learn this client's identity?"

Christian smiled and swiped a strand of blond hair out of his eyes. "Encryption, you say? So, what? You want me to hack her company's online program?"

"Is it possible?"

"To hack into this company's system? Of course it's possible."

"So will you do it? *Can* you do it?"

"Those are two different questions. *Can* I do it?" Christian made an ugly face. "Please. I wrote the encryption code for CramCase, and we've never been hacked. I know more about cyber security than the dorks who do it for a living. Of course I can do it. *Will* I do it? That depends."

"On what?"

"You promising me in some formal way that I won't eat shit for it. Listen, Doc, I don't mind digging through a dead girl's phone for you. But I came to Cherryview to get away from shit storms, not bathe in them. I'm enjoying my anonymity. No one knows me here except a few pickleball pals, and the last thing I need is a fat, ugly lawsuit shining a bright light at the shadow I'm hiding in. And that's what's waiting for me if I get caught hacking a nationwide company's online portal."

"You've got the CEO and founder's approval."

"I'll need that in writing and something from the higher ups. And this is nothing personal, Doc. I'm just telling you what my lawyers are going to tell me."

Ethan nodded. "So you want some *real* protection?"

"I want some sort of formal immunity that whatever I find won't blow back on me."

Ethan grabbed his phone from his pocket and dialed, putting the phone on speaker while it rang.

"Hello?" came the voice from the other line.

"Governor Jones, it's Ethan Hall. I think I'm close on Callie's case, but I need a favor."

CHAPTER 56

Nekoosa, Wisconsin
Thursday, July 31, 2025

SHE PULLED THE BLOND WIG OVER HER HEAD BEFORE LEAVING THE house on Thursday morning. She walked out the back door and across the street behind the home, clicking her key fob as she went. The Range Rover chirped as the doors unlocked and she climbed behind the wheel. She pulled away and doubled back through the neighborhood just to be sure. As she drove past the house, she offered no indication that she was aware of the unmarked police car parked down the street. It was the older gentleman with a limp again. The name *Eugenia Morgan* had appeared in Francis's visitor's log, and there was no doubt the DCI was working hard to figure things out. She needed to be careful. There were just a few days left.

On Tuesday, she had allowed the undercover officer to follow her to Milwaukee, where she made stops at the gun shop and tactical store. There was no harm in allowing him to see her purchase a gun and Kevlar vest. In fact, Francis wanted the authorities to know about those purchases. But for the final details she had been tasked with, she couldn't be followed. Hence, the blond wig and the second vehicle. They were looking for a tall, lanky woman with jet-black hair who drove a Ford Focus. The man behind the wheel of the unmarked DCI car was wholly uninterested in the blond woman driving past Eugenia Morgan's home in a Range Rover.

She slipped on her sunglasses as she passed the unmarked car without offering so much as a sideways glance. A peek in the rearview mirror confirmed that Special Agent Kramer was not interested in her. His car did not move. She drove toward Milwaukee and sped up and down Interstate 794 until she was convinced no one was following her, then took the exit and found Veteran's Park. She pulled into a spot in the north lot, a considerable distance from her destination. The walking path that meandered through the woods on the north edge eventually led to the lakefront. Lake Michigan offered a gentle breeze across her face, a delightful contrast to the torrid afternoon.

She found a bench near the water, took a seat, and pretended to scroll through her phone while she looked for anyone who might have followed her. She saw no one. Finally, she stepped back onto the walking path and made her way to a Little Free Library. The stand looked like a large birdhouse. The triangular structure was perched on an oak pole and housed a variety of free books for anyone to take.

She walked to the library stand and opened the door. From her purse she retrieved a paperback novel and set it on the shelf. In one swift motion she removed the envelope she had placed between the book's pages and secured it with tape to the inside of the library, fastening it to the ceiling. She perused the collection of books, finally settling on a Danielle Steel novel. She made sure the envelope was flat and secure against the ceiling.

Satisfied, she closed the door to the Little Free Library and walked back to the bench with her romance novel. She read the first three chapters while watching the park. When she was sure no one had followed her, she headed back through the woods to her Range Rover.

She put the address into the GPS and settled in for the five and a half-hour drive north to Ashland. The town was near Lake Superior and the Wisconsin-Minnesota border. There, just east of town, she'd find Lake Morikawa. Francis told her there were only eight homes on the expansive lake. One of them belonged to an elderly couple named Hugh and Ruth Winchester.

She was due to visit the Winchesters later that night. Although, they weren't expecting her. It was better for everyone that she arrive unannounced.

CHAPTER 57

Boscobel, Wisconsin
Thursday, July 31, 2025

FRANCIS WAS SITTING ON HIS BED IN THE WINDOWLESS CELL WHEN the buzzer rang, indicating that his door was about to be opened. This was the formal way prison guards entered his cell, not the way Andre Monroe did late at night. Since early summer, the head guard had been sneaking into Francis's cell and offering a continuous flow of news on Ethan Hall's investigation into Callie Jones, and updates on the latest developments with the Portia Vail case. In exchange, Francis gave Andre Monroe what he wanted. Refusing Mr. Monroe would bring a beating that Francis could not chance. An extended stint in the infirmary would disrupt his plans, so Francis had succumbed to Andre Monroe's demands. Today, though, something else was happening.

"Kneel in the corner," a guard yelled through the intercom system.

Francis stood from his bunk.

"Face the wall and place your hands behind your back."

Francis knelt in the corner, placed his forehead against the wall, and extended his hands behind him. Guards entered and cuffed his hands before lifting him off his knees. When he turned around, Andre Monroe was in his face.

"You've been summoned, Francis."

Francis stayed silent. An image from two nights earlier flashed in his mind of Andre Monroe with his pants to his knees grunting as he stood over Francis.

"The shrink wants a word. Probably worried that you're going to kill yourself."

The head guard leaned closer.

"Do you want to kill yourself, Francis?"

Francis stared past him and did not answer.

Andre Monroe's voice took on that of a child. "Do you need to talk to someone about your feelings?"

No answer.

"Get him out of here," Andre said.

The two guards on Francis's arms led him out of the cell. As he passed through the threshold, Francis knew Ethan Hall had started the transfer process. He had three more days in this hellhole.

CHAPTER 58

Lake Morikawa, Wisconsin
Thursday, July 31, 2025

THE LONG SUMMER DAY WAS COMING TO AN END BY THE TIME SHE reached Lake Morikawa. The horizon glowed with a cherry dusk. Clouds hung over the lake, their undersides burning with a blood-red tone. She couldn't help but think it was appropriate for what was about to happen.

She drove around the north side of the lake and started her way down the east edge. She found the driveway belonging to Hugh and Ruth Winchester and pulled in. A rest stop thirty minutes earlier assured that her legs were fresh after the long drive. The couple was elderly, but she still needed to be nimble. She was taking nothing for granted this late in the game. Mistakes needed to be avoided at all costs.

Stepping out of the car, she checked her purse for the knife. The closest neighbor was a long way off, but she couldn't risk using her Sig Sauer for fear that the shots would be heard. The knife would be messier and more work, but safer in the long run. She walked to the front door and rang the bell. A moment later, Ruth Winchester answered.

"May I help you?" the elderly woman asked.

"Yes. My name is Eugenia Morgan, and I'm hopelessly lost. I'm trying to find my way into town, but my navigation system isn't working, and, for the life of me, I can't make my way out of this area."

"Oh," Ruth said with a nod, "it can be confusing. And cellular service, or satellite signals, whatever makes those maps work, is always spotty around these parts. Let me get my husband. He'll be able to explain the route into town."

"Thank you. And sorry to intrude. It's getting dark and I just knew I'd have no chance once night came."

"Wait just a sec, hon. I'll grab Hugh."

She waited on the front porch as the woman retreated into the home, then reached into her purse and removed the knife. She held it down at her side. After a minute, Hugh Winchester came to the door. The man was old and feeble, the decades bending his spine into a hunched posture. He pushed open the screen door.

"What can I help you with?"

He'd barely gotten the words out before she lifted the knife and dragged it across the left side of his neck. The sheer volume of blood that poured over the man's shoulder and down his chest told her she'd severed his carotid artery. Hugh Winchester offered a confused expression before he grabbed his neck, recognized the blood, and collapsed.

She wasted no time stepping over his body and entering the home. She found the wife standing at the kitchen sink. She walked up behind her and repeated the process. Two minutes after she arrived, the Winchesters were bleeding out. Hugh in the front hallway; Ruth on the kitchen floor.

The faucet was still running. She dipped the knife under the stream before returning it to her purse. Then she drank a glass of water and started the cleanup. An hour later, the hallway to the garage was streaked with blood and the bodies were stacked in the subzero freezer. She made sure the front door was closed, and then climbed back into her car for another long drive. This time she was headed to the Mexico border.

CHAPTER 59

Madison, Wisconsin
Friday, August 1, 2025

THE MEETING WAS ORGANIZED AGAIN AT THE EDGEWATER HOTEL IN Madison. It was Friday afternoon. Ethan stood with Pete Kramer as the door to the suite opened and Mark Jones walked in. He held a manila file in his hands.

"Gentlemen," Mark said. "Let's sit."

They all took seats around the conference table.

"Ari Cutlass is the warden over in Boscobel. He and I go back a ways so I called in a favor. He agreed to the transfer on Monday, but only if he could get one of the prison shrinks to sign off on it."

"In case there's blowback?" Pete said.

"Exactly. Ari's worried that after so many years in solitary confinement Francis will lose his shit when they place him in gen pop. And if he kills someone, Ari doesn't want to be on the line for the repercussions."

"Did you arrange the psych eval?" Ethan asked.

"Yesterday," Mark said. "The son of a bitch not only passed, he did so with flying colors."

"So we have everything we need to process the transfer?" Pete asked.

The governor looked at Ethan. "Almost."

Ethan nodded, pulled an envelope from his back pocket, and slid it across the table.

"My letter," Ethan said. "To the parole board, the warden, and the Wisconsin Department of Corrections expressing my wish for

Francis Bernard to be transferred from the Wisconsin Secure Program Facility to Columbia Correctional Institute in order to provide him with better living conditions and more freedoms after thirty-two years of rehabilitation."

Ethan swallowed down the rancid stomach acids that climbed his esophagus.

The governor took the envelope.

"Thank you," Mark said. "I know writing that letter was not easy."

"The bottom line is that the scumbag is still going to be behind bars," Ethan said. "And if this gets us information on your daughter's killer and the location of Portia Vail, it's worth the pain it caused to write it."

Ethan didn't mention that in the back of his mind existed the hope that Christian Malone would come through for him and find the identity of Lindsay Larkin's anonymous client before Monday morning. There was still a chance he'd stop Francis from going anywhere.

The governor placed Ethan's letter into the folder, adding it to Francis Bernard's psychiatric evaluation and the formal letter from the governor's office. It completed the file and, once delivered to the prison, would begin the expedited process of transferring Francis Bernard to Columbia Correctional on Monday.

"So how is this going to work?" Pete asked.

Ethan cocked his head. "Francis said that once the transfer order is complete and he's on his way to Columbia, he'll tell me everything he knows about Callie's killer and Portia Vail's whereabouts."

"Bastard is going to wait to the last minute," Mark said. "And according to Ari Cutlass, Francis is going to have his attorney look over the documents to make sure the transfer happens and we're not just baiting him into giving up information."

"What a wonderful justice system we have," Pete said. "Where a cop killer can manage to wield such power from inside a prison cell."

Mark looked at Ethan.

"Any movement on figuring out how Francis knows anything about my daughter or Portia Vail?"

Ethan shook his head. "Nothing so far. Pete's been keeping an eye on Eugenia Morgan."

"Not much there," Pete said. "She purchased a gun this week but hasn't gone near the warehouse that Francis sent Ethan to. If the woman has anything to do with feeding Francis information, we can't figure out what it is. And Eugenia Morgan has been a dead end when it comes to linking her to Portia Vail in any meaningful way."

The room went silent for a moment as they all allowed the weight of the situation to sink in.

"What's our play here, gentlemen?" Ethan asked.

"I'll formally put the transfer through," Mark said. He looked at Ethan. "I'll need you in Boscobel Monday morning to speak with Francis before the transfer and get the information he's dangling in front of us."

Ethan nodded. *Come on Christian. Work your magic.*

CHAPTER 60

Hachita, New Mexico
Saturday, August 2, 2025

ANTELOPE WELLS, NEW MEXICO WAS THE LEAST TRAFFICKED PORT of entry along the U.S.-Mexico border. Forty-five miles north of Antelope Wells was Hachita, New Mexico—the last smudge of civilization before the United States banked up against Mexico. Hachita was a twenty-four hour drive from Nekoosa. The route down took her through five states—Iowa and Missouri first, before she drove diagonal across the entire state of Kansas. She stayed at a cheap hotel in Dodge City Friday night.

Up early on Saturday morning, the second leg of her journey took her across the panhandle of Oklahoma and the northwest tip of Texas before she entered New Mexico, where she drove for hours without stopping. The schedule Francis had her on left no room for unnecessary stops, which was why she wore an adult diaper for the hours-long voyage.

She pulled into the dusty town of Hachita at 4:30 p.m. on Saturday afternoon, and her timing could not have been better. She found the post office, parked in front of the small building, and waited. She watched a postal worker emerge just before 5:00 p.m. and walk to the mailbox at the end of the parking lot. The man keyed the box and removed the tray inside that had caught the envelopes dropped into the slot throughout the day. She watched the man place a new, empty tray inside the box before walking back into the post office.

She lifted the packet from the passenger seat. The tan manila envelope had kept her company for the long drive from Wisconsin. It was addressed to Eugenia Morgan and had arrived in Nekoosa earlier in the week. It carried Francis's familiar cursive, and her insides stirred when she looked at his handwriting. Francis had been strict with his orders on how she should handle the envelope, and she followed his instructions to a tee.

Before touching the package, she slipped her hands into latex gloves. She unclasped the gold metal clip that kept the envelope closed and tore through the adhesive seal. She looked inside and saw a single, unsealed, white envelope. She pinched the corner with her thumb and index finger and drew it out of the larger manila packet.

The name on the envelope was again written in Francis's immaculate cursive.

Special Agent Ethan Hall

There was a letter inside, but she didn't bother to read it. Francis had not instructed her to do so. She reached into her purse and found the key to the storage unit she had rented, which she dropped into the envelope before sealing it closed using a damp cloth, not her own saliva. She climbed from her car and hurried into the post office. The mail carrier was sorting packages behind the counter when she approached.

"Hi there," she said.

The man turned, clearly shocked by the tall, beautiful woman with jet-black hair and burning brown eyes.

"Hi," he said. "We're just about to close."

"Oh, good. I made it just in time."

Still wearing the latex gloves, she held up the envelope. "I need to mail this, but I'd like it to go out in a few days from now. Is that possible?"

The man bobbed his head back and forth. "I can put a delay on it. When did you want it postmarked?"

"Thursday. You can do that?"

"Sure," the man said, reaching for the envelope. "I can do that."

If he noticed her latex gloves, he never showed it. He placed the envelope on the scale and checked the postage.

"You've got plenty of stamps on it, so you're good to go. Is that all you needed?"

"That's it. I appreciate your help."

"No problem."

She smiled and twisted her head a bit. "You're sure it will go out Thursday?"

"I'll mail it myself. It's in good hands."

Another smile. "Thank you," she said before leaving the post office and climbing back into her car.

The package would start its voyage north on Thursday and would not arrive at Ethan Hall's home until next weekend. By then, she and Francis would have already started their new life together. Just a few more days, but so much to do.

Another few minutes passed until she saw the postal worker leave for the day. He locked the front door to the post office before climbing into the only other car in the parking lot and driving off down the dusty road to nowhere.

With the post office parking lot abandoned, she reached into the backseat and grabbed a new adult diaper. Stepping out of the car, she quickly lifted her skirt and pulled the wet, sagging diaper she was wearing down her legs and stepped out of it. She yanked the new one into place and felt immediate relief. Inside the car, she found her Adderall in the glove box and swallowed two tablets. She would not have the luxury of a hotel stay on the way back to Nekoosa. She had too much to do before Monday morning.

She pulled out of the parking lot, leaving a trail of dust in her wake and the wet diaper on the pavement.

CHAPTER 61

Cherryview, Wisconsin
Sunday, August 3, 2025

IT WAS SUNDAY EVENING WHEN ETHAN FINALLY GOT THE CALL FROM Christian.

"Got it?" Ethan said when he answered.

"Unfortunately, no. Dr. Larkin wasn't kidding when she said she had top-notch encryption in place. It's taking me longer than I had anticipated to crack. I'll get through it, but not before Monday, Doc. Sorry, pal."

Ethan took a deep breath. "No worries. I know you're doing everything you can. Keep at it. Even if it comes after tomorrow, I need to know what you find."

"Will do. But on a side note," Christian said. "I was finally able to recover Callie Jones's text messages from her SIM card. And I think you're going to want to see them."

"I'll be over in a few."

Christian handed Ethan a Spotted Cow when he answered the door.

"Come on in. The text threads are pretty garbled up, but I think I got most of what's left of them."

Ethan took a sip of beer as he followed Christian through the palatial home and into the man's tech lair, where the air was considerably cooler than the rest of the house to keep the bank of computers and processors working efficiently. Screens glowed and blinked from every corner. Christian sat in front of one of the monitors and attacked the keyboard in impossibly quick strokes.

"I told you that the girl used an app to encrypt her texts, and then delete them after they were sent. The application she used no longer exists, which is why it took me so long to recover the texts. I had to reverse engineer the old technology in order to gain access. And even now, I don't have everything. But I found the thread from Saturday, July 18, 2015. That's the night she disappeared, right?"

Ethan remembered touring The Crest with Lindsay Larkin and hearing that Callie had left abruptly after receiving a text. No one had seen her since, other than Jaycee Jones, Callie's younger sister, when Callie stopped home briefly for a sweatshirt.

"Yeah, that's the night."

"I figured," Christian said. "Because it's the last text thread that showed up on her phone. Came in at 9:02 p.m."

Christian pecked at the keyboard for another second until the text thread appeared. He pushed against the desk and sent his wheeled chair sliding to the side to give Ethan access. Ethan moved closer and read the thread.

What's wrong?
I need to see you.
Where are you?
The Crest.
You okay?
I need to talk to you about the baby. I'm keeping it.
You didn't go through with it?
No. I want this baby WITH YOU. I want to start a life with you. I need to see you tonight.
Do you have your parents' boat?
Yes.
Meet me at North Point Pier. I'll be waiting on the dock.
I love you, Blake.
I love you, too.

Ethan looked up from the monitor.

"So," Christian said. "The million dollar question is: Do you know who *Blake* is?"

Ethan put the beer on the desk and ran for the door.

"I do."

Summer 2015

Cherryview, Wisconsin

*T*HE LAKE WAS LIKE GLASS. CALLIE CUT ACROSS THE SURFACE IN HER PARENTS' *Malibu 20 VTX Crossover as the horizon glowed lavender—the final efforts of a long summer day. After she left The Crest she stopped home, a brief detour to grab a sweatshirt in case she and Blake decided to cruise the lake while they talked. Her mother and Damien were out, so Callie had only to fend off her younger sister. Jaycee wanted to know where Callie was heading, if not back to the party at The Crest.*

"Out," Callie said.

"Out where?"

"Just out."

The encounter was brief, and Callie knew her curtness might backfire. If Jaycee was in a mood, she'd call their mother and tell her that Callie was up to no good. Then, Callie's phone would ring relentlessly from her mother's calls. But she had no time to talk to her younger sister. And some part of her didn't care if her mother knew what she was doing or who she was meeting.

Now, as she cruised across the lake she felt free and light. Her parents' scorn seemed to drown in the wake behind her. Callie suddenly cared little about what her mother might say when she heard about the pregnancy or her decision to keep the baby. Or what her new life would mean for her father's political career. Or about college or medical school or her scholarship or winning the state championship for a third straight year. All those things had fallen into the shadows, outshined by the joy of her baby and the life she and Blake would have together.

As she approached North Point Pier, the dock came into view. The glow on the horizon was just bright enough to light her way. She cut the Malibu's engine, the wake splashing behind her as she cranked the boat into reverse to slow her momentum and maneuvered next to the long dock. It was empty.

"Where are you?" she whispered into the night.

The length of the dock glowed in the moonlight as Callie stepped onto it. The tarnished burn of the moon lay across the surface of Lake Okoboji. From the middle of the lake, the lights from The Crest were visible. Echoes of music gamboled across the water's flat surface. As she tied off the boat, she squinted into the parking lot but saw no cars. North Point Pier was used as a boat launch, and as Callie walked down the dock she expected to see him waiting for her in his car.

She placed a hand on her stomach and closed her eyes, imagining the child that was growing in her womb. It had been just two days since she visited the Planned Parenthood clinic, where Cheryl the nurse convinced her to take a moment before making a decision that she couldn't undo. The plan was to take a day or two to think about things, and if Callie still wanted to go through with the procedure then she'd come back, and Cheryl would help her through the process.

But from the moment Callie left the clinic, she knew she could never go through with it. A strange but magical connection had developed between her and her unborn child. It was something she didn't understand and could never explain, but that connection had brought her here to North Point Pier to meet the person she wanted to start a life with.

Would everyone agree with her decision? Callie was sure not. But it was her decision to make, and hers alone. Not her mother's or her father's or any of her friends'. It was her life, and no one would tell her how to live it any longer. She'd spent years listening to the plans other people made for her. From volleyball and how to spend every waking moment—at the gym or on the court—to her studies and her future. But with the life growing inside of her, she was ready to leave it all behind. Her parents would argue that she was throwing away an opportunity of a lifetime. But really, she was simply choosing another path. That of motherhood, and it felt so perfectly right. She sensed the heavy burden of the past few years lift from her shoulders, and, for the first time in many years, Callie Jones was excited about her future.

She walked to the end of the pier and stepped off the dock. Cicadas buzzed and echoed into the night. A dog barked in the distance. And a twig snapped behind her. Before she could turn around, she felt a crack on the back of her skull. The impact was jarring—stunning her and stopping her in her tracks. She had the wherewithal to turn around, her eyes wide and unblinking as she spun. Another blow followed. This one to the crown of her head. A stream of warmth flowed from her hairline and ran the length of her cheek. She put her hand to her face. When she pulled it away, thick red blood covered her fingers.

A third blow came and brought blackness to her world.

CHAPTER 62

Beaver Dam, Wisconsin
Sunday, August 3, 2025

ETHAN LEFT CHRISTIAN'S HOUSE AND CLIMBED INTO HIS WRANGLER. It was close to eleven o'clock when he turned onto Highway 151 and headed north toward Beaver Dam. He twisted the Jeep off the highway fifty minutes later and took backroads until he reached Prescott Estates. He drove past the main gate and the security booth where he and Maddie had passed through a week ago, opting instead to pull onto the shoulder a half mile down the road.

He killed the engine, cut the headlights, and stepped out into the humid night. The sky was pocked with stars, and cicadas buzzed from the darkness. He walked to the white wood lap rail fence that enclosed Prescott Estates, and which ran as far as the moonlight allowed him to see. Ethan made quick work of scaling it. He walked across a large field until he found a trail that ran parallel to the road he and Maddie had driven Monday. He walked a half mile until the horse stables came into view, continuing on until he saw Blake Cordis's cottage in the distance, warm yellow light spilling through the windows.

Ethan stopped at the edge of the drive that led to the cottage and took a quick look around before continuing on. He climbed the three steps to the front door and was about to knock when he heard the snap of a shotgun closing. He didn't bother raising his hands or looking anything other than relaxed as he turned around to see Blake Cordis standing at the bottom of the porch with a

12-gauge firmly planted in his right shoulder, the barrel staring Ethan down. When Blake recognized him, he lowered the gun.

"You trying to get yourself killed?" Blake asked.

"Just came to ask some follow-up questions."

"Really? At midnight? You're trespassing."

"Call the cops," Ethan said.

Blake further lowered the shotgun until it hung from his right hand and pointed at the ground.

"Callie Jones purchased a prepaid cell phone so you two could communicate."

Blake lowered his head, and his shoulders slumped.

"She received a text from that phone at nine o'clock the night she disappeared."

Blake shook his head. "I had nothing to do with Callie going missing."

"The evidence I've uncovered tells a very different story."

"There's no evidence that I did anything to her."

"Because you got rid of it?"

"Because there was never any to find."

"Callie was pregnant," Ethan said.

When Blake said nothing in response, the buzzing cicadas suddenly sounded louder than just a moment before.

"You were the father."

The cicadas continued on as Ethan paused.

"She decided to keep the baby rather than go through with the abortion down in Chicago."

Blake ran his left hand through his hair while continuing to hold the shotgun with his right.

"How the hell do you know all that?"

"I was hired to look into her case. That's what I've been doing."

Blake took a deep breath and pointed at the door behind Ethan. "Let's go inside."

Ethan nodded. Blake walked up the steps and opened the front door. Ethan followed him inside and felt the cool reprieve of air conditioning when he walked into the cottage. Blake set the shotgun against the wall and walked into the kitchen.

Ethan lifted the gun and cracked the barrel open. "Do you mind?"

Blake waved his hand. "Help yourself."

Ethan removed both shells and dropped them in his pocket before returning the shotgun to the corner.

"Beer?"

"Yeah," Ethan said.

Blake grabbed two Coors Lights from the fridge and placed them on the kitchen table as he took a seat. Ethan sat down across from him. They both opened their beers and took a sip.

"Yes," Blake said. "Callie was pregnant. And, yes, I was the father."

"She went to Chicago to have an abortion."

Blake took another sip and then stared at his beer can as he spun it in the circle of condensation that formed on the table.

"She went to the clinic, but never had an abortion. I told her I wanted to keep the baby, but I understood if she didn't. She had so much going on, and I told her it was her call."

"You ever tell Pete Kramer any of this back in the day when he was investigating?"

Blake shook his head. "No. He never asked, and I never offered. I knew coming forward about my relationship with Callie would paint me as the main suspect. And since I had nothing, and I mean *nothing*, to do with Callie going missing, I stayed quiet."

Ethan considered Blake Cordis as he took a sip of beer. Just like during his visit with Maddie, Ethan considered that the man was either a very good actor or telling some form of the truth.

"Let's do this," Ethan said. "I'll tell you what I think happened, and you tell me if I'm right or wrong."

Blake nodded.

"You were having a sexual relationship with Callie Jones, one of your student athletes. You were a legal adult, twenty-one years old in July of 2015. You'd be twenty-two in September. Callie was seventeen. You got her pregnant, and an abortion was the only way to keep your relationship secret. But after thinking about it, Callie decided to keep the baby. On Saturday night, July 18, 2015, she texted you to tell you. You texted back and forth using the prepaid Samsung phone, and she told you she was keeping the baby and wanted to start a life with you. With nowhere left to go, you took matters into your own hands. You told Callie to meet you at North Point Pier, where you killed her."

Blake smiled and finished his beer in one long swig, then cocked his head.

"Wrong, wrong, and let's see, oh yeah, wrong again."

"You and Callie used a text encryption app to communicate and erased your text threads after you sent them. You were clever and careful, but I was able to recover the texts, Blake. I saw the thread from the night Callie disappeared."

"Maybe you did. And that probably explains a lot. But it doesn't mean I killed her."

"Then explain what I'm getting wrong."

"You've got most of it right. I was in love with Callie Jones, no doubt about that. I still love her to this day. I talked her *out* of having an abortion, not into having one. I wanted to start a life with her. But she had her whole life in front of her—college and medical school, and she felt the pressure of the world on her shoulders. Her parents were lunatics. Her father, our great Wisconsin governor, was MIA during her high school years, more interested in his career than he ever was in Callie. Her mother was bipolar and lived vicariously through Callie, as if Callie's successes were her own. If Callie didn't thrive in every way—academically, athletically, socially—her mother would go into deep bouts of depression. And Callie had to carry all that around. So I told her that I understood if she didn't want what I wanted."

"But to the contrary, Blake. Callie texted you that night. Told you she wanted a life with you. You told her to meet you at North Point Pier. What happened after that?"

Blake shook his head. "You see, that's where you've got things wrong."

"Enlighten me."

Blake tossed his empty beer into the garbage and grabbed another from the fridge.

"I lost the prepaid. I had it Friday night when Callie and I texted. But sometime on Saturday, the phone disappeared. I wanted to tell

Callie but couldn't risk texting her from my own phone. I knew she was going to a party with her friends on The Crest Saturday night, and we had plans to see each other Sunday. I figured if I didn't find the phone by then, I'd tell her Sunday, and we'd buy another one."

Ethan squinted his eyes. He tried to read the man across the table. Although it had been a decade, Ethan had conducted many such conversations with kid killers in the past, and none had been as convincing as Blake Cordis was tonight.

"You didn't have the Samsung on Saturday? The day Callie went missing."

"No, sir, I did not. And if you're claiming someone texted Callie that night to lure her to North Point Pier, I believe you. But it wasn't me."

Blake took a sip of beer.

"I swear to God. It wasn't me."

Ethan jumped the rail fence and headed toward his Jeep. He climbed inside and started the engine. The headlights illuminated the gravel shoulder in front of him, and the bugs swirling in the night. The hum of the cicadas was audible even inside the Wrangler. But all of it was lost on him. Ethan's mind was churning, and his gut was telling him that he had things wrong. That Blake Cordis was not the man he was looking for, and that some other insidious puzzle was unfolding in front of him. The time he needed to unravel the mystery, he knew, was gone. Francis was set to be transferred in the morning, and Ethan was no closer to finding Callie Jones or Portia Vail than he had been when he started looking.

He had no choice but to go to Boscobel and grovel for answers.

CHAPTER 63

Nekoosa, Wisconsin
Sunday, August 3, 2025

AFTER THE NECESSARY GAS STOPS AND A FOUR-HOUR NAP AT A TRUCK stop, she arrived back in Wisconsin at 10:00 p.m. on Sunday night. She followed her Range Rover's GPS past Boscobel and turned onto Wisconsin Highway 58 north of Ithaca. There, she found a lonely stretch of road just past a bend in the highway. She steered the Range Rover onto the shoulder and continued onto the grassy embankment until she pulled into the foliage that flanked the highway. She grabbed the bag of fast food off the passenger's seat and exited the vehicle on stiff and aching legs. She discarded the diaper in the woods and limped back to the road. Surveying her work, she was satisfied that the Range Rover was hidden well enough.

She walked two miles to a gas station and called an Uber for a ride back to the house in Nekoosa.

She paid the driver and walked up the driveway. She looked down the street, but the unmarked cruiser was gone. Special Agent Kramer had never watched Eugenia's house overnight. He usually showed up in the mornings to poke around and keep tabs on her, but by mid-morning tomorrow she'd be long gone. It was just before midnight when she punched the code to open the garage door. She stepped inside and saw the Ford Focus parked in the second bay. She allowed the feeling of satisfaction to course through her body. But only for a moment. There was still much to do.

She dropped the car keys into the bowl on the kitchen table and opened the door to the basement, slowly descending the stairs and making sure nothing was out of order. In her hand was the grease-stained fast food bag, whose contents had long since run cold. The journey to the southern border had taken more than two days, and she knew the woman would be starved. She needed her to be calm and docile in a few hours, and the sedatives in the food would assure as much.

When she reached the basement landing she headed to the door and peeked into the room. The woman was lying on the bed, shackles attached to her wrists and ankles. She threw the bag of food into the room and then hurried up the steps to bed. Francis had insisted she find time for sleep so that she was as fresh as possible when he needed her most.

Perhaps it was because the end was so near, or because her new life was about to start. Whatever the reason, when her head of jet-black hair hit the pillow, she fell fast asleep and dreamt of Francis during her slumber. Months of planning had shrunk to weeks. Weeks to days. And now mere hours stood in the way of their new beginning together.

PART VI

Transfer of Power

CHAPTER 64

Boscobel, Wisconsin
Monday, August 4, 2025

FRANCIS LAY ON HIS BED WITH HIS HANDS BEHIND HIS HEAD AND LEGS crossed. He'd been awake since 4:00 a.m. He looked around the cell and took inventory of his meager belongings. His entire life consisted of a single, tattered paperback novel, a week-old newspaper, and three pieces of prison stationery. But all of that was about to change.

The muted buzz of his prison cell door unlocking echoed through the hollow space where he had spent the last many years of his life. He quickly sat up on his bed.

"Stand up," a guard said through the intercom system. "Kneel in the corner and put your hands behind your back."

It was the first time Francis was happy to go through the rigmarole. He knew today would be the last time he'd have to tolerate such a demeaning task as kneeling in the corner of a room. He did as instructed and placed his hands behind his back. A guard entered the cell and handcuffed him. The guard leaned over his shoulder and whispered into his ear.

"Don't know who you serviced to pull this off, but your ticket somehow got stamped for Columbia."

The guard took him by the elbow and lifted him to his feet.

"Let's go. Gotta get you into the transport suit."

Francis allowed the guard to lead him out of the cell and through the prison. He felt the eyes of the other inmates as they watched through the slatted glass windows of their cell doors.

Poor bastards, Francis thought. They had no freedom and no hope of ever acquiring it. Hope had kept him alive all these years. Hope and the determination to think his way out of this place. Boscobel was designed to ruin both the mind and the spirit, but Francis had found a way to stay sharp and active. Hope had been his savior to this point. He had faith that the one person he trusted would get him through this day and beyond.

When they reached the staging area, three additional guards waited for him. The red transport suit hung on a heavy-duty rack. Made of reinforced foam-dipped neoprene, the suit protected both the inmate being transferred and the guards who were transferring him. Once the suit was in place, Francis would barely be able to move. It consisted of several pieces, each of which was secured by a separate locking mechanism. A padded sleeve was fastened around each of his arms and legs. A vest was tightened around his chest to the degree that it restricted his breathing. And finally, a red, padded helmet with a single horizontal slot for his eyes was placed over his head.

"Looks like the Michelin Man," one of the guards said before they all laughed.

Francis heard a door hiss open, and the guards quickly went silent. He was unable to move, and the helmet restricted his vision, so all he was able to do was stand and wait. Finally, from his right field of vision a face emerged. It was Andre Monroe.

The head guard smiled as he stared at Francis.

"Time to hit the road, big boy. I've been assigned to take you to Columbia."

Monroe lowered his voice.

"Don't worry, though. I called my buddies up in Portage to let them know how accommodating you are to the guards, especially late at night. You're going to be a big hit, and my friends can't wait for you to arrive."

Francis said nothing. He wouldn't give the man any reason to impede the transfer.

"I've got some bigwig here who says he needs to talk with you before the transfer. He's from the governor's office or some shit. You talk to him here and then we move."

Monroe turned his head and whistled. Francis heard the door hiss open again, followed by slow and methodical footsteps, and then Ethan Hall's face came into view through the eye slot of the transport helmet.

For the first time in days, Francis allowed himself to smile.

CHAPTER 65

Nekoosa, Wisconsin
Monday, August 4, 2025

HER PHONE BUZZED WITH THE SONG SHE HAD SET TO WAKE HER—
"Goodbye Yellow Brick Road" by Elton John.

Her eyes did not flutter open. They did not squint to fight off
the morning light. Instead, her eyelids bolted upward, wide and
alert, her veins filled with adrenaline. It was as if she had slept for
twelve hours rather than four. She jumped from bed and felt the
freedom of leaving it all behind. The impulse to make the bed was
replaced by the notion that after today she would never be back inside this house. Abandoning the messy sheets left her feeling giddy
and reckless.

She turned on the home's entertainment system, which had
speakers in every room, and set "Goodbye Yellow Brick Road" on
repeat. She turned up the volume as Elton John crooned through
the speakers of the home, loud enough to drown out the whispers
of doubt and regret she knew would begin echoing from the dark
corners of her mind, but not so loud to alert the neighbors.

She hurried to the bathroom and looked in the mirror. She had
removed the brown-colored contacts the night before, bringing
her irises back to their natural blue tone. The color remover waited
on the vanity. She mixed it with baking soda until the bowl was
filled with a thick, bubbling paste that she massaged into her jet-
black hair. The lather foamed and stung her scalp, but she continued until the mixture began to froth with the black dye in her hair.

She climbed into the shower and put her head under the spigot, watching a stream of black water run over her flat stomach and down her legs until it spiraled into the drain. She repeated the process three times until the jet blackness of her hair was gone and the natural blond reappeared.

Back at the mirror, she unwrapped the blond hair coloring and followed the instructions. She knew the process of returning her hair to bright yellow blond would take an hour. She set the foil highlight tags in her hair as close to the roots as possible. It wouldn't be perfect, but it would be better than the jet-black coloring she had endured for the past month.

In the bedroom, she pulled an old T-shirt over her head but didn't bother with pants or underwear, opting to complete the final task Francis had asked of her wearing as little as possible, for fear of staining her clothes with blood. She walked down to the kitchen and checked the microwave clock. She was on a tight schedule this morning, and that was a good thing. Too much time would allow her to contemplate what she was about to do. Too much time would allow her mind to wander and permit her thoughts to work against her. Too much time and she may back out of this whole thing and run. But she had no time to think or contemplate or change her mind. If she wanted a life with Francis, she needed to move, move, move.

She grabbed the canvas duffle bag that she'd packed the previous night and carried it to the garage, where she deposited it in the front seat of the Ford Focus. She grabbed the knife from the bag and walked back inside. She paced the kitchen for a few minutes as Elton John continued to drown out her worries. When the clock reached 8:45 a.m., she knew she could wait no longer.

She walked to the basement door and thundered down the steps. She peeked into the room to make sure the woman was still shackled to the bed. Even better, she was sleeping. The fast food had satiated her into a slumber, and the sedatives stuffed into the burger had kept her there. She unfolded the Victorinox Swiss Army knife she had purchased at the tactical store, opened the door, and hurried to the bed. In a quick slicing motion she drew the knife across the woman's neck, ignoring the reverberations that vibrated the handle as the knife sunk through cartilage and bone. The woman's eyes opened briefly as a mist of blood sprayed from the wound. She dropped the knife onto the ground and raced out of the room, slamming the door shut on the way out and, hopefully, leaving all the memories of that moment behind.

She raced up the steps, through the kitchen, and climbed the stairs to the second floor. When she reached the bathroom and looked in the mirror she was shocked to see that her white T-shirt was spattered with blood, and that her face, too, carried red freckles from the woman's last breath.

She stripped out of the T-shirt, pulled the foil from her hair, and stopped for a moment to admire herself. To her eyes, the blood covering her face disappeared, and all she saw was her new self. The blond woman who Francis Bernard loved, with the python tattoo that slithered around her thigh, and the black heart on the right side of her ribcage. She turned from the mirror and climbed into the shower, lathering her face and hair for several minutes. She toweled dry, dressed, and exited the home.

As she pulled away in the Ford Focus, Elton John echoed from inside the home.

When are you gonna come down? When are you going to land?

CHAPTER 66

Boscobel, Wisconsin
Monday, August 4, 2025

THE ELECTRONIC LOCKING MECHANISM OF THE DOOR HISSED AS IT disengaged. A prison guard pushed the door open, and Ethan walked into the staging area. As he passed through the threshold, he saw Francis Bernard in a red, padded transport suit. The suit was so restrictive that Francis's hands were shackled together with a long length of chain because his arms could not come together.

On his head was a round, red helmet that had no openings other than a horizontal slot at eye level. Ethan walked until he stood in front of his father's killer. Although he could not see the man's face, the wrinkles at the corners of Francis's eyes told Ethan that he was smiling.

"You got what you wanted, Francis. But the transfer is not yours yet. The governor can still pull the plug on this whole thing if you don't give us the information you promised."

"Ethan, do you think I'd be so stupid as to offer something I couldn't deliver?"

"Tell me where Portia Vail is being held."

"Everything you need to know can be found in the Little Free Library located on the north end of Veteran's Park in Milwaukee. There's an envelope there, Ethan. It's taped to the top of the library."

"You tell me here and now, or this transfer doesn't happen."

"If the transfer van doesn't leave this morning, the girl will die. That's how this works, Ethan. I can't change it now."

"Who's helping you, Francis?"

"Hurry, Ethan. The girl won't make it much longer."

Ethan stared through the slot a moment longer before he turned and ran.

CHAPTER 67

Boscobel, Wisconsin
Monday, August 4, 2025

ETHAN SPRINTED THROUGH THE DOORS OF THE PRISON AND INTO the parking lot. Maddie waited in her unmarked squad car. Ethan jumped in and slammed the passenger door shut.

"Veteran's Park in Milwaukee," he said.

They tore out of the parking lot of the Wisconsin Secure Program Facility in Boscobel and sped east. This time they were on official business and Maddie had the lights flashing and the siren blaring.

"What the hell is a Little Free Library?" Ethan asked.

"It's like a need-a-penny-take-a-penny you see at gas stations, but for books. They're all over the place. Want to get rid of a book? Stick it in a Little Free Library. Want to grab a free book? Go to a Little Free Library and take one."

"Really? I've never seen one."

"Yes you have, you've just never noticed them."

With Maddie reaching top speeds of 100 mph, and traffic pulling to the side to allow the police cruiser to speed past, they made it to Milwaukee in just over two hours. They found Veteran's Park and skidded to a stop in the parking lot. They jumped from the car and sprinted through the woods on the north end. Ethan spotted the Little Free Library—a wooden structure that was the shape of an A-frame cabin and positioned on a wooden post secured into the concrete.

He was breathing heavily when he pulled open the door to the small structure. It was filled with hardcover and paperback books that lined the single shelf. He swiped the books away and reached inside. Brushing his hand back and forth along the top, he felt the corner of an envelope and pulled it free from the tape that held it in place.

He looked at Maddie as he produced the envelope. He pushed the distracting thoughts from his mind about how Francis was orchestrating it all. Ethan ripped the envelope open and pulled a single index card from inside.

> *Portia Vail*
> *286 Summerset Lane*
> *Lake Sherwood*
> *Rome, Wisconsin*

"Address in Rome," Ethan said.

"Where's that?"

Ethan typed the address into his phone. "Looks like a small, unincorporated town near Nekoosa."

He remembered that Eugenia Morgan lived in Nekoosa, and Pete had been running surveillance on the woman's house.

"North of Madison," he said. "Two and a half hours from us."

"Let's go!" Maddie said.

They sprinted back toward Maddie's cruiser.

CHAPTER 68

Ithaca, Wisconsin
Monday, August 4, 2025

SHE FORCED HERSELF TO DRIVE SLOWLY. THE LAST THING SHE NEEDED was to be pulled over for speeding. She glanced in the rearview mirror and blinked away the guilt that attempted to distract her. Over time, she hoped she could forget about what had happened in the basement. Hours and days would sand the edges of her memory of the knife slicing through the woman's neck. Months would erase the sickening feeling that remained in her hand from when the knife struck bone and cartilage. And eventually years would wash away the sadness and swirl her melancholy down the drain of time. She regretted none of it. None of what she had done Thursday night to the elderly couple in their Lake Morikawa home. None of what she had just done in the basement in Nekoosa. And none of what she was about to do on a lonely stretch of highway. Francis had called upon her, and she knew every bit of it was necessary.

She found Highway 58 north of Ithaca and the small two-lane stretch of road where she had ditched the Range Rover the night before. It was the route the transport van carrying Francis would take up to Columbia Correctional Institute. Now that she saw the road in the daylight, she was even happier with the location. Just south of the bend was a long stretch of road that ran for two miles before banking into a tight right turn where yellow traffic arrows pointed potential wayward drivers away from the guardrail and the ravine below. The bank forced vehicles to slow from 55 mph to thirty in order to manage the curving highway. It was the perfect spot.

She drove through the bank, pulled a U-turn so that the Ford Focus was facing south, and parked on the shoulder. The transport was scheduled for late morning, but she had no way of knowing if they were running on time. She'd have to stay alert. She should be exhausted after her trek back from the Mexican border the day before, but she was surprisingly awake and alert, almost buzzing with energy.

She exited the car and walked a few paces around the bend so she could see the long stretch of highway to the south. She stood and waited. Two hours passed but she saw no transport van. Anxiousness and doubt began to descend, but she refused to let it deter her. To occupy her thoughts, she went through the plan again. In the front seat of the van were two prison guards, each armed with pepper spray, a Taser, and a side arm. A 12-gauge shotgun was mounted behind the front seat. And in the holding block in the rear of the van was the man she loved.

As she played through the steps of the plan, she saw it. Like a mythical carriage emerging from the horizon, the Wisconsin Bureau of Prisons transport van appeared in the distance, speeding through the heat fumes that rose from the highway pavement. She hurried back to the Ford Focus and started the engine. She crept along the shoulder until she reached the edge of the bend, then pulled out into the middle of the road, turned on her hazards, and popped the hood.

She checked her purse for the handgun she had purchased earlier in the week and adjusted the Kevlar vest she wore under her shirt. There was no more time to go through the details of the plan again. Ultimately, her job was simple. Do whatever it took to get Francis out of that van.

CHAPTER 69

Ithaca, Wisconsin
Monday, August 4, 2025

ANDRE MONROE SAT BEHIND THE WHEEL OF THE PRISON VAN. He had requested a low-level guard who was under his tutelage to accompany him on the transport. They were moving Francis Bernard to Columbia Correctional Institute. Somehow, the son of a bitch had managed to pass a psych eval and convince the governor to sign off on the transfer. He must have some damn good lawyers, Monroe thought, although he wondered who the hell was paying them. Bernard had been behind bars for over thirty years, and any money he might have saved before he went to prison was surely gone now.

However he'd managed it, life was about to get considerably better for good ol' Francis Bernard. Monroe knew the isolation had been getting to him. Francis was on the brink, and those were the best kinds of inmates. They were broken and obedient, desperate for anything that might make their life even a hint better than reality. Monroe had enjoyed his late night visits with Francis. It was a shame to see him go.

Monroe glanced at the black-and-white monitor stationed on the dashboard. It displayed a real-time image from the camera positioned in the corner of the van's holding block. Francis stood because the transport suit prevented him from sitting. He was secured with a tether clasped to the ceiling and both sides of the van.

"What the hell?" the guard next to Monroe said as he squinted through the windshield. "Should I call it in?"

Monroe looked away from the monitor and back through the windshield. Up ahead was a disabled vehicle blocking the highway.

"Yeah," Monroe said. "Call it in."

He swiped a switch near the steering wheel that activated the van's dashboard camera. As he approached, Monroe saw a young-ish woman in short shorts bending over as she inspected the en-gine of her car, the hood popped open. He slowed the van, and she emerged from under the hood, a bottle of motor oil in one hand and a cell phone pressed to her ear.

Monroe pulled up next to her. She was very attractive. She had bright, blond hair and was a sweaty little mess out here in the heat of the late morning. The tattoo of a snake twisted around her thigh and disappeared up her jean shorts.

"What's the problem, young lady?" Monroe asked with a smile. "Don't tell me you got a flat tire out here in the middle of no-where."

"Not a flat, but my engine overheated," the woman said, taking the phone from her ear. "I just called Triple A, but they said they'd be an hour or more to get out here."

She walked to the driver's side window.

"I don't suppose you two strapping gentlemen would have time to help me, would you?"

CHAPTER 70

Hancock, Wisconsin
Monday, August 4, 2025

MADDIE HAD THE LIGHTS FLASHING AND SIRENS BLARING AS THEY raced north on Interstate 39 through the town of Hancock. Ethan was studying the map on his phone.

"There's a small lake in Rome," Ethan said. "Lake Sherwood. Looks like the address is to a house on the north side of the lake."

"How far out are we?"

"Thirty minutes."

"Should I ask for local backup from Nekoosa?"

"Your call. But the information is coming from the most deranged man I've ever met. I don't know how accurate it is, or what we're going to walk into when we enter the home."

"You're worried about a setup?"

"I don't know. Booby traps, maybe. A wild goose chase more likely."

"Okay," Maddie said. "We'll keep it to ourselves until we know what we're dealing with."

Ethan watched through the windshield as traffic braked and pulled to the side of the highway as he and Maddie sped past. He looked down at the address on the index card. A sickening feeling came over him. He looked at Maddie.

"We've gotta hurry."

Maddie pressed harder on the accelerator.

CHAPTER 71

Ithaca, Wisconsin
Monday, August 4, 2025

MONROE TOOK HIS EYES OFF THE WOMAN WEARING THE SHORT shorts and sporting a sexy tattoo on her leg to look at his partner. He smiled and arched one eyebrow. But before his partner could smile back, his face disappeared in a plume of red. Monroe blinked a few times until his brain processed the situation. Only then did he notice the hole in his colleague's forehead, just above his right eye. When he cocked his head back to the woman, he was staring down the barrel of a Sig Sauer P365, a stream of smoke spiraling from the barrel.

"If you even *think* about reaching for your gun, I'll kill you like I killed your partner," the woman said. "Now get out of the van."

Monroe lifted his hands from the steering wheel.

"I already called it in," he said. "Backup is on the way."

The woman smiled. "Better hurry then."

She pulled open the van door and gestured for him to exit. He did, and she grabbed his gun from his belt.

"Turn around."

Monroe did as he was told.

"Open the back of the van."

He shook his head. "I can't do that."

Without hesitation, he heard the Sig discharge and felt a searing pain in the back of his left leg. He collapsed as his knee exploded, howling in agony as he rolled on the ground.

The woman stood over him.

"There will be no more negative answers this morning. You will open the back of this van, or I will shoot you in the forehead and figure out how to open it myself."

The woman pointed the gun at his face and Monroe held up his hands.

"Don't shoot."

"Open the van!"

"Keys are on my belt."

"Give them to me!"

He reached for his belt. The pain in his knee had sent his body quivering. With trembling hands he found the key ring and pulled it from his utility belt. He held the keys up, noticing that his hand was covered in blood from grabbing his wounded leg.

The woman took the keys and hurried to the back of the van. When she was out of sight, he rolled onto his stomach and used his elbows to army crawl for the driver's seat. If he could manage to get himself into the van, he'd gun the engine and run for his life.

He grunted with each pull of his arms, snot and saliva pouring from his face. He reached the open door and started the painful rise to his feet. His body dripped with perspiration—partly from the heat of the morning, mostly from fighting the misery. Light-headedness threatened to topple him back to the ground as his vision constricted. He grabbed the seatbelt and used it to pull himself up. Just as he managed to get his chin over the driver's seat, he looked across the console. The passenger's side door opened, and the woman leaned over his dead colleague.

She reached into the van, pressed the ignition button to kill the engine, and lifted the key fob from the dashboard. "You didn't think I was going to let you leave without Francis getting a chance to say goodbye, did you?"

Over the woman's shoulder, Francis Bernard's face appeared. The woman had removed the transport helmet and Francis's expression offered neither anger nor concern. It was simply matter-of-fact serious. And then he smiled.

CHAPTER 72

Rome, Wisconsin
Monday, August 4, 2025

THEY EXITED THE HIGHWAY AND FOLLOWED THE GPS ALONG A FRONTAGE road, eventually fishtailing into a small residential lakeside community whose homes butted up against the lake.

"Two eight six," Ethan read from the card as Maddie turned onto Summerset Lane.

Maddie slowed as they looked at the address numbers, which were stenciled onto red plaques mounted in the front yard of each home.

"There," she said, pointing up ahead.

She pulled to a stop outside a home that had been clearly abandoned. There was no driveway, and the yard was a mess of overgrown grass and weeds. The vinyl siding had warped from years of summer heat, and paint was peeling around the windows and shutters. They both looked at each other and nodded before they exited the vehicle.

Maddie placed her palm on the handle of her service weapon. Ethan was less cautious and simply pulled his Beretta from his waistband as they approached the front door. They peeked in the windows. Dirty curtains blocked their view. The inside of the house was dark and quiet. Maddie pounded on the front door.

"Police! Open up."

When there was no answer she pounded again. Nothing. She tried the handle, but it was locked, although the door rattled with frailty.

"There's nothing to this door," Ethan said. "I could be through it with one kick."

Maddie seemed to think a moment. "We don't have a warrant."

"We're not looking for evidence. We're looking for a missing girl, and she's been gone a while."

Maddie nodded and backed away. Ethan lifted his leg and kicked the door, his foot striking close to the door handle. It splintered open and they both charged in, pointing their weapons at whatever waited for them.

CHAPTER 73

Ithaca, Wisconsin
Monday, August 4, 2025

FRANCIS WATCHED ANDRE MONROE'S BLOODY HAND SLIP FROM THE seatbelt as the man fell to the pavement, out of view.

"Hurry," he said.

He waited for her to finish unlocking the harness of his transport suit. When the final clasp gave way, his chest expanded as his lungs were finally able to fill with air. He shed the red suit onto the ground and took a moment to kiss the woman in front of him. He kissed her deeply on the mouth. It had been forever since he'd kissed a woman.

"Get the car," he said. He pointed to the ground. "Leave the gun. They need to find it."

She dropped the Sig on the ground next to the van.

"He's the one?" she asked of Andre Monroe, who moaned in pain from the other side of the van. "The one who visited you at night?"

Francis nodded. "Go."

He watched her hurry away from the carnage of the van and toward the Range Rover he had told her to hide in the woods. When she was around the bend, Francis reached into the van and pulled the 12-gauge shotgun from the cage behind the seats. He checked to make sure the gun was loaded, then walked slowly around the front of the van. He found Andre Monroe lying next to the open driver's side door, writhing in pain from a leg wound. His accomplice was a smart woman. He'd told her to do everything necessary to get Mr. Monroe to open the back of the van, but to make sure she didn't kill him. Anyone else in the van was dispensable, but not Monroe. Francis had plans for the guard who had tormented him.

Free from the constricting transport suit and so focused on the task at hand, Francis never considered that he was wearing just underwear and a white T-shirt. When he reached Monroe, the guard looked up at him. Francis noted the defeat and resignation in his eyes. He had seen the look before, although it had been quite some time. The women he had killed on the banks of Lake Michigan had offered similar expressions when they knew the end was near. When they knew pleading and begging would get them nowhere.

"Open your mouth," Francis said. "It's my turn."

He stuck the barrel of the shotgun to Monroe's lips and pressed incessantly until the man's mouth opened and the tip of the shotgun entered his mouth. With his lips sealed around the barrel, Monroe's cheeks ballooned with each breath he tried to expel. The man's eyes were wide and panicked just before Francis pulled the trigger.

CHAPTER 74

Rome, Wisconsin
Monday, August 4, 2025

ETHAN AND MADDIE CLEARED THE FIRST FLOOR OF THE RANCH-STYLE cabin. Maddie came out of the bedroom.

"Empty," she said.

"Nothing here, either," Ethan said as he lowered his gun and looked around the kitchen. On the table something caught his eye. He walked over and reached for the package of cigarettes that rested there. He held them up for Maddie to see.

"Saratoga 120s," Maddie said.

The off-market cigarettes Blake Cordis smoked when Ethan and Maddie first interviewed him.

"Should I make a call?" Maddie said. "Have someone pick up Blake Cordis?"

Ethan licked his lip and slowly gazed throughout the cabin. "Hold off on that until we know what's happening," he said.

Ethan cocked his head.

"What's that noise?"

They both stopped and listened.

"Is it music?" Maddie asked.

The sound came from somewhere in the cabin. Since they'd cleared the first floor, the only possible source was the basement. Ethan lifted his chin to the door off the kitchen. Maddie opened it. A flight of stairs led down to a dark cellar.

Ethan walked over, squinted into the staircase and listened. The music emanated from the darkness below. The last time he was involved in madness like this was a decade ago, and he suddenly preferred the chaos of the ER to the thought of descending into the dark cellar of an abandoned lake home with no idea what waited for him.

Ethan was first down the stairs with Maddie following. Ethan kept his arms locked with his Beretta pointed at the ground. The farther they descended, the less ambient light from the kitchen followed, until they reached the basement landing and stood in total darkness.

Ethan listened. The music was louder now, but still muffled. He found a light switch on the wall and clicked it on. Overhead bulbs blinked to life and brightened the space. Across the basement was a door with a horizontal slat cut in the center of it like a mail chute. The noise was coming from beyond the door.

Ethan hurried over. He and Maddie crouched into shooter's stances as he tried the handle. It was locked. He slowly lifted the flap on the door slat and looked into the room. He immediately recognized it as the room from the photo of Portia Vail, where the woman had been cuffed to a door while holding a newspaper. He saw a woman lying on a bed. The source of the music was the television that played from inside the room.

"Portia?" he said through the slot.

The woman did not move.

"Portia Vail," he said again, louder this time. "I'm Ethan Hall with the Department of Criminal Investigation, along with Detective Jacobson of the Milwaukee PD. We're here to help."

He continued to look through the slat, but the woman did not move. He put his shoulder into the door, but unlike the entrance to the cabin, this door was reinforced and sturdy. There was no breaking through it. They looked around and found a key hanging from a wall hook. He grabbed it and inserted it into the lock. The dead bolt twisted, and the door swung open.

He and Maddie raced into the room. Ethan kept the Beretta in front of him and made sure the room was empty, clearing the bathroom as Maddie ran to the woman on the bed.

"Portia?" Maddie said.

Finally, miraculously, Portia Vail sat up and squinted at Maddie.

"Am I dreaming?" the woman said.

"No. You're safe now. I'm Detective Jacobson and this is Special Agent Hall. We're going to get you out of here."

Portia Vail reached out her arms and Maddie embraced her in a hug as the woman sobbed. Ethan's phone rang. He stuck his Beretta into his waistband and pulled his phone from his back pocket. The caller ID told him it was Pete Kramer.

"Pete, we got her. Portia Vail is alive."

"Ethan, listen to me!" Pete said. "Francis Bernard escaped from the transport van that was taking him to Columbia."

"Escaped?"

"Yeah, we're just getting word now."

"How?"

"We're still getting updates, but it looks like the van was intercepted en route to Columbia by a stalled vehicle. Both guards are dead. One shot in the forehead, the other at close range with a shotgun. The stalled car on the scene is a Ford Focus registered to Eugenia Morgan."

"Damn it! Find her, Pete."

"I'm at her house in Nekoosa now and about to go in. I wanted you to hear about Francis from me, though, not on the news."

"I'm close to Nekoosa, Pete. Portia Vail was being held in an abandoned house in Rome. I'm heading over to you now."

"I'm going in, E. I'll see you when you get here."

"Be careful."

"See you in a while, partner."

CHAPTER 75

Nekoosa, Wisconsin
Monday, August 4, 2025

PETE KRAMER ENDED THE CALL WITH ETHAN AND SLID HIS PHONE into the breast pocket of his suit coat. He stared at Eugenia Morgan's house. Backup was on the way, and he considered waiting for the cavalry to arrive or at least for Ethan to show up. But there was a very realistic possibility that Eugenia Morgan and Francis Bernard were inside the home, and waiting was not an option. The garage door was open, although the garage itself was empty.

He stood from his car, leaving the cane behind. He pulled his Glock 45 from its holster and steadied himself on his good leg before limping up the driveway. He looked around the quiet neighborhood, knowing the place would soon be teeming with police cars and news vans.

He staggered another few steps up the driveway before noticing that not only was the bay door to the garage open, but so, too, was the door inside the garage that led into the house. He stopped when he heard it. He listened to make sure. It was music, and it was coming from inside the house. After another few more steps he reached the garage, and recognized the song—"Goodbye Yellow Brick Road" by Elton John.

CHAPTER 76

Nekoosa, Wisconsin
Monday, August 4, 2025

THE SUN WAS SETTING MONDAY NIGHT. YELLOW CRIME SCENE TAPE squared off the perimeter of Eugenia Morgan's home. Parked at odd angles were all sorts of vehicles—police cruisers, detective's unmarked cars, a morgue van, and a CSI truck in the driveway. Turf wars had started between the many jurisdictions involved in the case. Since Pete Kramer had been first to the scene and the one to find Eugenia Morgan's body—throat freshly sliced and lying on a bloodstained mattress in a basement eerily decorated in a shrine devoted to Francis Bernard that included a wall covered with photos of the man and a white flag decorated with a black heart—the Department of Criminal Investigation had claimed the scene as their own. But the Wood County Sheriff's Office was also flexing its muscle and taking as much control as possible. Since the scene was believed to be linked to the disappearance and miraculous recovery of Portia Vail, rescued in the next town over by Detective Maddie Jacobson, folks from the Milwaukee PD were also poking around. And, finally, because the puzzle pieces were still being assembled about what role Eugenia Morgan played in Francis Bernard's escape, officials from the Wisconsin Department of Corrections were also present.

Ethan spent the afternoon being debriefed after he and Maddie had found Portia Vail alive and well in an abandoned cabin mysteriously close to where Eugenia Morgan's home was located in Nekoosa. Portia was in remarkably good shape, had not been abused in any way, and told a story of being held captive but with access to a shower, toilet, daily food delivery, and a television and books to pass the time. All Portia could offer about her abductor was that she was a tall woman who delivered her food each day through the slot in the door. Her captor had always worn a mask and hoodie, adding sunglasses to hide her eyes the day she snapped a photo of Portia holding a copy of the *Milwaukee Journal Sentinel* and handcuffed to the bathroom door.

Ethan stood inside the crime scene tape but away from the activity inside Eugenia Morgan's home. Pete and Maddie were with him.

"What have you heard about the escape?" Ethan asked.

Pete shook his head. "Still piecing it together. But what we know for certain is that Eugenia Morgan's Ford Focus was found in the middle of the road with the hood up. The guards called it in. We suspect that the van stopped or at least slowed down due to the disabled vehicle. Then Eugenia shot and killed the guards. How, exactly, that went down is still being investigated. One of the guards was shot with a Sig Sauer that was recovered from the scene. We're running ballistics on it now, but we think it was the Sig Eugenia purchased at the gun shop in Milwaukee."

"And the other guard?"

"He was hit with the shotgun that was mounted inside the van. It looks like . . . what I'm hearing is whoever killed the guard put the shotgun in his mouth and pulled the trigger."

Ethan let out a long breath. "So, what do we have? Eugenia Morgan visits Francis in Boscobel. She's the only person on his visitor log other than me in the last three years. Her basement is decorated with a shrine dedicated to Francis and a flag with a black heart, so she was clearly obsessed with the man. Her car is found at the scene where the transport van was intercepted. The gun she purchased is the one used to kill the guard. And then what? After she helps Francis escape, he brings her back here and slices her throat?"

Pete shook his head. "I don't know, E. None of it makes sense yet, but we're trying to piece it together. Here's the kicker," Pete said, opening a manila folder. "And this is new, so don't share it with anyone."

Pete looked at Maddie. "We don't want Milwaukee in on this until we know what we're dealing with."

Maddie nodded. "I'll keep it quiet."

Pete pulled black-and-white photos from the folder.

"These were taken from the dash cam on the transport van."

Pete handed one of the photos to Ethan. He and Maddie scrutinized it.

"The guard called in the disabled vehicle, as was protocol, and gave a brief description of the woman to dispatch. The guard's exact words," Pete said, looking down at notes in the file. "Tall, white female with blond hair and a snake tattoo running around her right leg."

Pete pointed at the photo that Ethan held. It was an image of the woman who had helped Francis Bernard escape.

"Eugenia Morgan is tall, but she's got jet-black hair and no tattoos."

"So who the hell is this?" Maddie asked, pointing at the photo.

"We don't know. The images are not the best. It could be Eugenia Morgan in disguise, but we can't be sure."

Ethan's phone rang.

"Ethan Hall."

"Hey Doc," Christian said. "I'm a day late and a dollar short, but I made it through the encryption."

"Find anything?"

"I found *everything*. Get over here."

"I'm up north with my hands full. But I'll be there as soon as I can."

Ethan hung up the phone and looked at Pete and Maddie. "Something's come up that I've got to take care of. Pete, can I take your car?"

"Something I need to know about?" Pete asked.

"I'm not sure yet."

Pete reached into his pocket and tossed his keys to Ethan.

"Need any help?" Maddie asked.

"Not until I know more. I'll call you when I'm done. Pete, keep an eye on her for me?"

"Maddie doesn't need a gimp DCI agent to protect her. She's got around-the-clock protection from Milwaukee PD. But the DCI is adding agents to her detail until we find Francis. The governor even offered a few DPU agents if she wanted them."

Maddie put her hand on Pete's shoulder. "I'd still take Pete any day of the week. But I already talked to my boys," Maddie said. "They're not letting me out of their sights until we have Francis back in custody."

"When you're finished here," Ethan said to Maddie. "Stop down at my place. I want you to stay with me tonight."

CHAPTER 77

Beaver Dam, Wisconsin
Monday, August 4, 2025

LINDSAY PULLED UP TO THE GATES OF PRESCOTT ESTATES. THE SECURITY booth was empty at this time of night, and the gates were locked. She pressed the button on the intercom system, knowing that it buzzed inside Blake's cottage. This was not the first time she'd been here late at night.

"Yeah," Blake's voice squawked from the speaker.

"Hey, it's me."

There was a short pause before the gates rattled open. Lindsay pulled past the cast iron and into Prescott Estates. She followed the winding road until she saw the shitty little cottage where Blake Cordis had been exiled to a decade earlier. It was bittersweet to see him there.

Blake opened the front door as she pulled up. The humidity of the night assaulted her skin as Lindsay climbed from her car.

"Hi," Lindsay said in her best seductive voice.

"Hey," Blake responded.

"Can I come in?"

Blake shrugged. "I'm not going to make you stand outside in this sauna we have for a summer. And we wouldn't make it five minutes with the size of the mosquitos out here."

Lindsay followed him inside, noting a hint of aftershave as she walked past him. The man had, ever since she first laid eyes on him in high school, spun her world in circles. And the scent of his aftershave, even this many years later, had never left her mind.

"Something to drink?" Blake asked as he closed the door.

"Sure."

"I've got beer or whiskey."

Lindsay shrugged. "Whiskey it is."

She sat on the couch. Blake poured two Proper No. Twelve whiskeys and handed her one.

"Cheers," he said, clinking her glass.

Lindsay smiled and took a sip.

"So what's up?" Blake asked as he sat on the end chair next to her.

"It's ten o'clock on a Monday night, Blake. What do you think's up?"

Lindsay smiled and raised her eyebrows.

"It's a bad idea, Lindsay."

"We're grown adults. We're allowed to make bad decisions."

Blake said nothing as Lindsay stood and placed her glass on the coffee table. She wore a sleeveless button down shirt, the top two buttons unclasped. She took the third in her fingers and opened it, exposing her cleavage and revealing that she was not wearing a bra.

Blake squirmed in his chair. Lindsay knew he was not going to put up a fight tonight. She walked closer and climbed onto his lap, straddling him.

"Why are we fighting this?" she asked.

Her lips were close to his.

"Why don't we just do what we've wanted to do all summer?"

Of course, Lindsay knew the reason why Blake had refused to sleep with her earlier in the summer. It was because he had started seeing another woman. But Portia Vail was out of the picture for the time being, and she knew Blake was going on five weeks without sex. It was likely a record for the man.

She pressed her lips to his and their mouths opened. The glass of whiskey fell from his hand and hit the ground just as Lindsay felt his hands grab the back of her thighs and slide up her shorts. This was going to be easier than she imagined.

Blake stood from the chair and lifted her as she wrapped her legs around his waist. They kissed all the way to the bedroom, where he laid her on the bed and fell on top of her. Lindsay quickly changed positions so that she was on top. She would be in control this time, taking back what he had stolen years before.

CHAPTER 78

Cherryview, Wisconsin
Monday, August 4, 2025

ETHAN WATCHED OVER CHRISTIAN'S SHOULDER AS THE TECH GURU typed at a mindboggling pace while three computer monitors blinked and registered white code against a black background.

"Ah, I see," Christian whispered as he raced through the computer code. "That's sort of clever, but not terribly sophisticated. Definitely something learned at a university and not in the real world. There's a workaround . . . that. I. Think . . ."

His fingers were like lightning strikes against the keyboard and Ethan would not have believed the violence could possibly produce anything intelligible but for the fact that the computer responded every time Christian's fingers touched the keys

"Yep, here we go! Voilà!"

Christian pushed his hands against the desk and sent himself wheeling away on his chair again.

"All yours, big boy."

Ethan pulled a chair over and sat in front of the computer.

"What am I looking at?"

Now it was Christian who was standing over Ethan's shoulder. He pointed at the screen.

"These are all of Dr. Larkin's consults in the last three months. They're listed by patient number and used to be encrypted and protected, but all you have to do now is click on the link and it'll show you everything you need to know. Do you have the date of the anonymous confession?"

"July thirtieth," Ethan said, scrolling down until he arrived at the correct date. There were several consultations listed that day. Ethan clicked on the ID number of the final patient of the day. Immediately, white letters appeared against the black background.

Blake Jaxson Cordis
DOB: September 4, 1993
IP: 192.458.177.296

Ethan shook his head.

"What's wrong?" Christian asked.

Ethan ran his tongue along the inside of his lower lip as he stared at Blake's name. Perhaps, he considered, being away from investigative work for so long had dulled his instincts.

"Not what I was expecting to see."

"I figured it wouldn't be," Christian said. "I just wanted to make sure Mr. One Hundred Percent was on the right track. Move over."

Ethan slid his chair to the side so that Christian could take control of the computer, which he did in the swiftest of manners.

"Whoever Blake Jaxson Cordis is," Christian said, "he's not the client who logged in on July thirtieth."

"No?"

"No. But someone wants you to think he is. Someone with some chill computer skills, too. But I see what they did. They reverse populated the IP address and then ran it through the online portal's encryption software so that if you looked but didn't dig too deep—or even if you *did* dig deep but didn't know what the hell you were doing, which most people don't—it would appear as if the video originated from Blake Cordis's computer."

"It didn't?"

"No."

"So where did it come from?"

Christian looked at Ethan. "Ever seen the movie *When a Stranger Calls*?"

"No."

"Really? It's good. You should check it out."

"Christian, I'm in a time crunch here."

"Sorry, I digress."

Christian attacked the keyboard again until the actual video of the session appeared. The patient's face was blurred beyond recognition, while Lindsay Larkin's image appeared in a small window on the top right of the monitor. A triangular "play" button was transposed in the center of the screen.

"It's about a stalker who terrorizes a woman with harassing phone calls," Christian said.

"What?"

"The movie. *When a Stranger Calls.* But the twist is that when police trace the calls, they figure out that they're coming from inside the house. Anyway. This reminded me of that movie."

Christian clicked the button so that the video played.

Lindsay Larkin spoke: *"Does, uh . . . this girl have a name?"*

"Yes. You know her."

The patient's voice was muffled and distorted into the digital, artificial intelligence tone.

"Her name is Callie Jones, and I need you to help me forgive myself for what I did to her."

Christian pushed himself away from the desk one more time. He pointed at the monitor.

"Press the escape button," he said, "and the filter will disappear."

Ethan looked at Christian for a moment before turning back to the keyboard. He pressed the button, and the encryption filter disappeared. The anonymous patient's image came clearly into focus on the screen. Ethan blinked a few times to clear his confusion. He was looking at Lindsay Larkin confessing to herself about having killed Callie Jones.

CHAPTER 79

Beaver Dam, Wisconsin
Monday, August 4, 2025

SHE MANAGED TO ORGASM, ALTHOUGH IT WAS SELF-ASSISTED. COACH Cordis did not have the same hold on her that he once had. Still, she made a point of satisfying herself, using him as a means to an end. It took much longer than Blake had lasted himself and their reunion was less than synergistic. But tonight was not about sexual satisfaction. It was about closure.

She stood from the bed and stepped into her bikini bottoms.

"Where are you going?" Blake asked in a playful tone, as if another round waited if she stayed the night.

"I've got a full day of clients tomorrow, and I'm quite certain you're going to be very busy yourself."

It took everything Lindsay had to say no more. Blake's sad life was about to come crashing down now that Portia Vail had been found alive. Lindsay hadn't seen any news reports yet about the girl's safe return, but Francis Bernard had been transferred that morning and the plan was for him to give Ethan Hall the address of the cabin in Rome where Lindsay had kept the girl over the last few weeks. Months earlier she had purchased the shitty fixer-upper cabin through a trust that she had registered in Blake's name. And Lindsay had left enough clues inside the cabin for police to find their way to Blake—the Saratoga cigarettes, which she still tasted in her mouth now from kissing him, were the easiest clues. But Ethan Hall would find the others.

This time around, Lindsay was taking no chances. She used Francis Bernard to deliver the prepaid cell phone to Ethan Hall. Alone, it might have been enough. But to be sure, she had put her computer coding skills to work and created the anonymous confession using the encryption technology at the office. Lindsay knew that trail would be difficult to follow, and even harder to crack. But once Ethan Hall made it through the cyber security fortress, she made sure the trail would lead back to Blake's computer. When it was all pieced together, it would end with police storming Blake's home on Prescott Estates sometime in the next day or two.

"You know," Lindsay finally said, a smile on her face as if reminiscing. "The last time we slept together, I didn't even know what to call you."

Blake sat up on his elbows and looked at her with a confused expression.

"You probably didn't even know how scared I was that night."

Lindsay pulled her shorts up her thighs and buttoned them.

"Do you remember the night you took my virginity? The summer you started coaching at Cherryview? The summer I turned seventeen, and you were the new, young, hotshot volleyball coach?"

She saw Blake swallow hard. His playful tone was gone when he spoke.

"I remember that night, Lindsay. It meant a lot to me."

"Did it?" Lindsay asked as she buttoned her blouse. "I wasn't sure because you started sleeping with Callie a week later."

"I didn't . . . Lindsay."

"Did you know I was a virgin that night? You had to know, right? I was seventeen and it wasn't exactly the easiest night of sex. I mean, you powered right through it like a typical man, concerned about nothing but yourself. But, yeah, I didn't know what to call you after you thrust yourself inside of me. I had only ever called you *Coach Cordis*, and that sounded so totally inappropriate in the moment. I made plans, though." Lindsay paused to laugh as she reminisced. "I *actually* made plans to whisper your name in your ear the next time we slept together. But that never happened. You took my virginity, allowed me to fall in love with you, and then ghosted me to run off with my best friend."

"We didn't run off, Lindsay."

"Of course you didn't. But you were about to. You two were in love, right? I mean, I saw your text messages. You and Callie wrote those words to each other. You can imagine my surprise when I read them."

Blake pushed off his elbows and sat up in bed.

"How did you read our text messages?"

"You took my virginity one week, and were in love with Callie the next?"

"That's not how it happened, Lindsay."

"I guess it doesn't matter all these years later. But just know that you're in a world of hurt, and the things that are about to happen to you . . . you deserve all of them. I mean, look at you and me. It's irony defined, isn't it? You once believed you had total control over me. You could take my virginity and break my heart, and not even talk to me about it. You could run off with my best friend and I was expected to just sit back and take it. You believed you were so superior. But look at us now. You shovel horse shit for a living, and I run an empire. The tides have certainly changed."

Lindsay smiled.

"And just so you're not confused. Tonight was about nothing more than me taking back what's mine."

Lindsay headed for the door, turning before she left.

"Enjoy your time in prison, *Coach*."

CHAPTER 80

Beaver Dam, Wisconsin
Monday, August 4, 2025

LINDSAY DROVE AWAY FROM PRESCOTT ESTATES FEELING SATISFIED, despite the lackluster sex. It had taken a decade, but things had finally come full circle. If Ethan Hall did his job, Blake would soon be behind bars. If Blake Cordis didn't want a life with Lindsay, then he would have no life at all.

As she drove through the night, her mind spun back to a decade earlier. She could hardly believe so many years had passed since that summer, or that it had taken her so long to pull the trigger on a plan she had considered many times. But Lindsay had lost her nerve back then, and couldn't go through with it. She naively believed that after Callie was gone she and Blake might still be together. Despite the fact that he had rejected her in the months after Callie was out of the picture, Lindsay still thought there was a chance for them. But in the years since, Blake had never succumbed to her advances. Until tonight. But tonight was too late.

The long game had been in the works for some time, and Lindsay believed she had played it perfectly. A light mist began to fall. It smattered her windshield and blurred the headlights of oncoming cars, allowing her mind to wander back to the fateful day it all began.

Ever since they'd slept together he'd been distant. She wondered if this was how all men acted after sex. But hers was a unique situation, wasn't it? It had to be. Blake Cordis was the hot history teacher and new volleyball coach all the girls had a crush on, but he had chosen her. They had flirted at practice until one day he offered to drive her home after she stayed late re-lining the courts on the gymnasium floor. But instead of taking her home, they had ended up at his apartment.

Lindsay was nervous when they went into his bedroom. She would never forget the moment he unclasped the button on her jeans. She knew then that there was no turning back, and she did her best to hide that it was her first time. She was happy it had not been with a random boy on prom night, or a friend after too many drinks. It had been with Blake Cordis, a man she was in love with.

But the things Lindsay expected to happen after that night never tran-spired. There was no budding romance. There was no courtship. There was no secret rendezvous where a forbidden love was too electric to ignore. In-stead, Coach Cordis ghosted her. He told her it had been a mistake to get in-volved with one of his players and that they needed to end things and go back to a strictly player-coach relationship.

Lindsay was heartbroken and not ready to give up on them. She decided to talk to him in his office Saturday morning after practice. It would ulti-mately become the Saturday Callie Jones went missing, although Lindsay didn't know that at the time.

She gave no warning. Lindsay simply waited until practice was over and her teammates were gone. Then, she walked to his office.

"Hey, Lindsay," Blake said after she knocked on the doorframe. "What's going on?"

"We need to talk."

"Okay. Does this have something to do with the team?"

"We need to talk about us."

Blake stood from behind his desk and glanced over her shoulder, looking out into the hallway. His voice was lower when he spoke again. "I thought we agreed to keep our relationship straight up. I'm your coach, you're my player. Remember?"

"I actually don't remember, because that was never my plan."

It was his, and he expected her to go along with it and ask no questions and make no trouble. He expected to take her virginity and never talk to her again.

"Look, Lindsay. We could both get in a lot of trouble for what hap-pened."

"It's not fair. What you did," she said as she walked into his office.

"Coach?"

Blake looked to the doorway and saw Curt McGee, Cherryview's athletic director, standing in the hallway.

"Hey Lindsay," Curt said.

Lindsay smiled. "Mr. McGee."

Curt looked at Blake and cocked his head. "We're supposed to go over the budget. Meeting's getting started now upstairs."

"Yeah, of course," Blake said. "Lindsay and I were just talking shop."

Blake turned and pointed at Lindsay.

"Great job today at practice. I'll see you Monday?"

Lindsay forced a smile and nodded. "See you then."

Blake walked out with the athletic director and left Lindsay standing alone in his office. When he was gone, tears came to her eyes. Her soft sobs were interrupted by a chirping noise. It was the muffled sound of a cell phone ringing. Lindsay listened for a moment and then walked to Blake's desk. She pulled the top drawer open and saw a Samsung flip phone lighted up with a recent text message.

She looked briefly at the open door to Blake's office, and then reached for the phone. A name glowed across the caller ID screen.

Callie

She opened the phone and read the text message.

I'm going to a party out on The Crest tonight. But I want to see you. I'll call you when I leave.

I love you.

Lindsay stared at the phone. She could hear her friend's voice echoing in her ears.

I love you.

Lindsay's stomach roiled. She slipped the phone into her pocket and, with tears streaming down her face, ran out of Blake's office.

Summer 2015

Cherryview, Wisconsin

*L*INDSAY STOOD IN THE SHADOWS OF THE RESTAURANT. MUSIC BLARED *from inside the bar as those who had ventured out to The Crest started their night of drinking. She looked toward the volleyball courts and saw Callie standing on the sidelines. The stadium-style lights that allowed volleyball to be played well past midnight on summer nights were bright as they fought against the coming darkness. Lindsay pulled Blake's flip phone from her pocket and saw that Callie had texted several times. She sent a reply text to Callie.*

What's wrong?
I need to see you.
Where are you?
The Crest.
You okay?
I need to talk to you about the baby. I'm keeping it.

Lindsay stared at the phone. Her breath caught in her throat, and she didn't inhale again until her lungs burned to the point of snapping her back from her trance. She paused before she typed back.

You didn't go through with it?
No. I want this baby WITH YOU. I want to start a life with you. I need to see you tonight.
Do you have your parents' boat?
Yes.

**Meet me at North Point Pier. I'll be waiting on the dock.
I love you, Blake.**

Lindsay didn't hesitate when she typed her response this time.

I love you, too.

Lindsay dropped the phone into her pocket and walked from the shadows. Her hands were shaking, and her breaths were shallow.

Callie was pregnant. Blake was the father. He'd slept with both of them. He was in love with Callie.

Lindsay walked up behind Callie, who was still staring at her phone.

"Who was that?"

Callie looked up from her phone as she turned.

"Oh, um, my mom. She wants me home."

Lindsay squinted her eyes and did her best to look disgusted. "It's nine o'clock on a Saturday."

"The regular crowd shuffles in."

Lindsay saw Callie push a smile onto her face.

"There's an old man sitting next to me . . ." Callie crinkled her nose. "No?"

"We're playing next."

"I can't, Linds. My mom's all over me about something."

"Why is your mom such a buzz kill?"

"You think anything my mom does makes sense? She's probably having a breakdown about something. I'm going to take the boat home. Be back in an hour. Then we'll play those guys. Kick their butts."

Lindsay was amazed at how easily her friend was able to lie. She saw a tear run down Callie's cheek.

"You sure you're okay?"

Callie quickly wiped it away. "Yeah. All good. I'll see you later."

Lindsay watched her hurry off. She stood on the sidelines of the sand volleyball court and watched Callie climb onto her boat and pull away from the dock. She turned and walked quickly toward the back of the restaurant. She knew from her guy friends on the football team who worked on The Crest that there was a fleet of five Polaris Ranger 4x4s they used to haul supplies along the small, unpaved access road that ran out to The Crest from the mainland.

Once she was beyond the crowd, she took off in a sprint. She hopped into one of the 4x4s. *The key was in the ignition, and she cranked the engine to life. The Ranger took off, bouncing along the narrow road as she raced to beat Callie to North Point Pier.*

Lindsay killed the Ranger's headlights as she pulled into the parking lot at North Point Pier. The pier was where those who did not own homes on Lake Okoboji launched their boats for a day on the water. On any given morning, the lot was crowded with pickup trucks and trailers. But they typically pulled their boats from the lake before dark. Tonight, the place was empty.

Lindsay pulled the Ranger into the shadows on the side of the parking lot and climbed out. In the storage unit on the back of the 4x4 was a Callaway 9-iron golf club. Lindsay had seen the football players driving golf balls off The Crest, attempting to hit a wooden raft that floated a hundred yards off the dock. With little thought, she grabbed the club and hurried along the side of the parking lot to the boat launch area and the dock that ran out into the water. Far out in the middle of the lake she saw The Crest and the lights of the volleyball courts. The occasional lyric bounced across the lake, and she could hear an old Tom Petty song playing from where she hid in the darkness. She waited only five minutes before she saw a boat approaching. It had to be Callie. Lindsay had beaten her here.

She stepped deeper into the woods near the end of the dock and watched as Callie approached in her parents' boat. Cloaked by darkness, Lindsay stood in the shadows as Callie tied off the boat and stepped onto the pier. Callie looked toward the parking lot, surely anticipating Blake's car being there, and slowly walked down the dock. Once she stepped onto the gravel at the end of the pier, Lindsay emerged from the shadows. A twig snapped under her foot, but before Callie could spin around, Lindsay lifted the 9-iron and, in one swift motion, brought it down on the back of Callie's head.

The thud was sickening as she felt the club insert itself into her friend's skull. She pulled it out, expecting Callie to fall to the ground. Instead, Callie turned around and locked eyes with her. Lindsay lifted the golf club again and struck Callie in the crown of the head. The blow seemed to turn Callie into a statue, until she reached up and touched the blood that poured like lava down her face. Lindsay lifted the club and struck her a third time. This time, her lifelong friend and teammate—and the girl who had stolen Blake from her—collapsed in a heap.

CHAPTER 81

Milwaukee, Wisconsin
Monday, August 4, 2025

THE MEMORY OF THAT NIGHT WAS STILL HEAVY ON HER MIND AS LINDsay pulled up to her house. Her training had taught her coping mechanisms and ways to compartmentalize her feelings about that time of her life. In the immediate aftermath, Lindsay had distracted herself by working hard to win Blake back. She gave him a month to grieve and get over the confusion that came with losing the mother of his child. Lindsay waited for the investigation to die down, too. Then, she tried to rekindle what had once been between her and Blake. When Blake rebuffed her efforts, she decided to give him more time.

She visited his apartment late at night during her junior year of college, only to find that he was wholly uninterested in her. She tried again after she graduated and started her business, stupidly believing that Blake would be impressed with her success. Eventually, though, over the years Lindsay understood that no matter how badly she wanted to recapture the magic they had once shared, Blake did not. So, after years of rejection, Lindsay's impetus morphed from lust to revenge.

She had treated clients over the years who suffered from OLD—obsessive love disorder—and she was not so blind as to miss the telltale symptoms of the disorder in her own life. She knew she was in the throes of the affliction, and decided the only way past it was to find closure. And closure would come only after she delivered justice to Blake Cordis. She thought long and hard about how to do it, settling on the idea that the prepaid cell phone she had kept hidden for years would be the perfect tool.

Lindsay knew the phone was the perfect way to exact her revenge, but still she had never been able to go through with it. Despite her frustration, there was an ember of love for Blake Cordis that remained insufferably glowing. It represented a tiny morsel of hope that perhaps they would someday get back together. That tiny ember had prevented her from pulling the trigger on her plan over the years. But it had finally gone dark when Lindsay learned of Blake's love affair with Portia Vail.

In one torrid night of alcohol and Valium, Lindsay formulated a plan to abduct Portia Vail and frame Blake for it. The scheme came fully together after Ethan Hall was tapped to reopen Callie's case. Suddenly, Lindsay knew whom she would give the prepaid Samsung to. And when she started seeing Eugenia Morgan as a client, the pieces of her revenge began to align. The poor woman was suffering from hybristophilia and in love with a convicted cop killer named Francis Bernard. When Lindsay looked into Francis Bernard's history, she learned that the man's past was intimately connected to Ethan Hall. It was then that Lindsay's plan took an unexpected, but utterly perfect, turn.

For years, *The Anonymous Client* had done pro bono work for prison systems around the country, offering psychological care to inmates. When she rooted through the requests waiting for her approval, Lindsay reviewed the list of inmates at the Wisconsin Secure Program Facility seeking mental health exams. On the list was none other than Francis Bernard. Lindsay took the pro bono case, and within a week was sitting face-to-face with the man who had killed Ethan Hall's father.

Only attorneys and doctors were allowed personal interaction with inmates at the maximum security prison in Boscobel. Lindsay's first session with Francis Bernard took place in a small conference room rather than at the visitation booth where a pane of glass would have separated them, and where their conversations might have been overheard through the prison's phone system. In that quaint meeting room, Lindsay had laid out the details of her offer.

She knew after a single session that Francis Bernard was desperate for a transfer to a more humane prison, and that he would do anything to be liberated from solitary confinement.

Lindsay informed Francis that for a chance at such a request, he'd need to pass a psychological evaluation, which Lindsay offered to facilitate if he gave her something in return. If Francis agreed to lead Ethan Hall to certain bits of evidence that Lindsay planted—specifically, the prepaid Samsung phone and Portia Vail's whereabouts, which Francis could use as leverage—then Lindsay would repay Francis by signing off on a psychological evaluation that would spring him from the WSPF and put him on his way to Columbia Correctional Institute.

Lindsay's plan was so meticulous that she never considered Francis had one of his own.

CHAPTER 82

Milwaukee, Wisconsin
Monday, August 4, 2025

L INDSAY PULLED INTO THE GARAGE OF HER HOME LOCATED IN THE Lower East Side neighborhood. She had purchased the custombuilt home the year before, after spending the last many years in the city. She let out a restrained laugh as she parked in the expansive garage that was larger than Blake Cordis's entire cottage. A home he didn't even own, but which had been bequeathed to him by the Prescott family in exchange for a lifetime of servitude looking after their stables. It was such a sad existence and was still more than he deserved.

She shut down the engine of her Mercedes and closed the garage door. Despite her excitement, she couldn't get ahead of herself. There was still much to do, but if her plan had gone according to schedule today, then Ethan Hall should have already found Portia Vail hidden away in the abandoned cabin in Rome. A cursory search would have turned up Blake's Saratoga 120s cigarettes, which Lindsay had planted when she was there over the weekend. She had taken the package of cigarettes the night she broke into his cottage to reroute the encryption software to the IP address of Blake's computer. Together with the prepaid phone she had planted in the warehouse, and the photos she had snapped of Portia Vail chained to the bathroom door, it would be enough for the authorities to take Blake into custody.

The final nail, of course, would be leading Ethan Hall to Callie's body. She had given the coordinates to Francis during their last session, and soon the authorities would find the location not far from North Point Pier. It was there, at an old, abandoned power plant that stood at the water's edge, where Lindsay had stashed Callie's body in a 55-gallon barrel before rolling it into the lagoon. An autopsy would reveal the cause of death to be trauma from a Callaway golf club. The same club Lindsay had hidden in the closet of Blake's cottage.

She'd checked on the barrel twice in the ten years that had passed. In a strange twist of fate, the Prescott family had purchased the land that included the decrepit building that was once a power plant, and the lagoon next to it. Consequently, the land had been uninhabited since, and the barrel had remained for ten years unattended and unnoticed just below the surface of the water.

She turned the garage lights off as she entered her home, simultaneously clicking on the kitchen lights. She screamed when she saw Francis Bernard sitting at her kitchen table. He wore a white T-shirt freckled with blood spatter. Lindsay could have no idea that the blood belonged to Andre Monroe, the other person who had tried to take advantage of him while he was in prison.

The edges of Francis's lips twisted into a tight smile.

"Hello, Dr. Larkin."

CHAPTER 83

Milwaukee, Wisconsin
Monday, August 4, 2025

ETHAN PULLED HIS JEEP WRANGLER TO THE CURB OUTSIDE THE Lower East Side home that belonged to Dr. Lindsay Larkin. He shut off his lights and waited. Within ten minutes two other cars had arrived—those belonging to Pete Kramer and Maddie Jacobson. Pete was in his unmarked DCI car; Maddie was in her Milwaukee PD squad car. Two other marked cars followed behind, filled with the four officers assigned to protect Maddie Jacobson—the only surviving victim of the Lake Michigan killings—until Francis Bernard was apprehended. Ethan had requested Milwaukee Police Department presence to take Lindsay Larkin into custody.

Ethan wanted to question Lindsay about how she had pulled it all off. How she had brought Francis Bernard into the picture, and what role she might have played in his escape. He also wanted to learn her motive for killing her best friend, and why she had chosen Blake Cordis to pin the blame on. The woman was a treasure trove of information, but not until they safely had Dr. Larkin in custody.

Ethan knew that everything he did from this moment forward would be scrutinized by law enforcement, district attorneys, and Lindsay Larkin's powerful defense attorneys, so he planned to make no mistakes. It was why he had called Maddie to make the formal arrest. There was a level of clandestine fogginess to his agreement with the Department of Criminal Investigation, and Ethan wanted to avoid a breach in procedural protocol. It was also why he left his gun in the glove box.

The three of them met on the street outside Lindsay's house.

"You take the lead," Ethan said to Maddie. "Everything's got to be by the book on this."

"Got it," Maddie said.

She turned and walked up the driveway with Ethan and Pete following. She started to knock on the front door, but the first knuckle-to-wood connection sent the door slowly gliding open. Maddie looked at Ethan and Pete. The Lower East Side was an affluent neighborhood. Residents were known to leave their doors unlocked, but they did not leave them *open.*

She removed her sidearm. Pete did the same. Maddie led the way into the home with Ethan and Pete close behind. Maddie pushed open the door and yelled into the darkened house.

"Dr. Larkin? Milwaukee PD. Are you in the home?"

No answer.

The entrance foyer was dark, but the light in the kitchen down the hall was on.

"Dr. Larkin!" Maddie yelled again.

When no answer came, they headed toward the kitchen, clearing the rooms to the left and right as they went. As they approached the kitchen, Ethan heard Maddie gasp.

"Oh my God."

Ethan hurried past her. Lindsay Larkin sat at the kitchen table with a garrote tight around her neck, her face bloated and her skin the color of white marble. Blood streamed down her neck from where the cord had been cinched into her skin. As Ethan approached, he saw that Dr. Larkin's blood had been smeared onto the white maple wood of the kitchen table.

Close Ethan, So Close

PART VII

Loose Ends

CHAPTER 84

Milwaukee, Wisconsin
Tuesday, August 5, 2025

THE TELEVISION WAS TUNED TO THE LOCAL NEWS AND PLAYED IN THE background as Maddie packed. Ethan had spent the night. He'd gotten almost no sleep, despite the officers posted outside Maddie's apartment. In total, four Milwaukee PD officers were assigned to keep tabs on Maddie's home and act on anything suspicious they saw. In addition to the cops, two DCI agents spent the night parked in the alley behind Maddie's apartment.

The death of Dr. Lindsay Larkin dominated the local news, and with the murder happening just miles from Maddie's apartment, Ethan knew Francis was close. He was taking no chances. He stepped from the closet and saw that Maddie had stopped packing to watch the news. On the television, the female reporter stood in front of Lindsay Larkin's home, yellow crime scene tape visible behind her, along with the police cruisers and crime scene investigation vans.

Dr. Lindsay Larkin, the founder of The Anonymous Client, *a leading online counseling company, was found dead in her Lower East Side neighborhood home late last night. Police have yet to offer details about Dr. Larkin's death, other than to say that it is an active homicide investigation. There has been speculation that a former patient of Dr. Larkin's has been implicated, but again, details are only just now coming in.*

The Milwaukee Police Department chief offered a statement early this morning but refused to confirm a connection between Dr. Larkin's death and Francis Bernard, a high-profile inmate who escaped while being transferred from the Wisconsin Secure Program Facility in Boscobel. Bernard was being moved to Columbia Correctional Institute in Portage when his transport van was ambushed and both guards were killed. And Dr. Larkin's death comes on the heels of another homicide that took place yesterday in Nekoosa, north of Madison. Francis Bernard is still on the loose.

The news anchor sent things back to the studio, which transitioned to a weather report about the coming storm that would finally break the record heat wave that had consumed the Midwest all summer.

"Maybe we should shut it off," Ethan said.

Maddie turned from the television. Her eyes were filled with tears.

"He's close. I feel it in my bones."

Ethan tossed the clothes he carried from the closet into Maddie's suitcase. "That's why we're getting the hell out of here. My cabin, through a loophole that's been passed down through three generations, is registered in a trust tied back to my great-grandfather's copper mining company that no longer exists. No one's going to find us there because no one knows I own the cabin. Lake Morikawa is the safest place for you right now."

Maddie nodded and continued to pack.

CHAPTER 85

Madison, Wisconsin
Tuesday, August 5, 2025

Ethan pulled back on the controls and the Husky lifted off from the runway. He banked slightly to the left as he climbed to eight thousand feet to join his course up north to the lake.

"Two hours out," Ethan said to Maddie through the headset.

Maddie nodded but kept her eyes closed.

"You didn't get much sleep," Ethan said. "Take a nap, you'll feel better."

Another nod.

With his route programmed into the GPS, he allowed the autopilot to take over. When he locked in his controls and dialed in his settings, Ethan settled back for the flight up to Lake Morikawa. He skipped playing Jimmy Buffett through the headsets. The "Leave All Your Troubles Behind" vibe seemed inappropriate for this trip up to the cabin, and he wanted Maddie to sleep. They'd packed for two weeks, but planned to stay up north as long as it took for authorities to find Francis Bernard.

CHAPTER 86

Lake Morikawa, Wisconsin
Tuesday, August 5, 2025

HARRIETT ALSHON WALKED OUT OF THE CABIN AND SAT IN AN Adirondack chair on the front porch, feeling liberated and peaceful. Her long, blond hair flowed on the shoulders of a light breeze that came off Lake Morikawa. But it was more than the beautiful surroundings that helped her feel at ease. Her journey as Eugenia Morgan had finally ended. Shedding the woman's identity after having assumed it for so long, and climbing back into her own skin, was more transformative than she predicted. She felt free and easy now that she was back to her old self. Some of her vigor, of course, came from finally knowing she and Francis would be together like they'd always planned.

Their relationship had started two years earlier with a simple letter. She had written to him but had never really expected a reply back. When one came, she was flabbergasted. She knew the ACLU had won a legal battle that allowed prisoners at the Wisconsin Secure Program Facility to use the postal system, but she never thought Francis would actually respond to her. But he had, and they continued to write back and forth until one day a long letter arrived from Francis explaining his vision for how they could be together.

He had been explicit that she should never attempt to visit him. It was important for Harriett's name never to appear on his visitor's log. When authorities looked, they would only see that Eugenia Morgan had visited him. They wouldn't know that it was not Eugenia who had made the trip to Boscobel, but Harriett. How could they? Harriett looked exactly like Eugenia. She had dyed her hair jet-black and used contact lenses to change the color of her eyes to match Eugenia's.

With the woman securely shackled to a bed in the basement of her home in Nekoosa, Harriett had taken Eugenia's driver's license and used it to check in at the Wisconsin Secure Program Facility when she visited Francis. She had used the same ID card to purchase the storage unit, to buy the gun Harriett used to kill the guard, and to purchase the Kevlar vest that thankfully hadn't needed to stop any bullets. Harriett had driven Eugenia's Ford Focus to intercept the transport van, and had left it there, along with the Sig Sauer Francis had told her to drop in the middle of the street. Both items would easily trace back to Eugenia Morgan.

Everything Harriett had done for Francis had been while assuming Eugenia Morgan's identity. Detectives and investigators could come to no other conclusion than that Eugenia Morgan, a woman who suffered from hybristophilia and had written Francis seventy-five times in eighteen months, was his accomplice. And then, early Monday morning, Harriett had sliced the woman's throat. According to news reports, police now believed that Francis was on his own. It could not be further from the truth. Harriett was with him today, and would be with him to the end—wherever that was and whenever it came.

She reached into her purse and found her wallet, removing the driver's license that she had placed there weeks before. She slid it from the protective plastic sleeve and held it in the early afternoon sun. Eugenia Morgan's face stared back at her. The resemblance was uncanny, and not for the first time she believed that fate had been on her side. She held the driver's license with her left hand and clicked a cigarette lighter with the thumb of her right. The flame licked at the corner of the license until the laminated edge curled. She stared at Eugenia Morgan's image until the flames melted the woman's face away and burned her fingers. When the pain became too great, she dropped the license onto the porch. But not before Eugenia's image had evaporated.

She took a deep breath, feeling unrestricted now that Eugenia

Morgan was finally out of her life. It would take time to fully shed the woman's persona from her being. But Francis had instructed her closely. She was to not only assume Eugenia Morgan's identity, but to physically *become* the woman. It was the only way for their plan to work. Only now was she realizing how taxing that process had been. Only now did she understand how far she had burrowed into the woman's life. At first she wasn't sure she could pull it off, but she knew that love gives you the power to do all things. Francis had told her as much in one of his many letters to her. And he was correct. Her love for him had taken her this far, and now she needed to go just a bit further for him. So much waited for her in the very near future. Stepping back into her old identity was exciting, but she was not striding back to her old life. That life was over, and a new one waited for her. A second chance at life, this time with the man she loved.

She unzipped the small compartment in her purse and removed her real driver's license. The name on the ID read HARRIETT AL-SHON. It felt good to look at a picture of herself, with blond hair and blue eyes. She had avoided looking at the photo ID of herself for the whole time that she had assumed Eugenia Morgan's identity. But she was happy now knowing she'd never have to go back to the jet-black hair and brown contact lenses she had worn for the last few weeks.

Lake Morikawa unfolded in front of her. Harriett sat on the porch and took in the scenery. The home belonged to Hugh and Ruth Winchester, the elderly couple she had visited on Thursday night. Their bodies were now frozen solid and stacked in the large freezer in the garage. Harriett had checked on them when she arrived earlier today.

Her job now was simple, and much easier than racing around Wisconsin and down to the southern border setting things up for Francis. Her only responsibility at the moment was to wait and watch for the plane—a red-and-white, two-seat Husky—to land on Lake Morikawa. After it did, the real work would begin.

CHAPTER 87

Lake Morikawa, Wisconsin
Tuesday, August 5, 2025

Ethan brought the Husky down in a smooth approach, the floats kissing the surface as the plane skimmed across the lake. The late afternoon sun cast long shadows of pine trees across the lake. He turned the plane left and taxied toward the dock in front of his cabin. He hadn't called ahead or told anyone he was coming, but still Kai was waiting at the end of the pier to welcome him. The Chippewa elder raised his hand in an amicable wave as Ethan approached. Ethan gestured through the window.

Kai cleated off the plane as Ethan popped the cockpit door open and threw his old friend another line of rope, which Kai used to secure to the rear float.

"You just made it," Kai said. "A storm is coming."

Ethan climbed down onto the deck. "Tomorrow, right?"

Kai looked to the sky and assessed what he saw and felt. "Tonight. Bad winds will start early this evening. You would not have been able to land in them."

Kai raised his chin to the east and then looked at Heaven's River, the current of which was raging.

"The rapids are loud and angry. We need to secure the plane tight. The storm will be fierce."

Ethan had learned to trust Kai when he mentioned anything weather related. The man had never been wrong about a meteorological prediction in all the years Ethan had known him.

"I'll haul our bags up to the cabin and then tie off the plane."

"Supplies, too?" Kai said.

"We're short on supplies. Left in a hurry."

Maddie pushed open the cargo door of the plane.

"Hey Kai."

"Hello, Maddie," Kai said, taking the bag she passed out of the plane. "Just a short stay, then?"

"No," Ethan said. "We're planning on a couple weeks."

"Or longer," Maddie added.

"Something I should know about?" Kai asked.

Ethan looked at Maddie, who nodded.

"Let's get our bags up to the cabin and get the plane secured," Ethan said. "Then we'll talk."

CHAPTER 88

Lake Morikawa, Wisconsin
Tuesday, August 5, 2025

I T TOOK TWO HOURS FOR ETHAN AND MADDIE TO BRING KAI UP TO speed on the developments of summer and the events that had unfolded since Memorial Day weekend, the last time they were at Lake Morikawa. Ethan told Kai about Francis Bernard and the man's haunting connection to both Ethan's and Maddie's lives. Kai listened as Maddie relived her harrowing story of escaping as a teenager from the man who brought her to the shores of Lake Michigan to kill her the way he'd killed eight other women that summer. Ethan and Maddie explained how they had met two years earlier at Francis's first parole board hearing and quickly fell in love. Maddie told Kai about the ten letters she had received—all postmarked in Boscobel and signed with a black heart—promising to finish what was started years ago.

"And this man," Kai said, "has escaped from prison?"

"Yesterday morning," Maddie said.

"And we believe he killed a woman down in Milwaukee. A doctor who had been treating him, and who helped facilitate his transfer. It's also possible he was involved in another homicide—a woman named Eugenia Morgan, who we believe was his accomplice in the escape. Authorities are still trying to piece it all together. But until they find him, I thought Lake Morikawa was the best place for Maddie."

Kai nodded. "It is. You'll be safe here. It's quiet and peaceful, and I hope you stay for a long time."

"As long as it takes for my colleagues to find Francis," Maddie said.

Kai looked out the front window. "You came just in time."

The wind had picked up and the lake swarmed with small white-caps that would have made landing the Husky impossible. The weather reports predicted winds gusting overnight. Kai had proven them wrong again.

"I'm heading home before it gets too nasty," Kai said.

Ethan stood. "I'll walk you out."

They left through the front door and stopped in the driveway. The Chippewa elder's long braid flew from his shoulder as a gust of wind skirted across the land.

"I have to head into town for supplies," Ethan said. "We came up unexpectedly and didn't have time to make our usual run before we left. We're going to need some food and water, especially if the storm prevents us from leaving the cabin tomorrow."

Kai looked to the sky. "You'd better hurry."

"I'll go now. Do you mind keeping an eye on the cabin and Maddie, in case she needs something? She can take care of herself, but she's still pretty rattled."

"Of course. I'll be right around the corner."

Kai's home sat on a bluff above Ethan's cabin. Tall lodgepole pines formed a barrier of privacy, but Ethan knew the foliage had never been much competition to Kai's vision and awareness.

"Thanks," Ethan said as lightning blinked far off on the horizon.

CHAPTER 89

Lake Morikawa, Wisconsin
Tuesday, August 5, 2025

"**S**URE YOU DON'T WANT TO COME WITH?" ETHAN ASKED AS HE stood at the front door of the cabin.

"I'm exhausted," Maddie said.

"I bet. I'll be back in an hour. Any special orders?"

"Wine. A cold sauvignon blanc so that I can sleep tonight."

"Done."

Ethan kissed her.

"You've got your Glock?"

Maddie nodded. "In my duffle upstairs."

"Keep it close. It'll make me feel better."

"We came up here so I wouldn't have to use it."

"Humor me?"

"I'll grab it. Hurry back."

Another kiss and he was gone.

Maddie watched Ethan climb into the old model Ford Bronco he kept at the cabin and drive off into the night. The wind howled and for the first time in weeks, as she closed the front door she felt a hint of coolness in the air. The relentless heat wave was coming to an end.

She locked the front door and headed up the stairs to the bedroom, where her duffle bag sat on the bed. She unzipped the top and removed her Glock 45 from the inside pocket, carrying it back downstairs. The windows blinked with a flash of lightning, and a crack of thunder followed. The wind whistled through the window-panes of the old cabin just as she heard the first drops of rain on the rooftop. Five minutes later there was a steady downpour. Ten minutes after that, the trees down by the lake were bent to the east and fighting against an angry wind that had brought the rain.

Maddie moved from the window and settled into the couch. She clicked on the television and tuned to local news out of Duluth, hoping for a weather report. Her Glock sat on the end table.

CHAPTER 90

Lake Morikawa, Wisconsin
Tuesday, August 5, 2025

ETHAN PULLED THE BRONCO ONTO THE MAIN HIGHWAY FOR THE fifteen-minute ride into town. The rain came from nowhere and fell in sheets, his wipers barely able to keep up.

"Damn," he said as he squinted through the windshield.

The pines that flanked the highway were bent against the wind, and he considered turning back. But it had been two months since he'd been up to the cabin, and the refrigerator and pantry were empty. He at least needed water and dinner for the night.

He tried the high beams but they lighted the falling rain and made visibility worse, so Ethan switched on his fog lights to help navigate the road. Headlights appeared in the distance. He was used to an empty road when he ventured into town and was surprised to see someone else braving the elements. He slowed the Bronco as the oncoming vehicle sped past, barely able to make out that it was a Range Rover.

CHAPTER 91

Lake Morikawa, Wisconsin
Tuesday, August 5, 2025

THE DULUTH STATION SHOWED A DOPPLER RADAR HIGHLIGHTING A thick band of quickly developing thunderstorms that ran northeast from Nebraska to Ontario, Canada. The line of storms was a slow-moving network that promised torrential downpours, violent lightning, and severe wind gusts for the next several hours. The good news, the cheery female meteorologist added, was that behind the storm was delightfully cool weather that would be a welcomed relief from the oppressive heat that had plagued the Midwest all summer.

"Awesome news," Maddie said, "for whoever survives this monsoon."

She changed the channel just as a bolt of lightning flashed through the windows, followed a second later by another crack of thunder that shook the cabin. A second later the lights went out.

"Come on," Maddie said. "Are you kidding me?"

She grabbed her phone, and the face lit up with the date and time. It felt like a lifeline to the world beyond the storm. Swiping the phone open, Maddie noticed that her hand was trembling and her heart was racing.

"Calm down," she whispered to herself.

She checked her signal strength and saw that she had a single bar of service. She rarely ever used her phone at Ethan's cabin. Mostly because she and Ethan were always together, unless Ethan was fishing on the lake. She dialed Ethan's number, and he picked up on the second ring.

"You okay?" Ethan asked.

The connection was staticky.

"The power went out."

"Okay. You know where the generator is?"

"Yeah," Maddie said. "I remember. It's out back."

"It should be gassed up. Just give the ripcord a pull and it should power everything back up. I'm almost to town. Want me to turn around."

"No. Grab what we need. But hurry back."

"Ok. Will do."

Maddie ended the call and stood from the couch. She placed the Glock in the back of her waistband. With the flashlight on her phone lighting the way, she headed through the kitchen to the back of the cabin. On the patio, under the carport, was access to the small crawl space where the gas generator was located. This was not the first time a storm had knocked out the power, and she was well versed on how to restore it. She had helped Ethan many times.

She twisted the handle on the back door, having to put some extra weight behind it to fight against the wind that pushed its way into the cabin. The rain roared as it fell against the tin roof of the carport. Maddie pulled the door closed behind her to stop the sideways rain from soaking the inside of the cabin. She crouched down and used her phone to find the handle to the crawl space. She opened the hatch. The generator was located inside, and she pulled it on wheels until it was under the carport.

Another strike of lightning illuminated the night, and Maddie braced for the crack of thunder. When it came, the ground shook and she felt a hand on her shoulder. Her scream blended with the roar of the rain. In one fluid motion she turned and pulled the Glock from her waistband. But her hand, slick with rainwater, could not grasp the handle and the gun clattered to the ground.

CHAPTER 92

Lake Morikawa, Wisconsin
Tuesday, August 5, 2025

Ethan parked the Bronco and ran through the parking lot and into the small grocery store in town. The store's lights were dim, with every other overhead fluorescent lighted.

"Ethan Hall!" the woman behind the register said. "You're either brave or stupid to come out in this kind of weather."

Uma Morris owned The Corner Grocer, and Ethan had known her for years.

"It wasn't raining like this when I left," Ethan said.

"Yeah, came in with a bang. Knocked the power out. We're on the generator, which is why it's so dark in here. I was about to close up when I saw you pulling in."

"Sorry to keep you. I'll just grab what I need. I won't be long."

"Take your time. I was about to lock the doors, but I'm not leaving until it settles down a bit."

"Thanks, Uma. I'll be quick."

Ethan pulled a grocery cart from the chain of others and hurried down the produce aisle.

CHAPTER 93

Lake Morikawa, Wisconsin
Tuesday, August 5, 2025

MADDIE SCREAMED AS THE GLOCK HIT THE GRAVEL. AS SHE SPUN around she saw Kai standing behind her. He raised his hands in fright when she shrieked.

"Kai! Oh my God. I'm sorry."

"No," Kai said, yelling over the roar of the pouring rain. "I didn't mean to startle you. I called your name, but you couldn't hear me. I decided to see how you were doing when the power went out."

"Thanks for checking on me. Ethan's not back yet."

"Can I help with the generator?"

"That would be great, thanks."

Kai bent over the generator and fooled with the gauges for a moment before pulling the ripcord. The engine hummed to life and the cabin's lights came back on.

"The tank is full," Kai said. "Should get you through the night, no problem. Might have to gas up tomorrow if the storm doesn't break, but the worst should be through by midnight. No telling how long it will take to restore the power, though."

Maddie crouched down and retrieved her Glock.

"Sorry about that."

"No worries," Kai said. "Do you want me to stay until Ethan gets back?"

"No," Maddie said over the echoing rain. "Get home to your family. Ethan will be back soon."

"I'll check on you both in the morning."

"Thanks, Kai. Be careful."

Maddie watched Kai hurry off into the storm, running through the rain and to the front of the cabin. She wheeled the generator back into the crawlspace to protect it from the rain and opened the hatch to allow the fumes to escape. She walked into the cabin and shut the back door, happy to be out of the storm. She placed her Glock on the counter by the back door. Opening the door just momentarily allowed the horizontal rain to come around the carport and soak the floor inside the door. She grabbed a towel to clean up the mess.

Her clothes were drenched, so she headed upstairs to change.

She paused at the front door long enough to see Kai back his pickup truck out of the driveway and pull away. Maddie turned from the window and jogged up the steps before a Range Rover pulled into the driveway.

CHAPTER 94

Lake Morikawa, Wisconsin
Tuesday, August 5, 2025

"**A**NYTHING I CAN HELP YOU WITH BEFORE I LEAVE?" ETHAN asked after his groceries were bagged.

"Only thing I have left to do is refuel the generator to make sure it lasts through the night," Uma said. "If my freezers go down, I'll lose my inventory."

"Need a hand?"

"Would you mind?"

"Of course not," Ethan said.

"Generator is in the back."

"Lead the way."

A few minutes later, Ethan lifted the heavy five-gallon tank to the generator and poured gas into the funnel. He filled it to the brim.

"That oughta do it," he said.

"Thank you. Storm is supposed to break overnight, but you know how slow they are to bring the power back around here."

Life on Lake Morikawa could not exist without a good generator, Ethan knew. It sometimes took days for the power to return after an outage.

"Want me to stop by tomorrow?" Ethan said. "In case you need to refill it?"

"No. I'll have my husband do it. Thank you, though."

"Have a good night."

"Stay safe, Ethan," Uma said as Ethan hurried into the storm with his bags of groceries weighing him down.

CHAPTER 95

Lake Morikawa, Wisconsin
Tuesday, August 5, 2025

MADDIE HAD ONLY THE BEDSIDE LAMP ON IN THE BEDROOM. SHE'D been up to Ethan's cabin before when the electricity had gone out, and she knew to draw as little power as needed from the generator. She pulled off her wet shirt and sorted through her duffle bag as she stood in her damp shorts and bra. Three loud bangs stopped her cold. She stood with her hands sunk in her bag and listened. The banging came again, and she thought that perhaps a tree branch was hitting the side of the cabin. But when the pounding came a third time, she knew someone was knocking on the front door.

"Kai?" she whispered in an attempt to calm her nerves.

She looked down at her waist and remembered that she had left her Glock on the counter by the back door. She found a T-shirt and pulled it over her head before exiting the bedroom and starting down the stairs. When she reached the landing, she walked to the front door and peeked through the side window. Standing on the front porch, barely shielded from the pouring rain, was a woman. She was backlit by the headlights of her car that was parked in the driveway. She wore a baseball cap—what Maddie suspected was a way to protect her from the rain.

Maddie slowly opened the door.

"Thank God," the woman said. "I am so sorry to bother you. I'm staying at one of the other cabins on the lake and my power went out."

"Ours, too. We're running on a generator."

"It's my aunt and uncle's cabin. I don't know if they have a generator. And if they do, I have no idea how to use it. I hate to impose," the tall woman said. "I was going to drive back to Duluth, but I don't think I can make it until the storm dies down. I turned around to hunker down in the cabin, but there's a downed tree in the road and I can't make it back. I saw your lights on and thought I'd take a chance."

Maddie pushed a hesitant smile onto her face and nodded. "Of course. Come in."

"I don't know how to thank you," the woman said as she stepped in out of the storm. "I'm *so* sorry to drip all over your home."

"Don't be silly. Let me get you a towel. I'm Maddie, by the way."

The tall woman with radiant blue eyes smiled. "Harriett. Thank you so much for opening your home to me."

Harriett stepped farther into the cabin as Maddie shut the door against the raging wind and driving rain.

CHAPTER 96

Lake Morikawa, Wisconsin
Tuesday, August 5, 2025

ETHAN MANEUVERED THE BRONCO AROUND THE FALLEN BRANCHES that littered the road. The rain came in sheets, and, had Maddie not been at the cabin alone, he would have pulled to the shoulder until the torrent subsided. Instead, he twisted the truck around a large tree limb that blocked the eastbound lane, splashed through a twenty-yard-long puddle, and continued on. He dialed Maddie's number again. On clear days, his phone rarely registered more than a single bar of service up at the lake. The storm was making things worse, and he gave up after the third time the call went straight to voicemail.

The fifteen-minute drive took thirty, and when Ethan turned onto the last stretch of road, he saw a vehicle pulled to the shoulder of the westbound lane. The headlights were on, and the driver's side door was open. As Ethan drove closer, he recognized that it was Kai's pickup truck. Ethan bounced the Bronco onto the breakdown lane on the other side of the road. The rain hindered his vision so he couldn't see what the problem was.

He reached into the middle console and grabbed the flashlight he kept there, clicked it on, and opened the Bronco's door. The rain demarcated the beam of the flashlight as Ethan stepped into the storm and shined the light onto his friend's truck. He saw that the driver's side tires were intact. No flats. He walked across both lanes of the road and checked the cab. Empty.

"Kai!" Ethan yelled against the driving rain.

He was soaking wet. Rainwater dripped from his chin and his T-shirt stuck to his chest. Ethan shined his light into the bed of the F-150. Also empty. But when he walked behind the truck, he saw Kai lying in the embankment on the side of the road.

"Kai?" Ethan said.

He ran to his friend and crouched next to him. The rain mixed with the blood that streamed from Kai's abdomen and mouth.

"Kai. You okay, buddy?"

Kai's eyes opened. A bubble of blood formed on his nostril when he tried to speak.

What's going on? Ethan said to himself as he examined Kai's body. *Where's the blood coming from?*

On the side of the road and amidst a vicious storm, Ethan morphed back into an emergency medicine physician, looking for the source of the blood and the best way to stanch its flow. But before he could make the full transformation, Kai spoke a single word that snapped Ethan back to his current role as an investigator.

"Francis."

Ethan stopped his exam.

"What?"

"Go," Kai said, his teeth red with blood. "Now! Maddie's in danger."

Off in the distance, in the direction of his cabin and through the pouring rain, a gunshot echoed into the night.

CHAPTER 97

Lake Morikawa, Wisconsin
Tuesday, August 5, 2025

"**W**HERE'S YOUR CABIN?" MADDIE ASKED. "ETHAN—THAT'S MY boyfriend, he owns this place—says there are only a few on the lake."

"Just around the bend," Harriett said. "On the northeast side. It belongs to my aunt and uncle. They offered the cabin for the week." She smiled. "I thought it would be a relaxing getaway until the storm hit."

Harriett used the towel Maddie had given her to wipe her face. The Minnesota Twins ball cap still covered her head.

"Can I get you a change of clothes?" Maddie asked.

"Oh, I don't want to be a problem. I'm already imposing."

"Stop. It's no problem at all." Maddie pointed outside. "It's going to be a while before the storm breaks."

"Are you sure?" Harriett asked.

"Absolutely. All I have are shorts and T-shirts. But they're dry."

"Thank you."

Maddie ran upstairs and rooted through her duffle bag. She grabbed a pair of jean shorts and the least ratty T-shirt she had packed. She headed down the stairs and handed them to Harriett.

"Bathroom is around the corner."

Harriett disappeared into the bathroom and Maddie removed two waters from the fridge. She checked her phone. There was still just a single bar of service and three missed calls from Ethan. She tried his number, but the call went straight to voicemail.

Maddie heard the bathroom door open. She put her phone back onto the table and grabbed a bottle of water for Harriett, but when the woman walked out of the bathroom Maddie's breath caught in her throat. The woman had changed out of her wet jeans and into the shorts Maddie had given her, revealing a spiraling black python tattoo on her right leg that started at her calf and twisted up her thigh, disappearing under the jean shorts. And the Minnesota Twins ball cap was gone, allowing the woman's long blond hair to corkscrew down her back.

"Is that for me?" Harriett asked, pointing at the water bottle in Maddie's hand.

Maddie's mind flashed to the still image Pete Kramer had shown her and Ethan from the dash cam of the transport van—the tall woman with blond hair and the snake tattoo who had helped Francis escape was standing in front of her.

Maddie smiled. "Yeah. Here you go."

She handed over the water bottle, swallowing hard in the process. She had left her Glock on the counter by the back door. Maddie gave nothing away as she slowly turned and walked through the kitchen toward the back entrance.

But when she made it to the door, the gun was gone.

CHAPTER 98

Lake Morikawa, Wisconsin
Tuesday, August 5, 2025

MADDIE'S FLIGHT OR FIGHT RESPONSE KICKED IN AND BLOOD pulsed through the vessels of her neck. When she turned from the empty counter, Harriett was smiling.

"Looking for your Milwaukee Police Department issued Glock forty-five?"

Maddie looked around the cabin. The woman was tall and young. Maddie was trained in close-quarters combat, and she could take care of herself if it came to that. But her first goal was to get out of the cabin. She turned and took two steps to reach the back door, but the woman was on her in an instant. Maddie felt her head snap backward as Harriett grabbed a handful of her hair and yanked her away from the back door.

Turning, Maddie bull rushed the taller woman, cramming her shoulder into Harriett's sternum and advancing forward until they crashed into the kitchen table and toppled over the surface. Maddie landed on top of her in a jarring manner that caused Harriett to release her grip on Maddie's hair. Maddie sat up and delivered two sharp strikes to the woman's face—one landed below her eye, the other square to the nose.

As Harriett cried out in pain, Maddie climbed off of her and sprinted for the front door. But Harriett caught her shin with her hand and Maddie went down hard. The woman climbed onto her back and wrapped her arm under Maddie's chin, tightening her grip in a chokehold that immediately restricted her breathing.

Maddie clawed at the woman's forearm but could not loosen the grip. Stars formed in her vision and the compartmentalized memories of her time as a sixteen-year-old girl came back to her, when Francis dragged her to the shores of Lake Michigan to kill her. Climbing first to all fours, Maddie next managed to get to her feet—Harriett on her back the whole time. She stumbled a single step forward before bracing herself and then rushing backward several steps and launching them both against the wall of the cabin where the fishing spear Kai had gifted Ethan hung. Maddie knew that the spear hung on three ivory tusks set firmly into the wood, and she prayed she'd find one of them.

As they crashed backward, Harriett collided against the wall with Maddie's weight and momentum adding to the force. Maddie knew she'd hit pay dirt. Harriett's scream was otherworldly as one of the ivory hooks pierced her back just below the scapula. Maddie felt the woman's grip loosen, and she managed to escape from the chokehold. As Harriett crumpled to the ground, Maddie staggered for a step or two as she sucked in air until the tunnel vision cleared. Then, she turned and ran for the back door.

When she reached it, Francis Bernard stood on the other side and smiled at her through the glass. Rain dripped from his face. His clothes were soaking wet and his white T-shirt stained red with blood. He lifted Maddie's Glock from his waist and used it to tap lightly on the glass.

CHAPTER 99

Lake Morikawa, Wisconsin
Tuesday, August 5, 2025

MADDIE BOLTED FROM THE BACK DOOR AND RAN THROUGH THE cabin. Harriett had made it onto her knees and tried to hinder Maddie's progress. But a visceral fear coursed through Maddie's body that made her feral and unstoppable. She ran through Harriett as if the woman were a sack of suds. She reached the front door and yanked it open before she heard the blast from her Glock and felt a searing pain pierce her left side.

The force of the bullet caused her to fall forward, slamming the front door closed. When she pushed away she saw the exit wound in her lower left abdomen where her T-shirt was painted red. Blood, too, spattered the door. The pain came and went, overshadowed by the adrenaline that flowed through her veins. She twisted the handle to the front door and started to pull it open again when she felt Francis grab the back of her shirt.

"Now look what you've made me do," Francis whispered in her ear. "This won't be nearly as fun if you die quickly. I was hoping to take my time."

Francis spun her around and, with a violent jerk, ripped the front of her shirt so that her breasts were exposed. His head tilted to the side as he examined her chest. Then, he traced the spot on her left breast where he had years ago etched a black heart into her skin. The heart was gone, replaced now by a jagged scar.

"You erased my work," Francis said. "We can't have that, now can we?"

The burning pain in her side had taken on a life of its own, and the blood loss was making her drowsy. As Francis continued to stare at the scar on her breast, Maddie reared back and drove her forehead into his nose. She heard cartilage crunch and bone break. Blood shot horizontally from Francis's nostrils as he stumbled backward. A stream of blood poured into Maddie's eyes from the newly formed gash that ran from her hairline to the bridge of her nose.

Combined with the bullet that had pierced her side, the concussion of the impact with Francis's skull made her dizzy. She staggered two steps forward until she was in striking distance again. Then, she delivered an upward kick to Francis's groin. He howled in pain and fell to his knees. Maddie turned and, like a drunk leaving the bar, zigzagged for the front door. Before she made it, though, Francis lunged forward and grabbed her ankle. It was all it took to send her face first into the doorframe.

Exhausted from blood loss, Maddie closed her eyes and willed her brain to power down and take her far away. She had nearly succumbed to the urge when she felt Francis pull on her leg as he dragged her back toward the kitchen.

His voice was nasally when he spoke. "I'm going to return you to the black heart club before I kill you," Francis said.

She felt him grab her by the hair as he lifted her off the floor and forcefully shoved her onto the kitchen chair. Maddie was helpless now as Francis secured her wrists to the chair with zip ties. She opened her eyes when she felt him unclasp the front of her bra. He touched a knife to her left breast.

CHAPTER 100

Lake Morikawa, Wisconsin
Tuesday, August 5, 2025

I T KILLED HIM TO LEAVE KAI BLEEDING ON THE SIDE OF THE ROAD, BUT he had no choice. Ethan jumped back into the Bronco and stepped on the accelerator, the tires spitting gravel as he fishtailed off the shoulder and back onto the road. Visibility was for crap, and he was driving much too fast for conditions. He'd be no help to Maddie if he flipped the Bronco into a ditch, but he couldn't help himself.

It took four minutes to reach the cabin and as he turned the Bronco wildly into the driveway, he collided into the backend of a Range Rover that was parked there. The airbag deployed and delivered a solid jolt to Ethan's nose, drawing blood. As he jumped from the truck and ran through the driving rain, he reached for his waistband but remembered that his Beretta was in his bag.

He ducked down below the Range Rover and changed course, running along the side of the cabin and then around to the back door, which had been left eerily open. There was no time to assess the situation or decide on the best tactical approach. Instead, he bolted forward and put his shoulder into the partially open door, sending glass shattering as he crashed into the cabin.

Ethan stumbled into the kitchen to find Maddie tied to a chair with Francis behind her, a garrote similar to the one he'd used on Lindsay Larkin around Maddie's neck. Her shirt was torn at the neck to reveal a crude black heart that had been carved into her left breast, blood oozing from her gouged and stenciled skin. There was no hesitation. Ethan lunged forward and clipped Francis with a clothesline forearm across the neck and both men went down.

He heard Maddie choke as she sucked air through her now-open trachea. Ethan climbed on top of Francis and pummeled him with several blows to the face. Years of pent up rage poured from him as Ethan bloodied the man's face with a relentless fury of strikes. When Francis's arms fell to his sides and the man could not defend himself, Ethan placed his hands around Francis's neck and began to choke the life from his body. The man's face turned to a deep purple and his eyes bulged as Ethan tightened his grip.

A violent blow to Ethan's temple stunned him. A second to the back of the head caused him to slump to the side and collapse onto the ground next to Francis. Ethan rolled onto his back and opened his eyes to see a tall, blond-haired woman standing over him and pointing Maddie's Glock down at him.

The woman squeezed the trigger, and he felt a searing pain in his left shoulder. The blond woman adjusted her aim, this time bringing the barrel of the Glock in line with Ethan's face. Before she could pull the trigger, though, Ethan saw the walrus tusk that tipped the end of his prized fishing spear pierce through the woman's chest.

CHAPTER 101

Lake Morikawa, Wisconsin
Tuesday, August 5, 2025

THE WOMAN'S EYES WENT WIDE AS SHE DROPPED THE GLOCK AND studied the spear that impaled her chest cavity. She grabbed it with both hands and, amazingly, drew it forward through her body, pulling it from her chest. Ethan lay on the ground, unable to do anything but watch it all unfold. Maddie stood behind the blond woman and released her grip on the spear as the woman pulled it through her body. Ethan knew, depending on which organs had been pierced, that there might have been a chance the woman could survive such a wound. But only if the spear had remained in place until she got to a trauma surgeon. Once she removed it, any chance of survival was gone.

Once the spear came out of her chest, blood spurted from the wound like an open spigot. Shocked and confused, the woman simply stared at the blood that flowed from her body and never attempted to stop it. Her face drained of color, and she slowly fell to the ground next to Ethan. Despite the ringing in his ears and the throbbing in his temple, Ethan was aware enough to feel the warm flow of the woman's blood as it pooled on the ground around him.

Maddie stumbled back into the chair, reached for her side, and collapsed into it. Ethan made it to his hands and knees and crawled over to her.

"What is it?" he asked.

"GSW," Maddie said in a hoarse voice, her vocal cords damaged by the garrote. "Through and through. Exit wound in front."

Ethan shook his head to clear the cobwebs. His left shoulder burned like hell as he ripped away what was left of Maddie's shirt to see the exit wound. It oozed with frothy red blood. He pulled his own shirt over his head, wincing at the pain in his shoulder, and stuffed it into the hole.

"Hold it there."

Ethan checked her back and found the entrance wound. The hole there was smaller and barely bleeding.

"Good," he whispered, wondering how long Maddie could withstand the internal bleeding. Could they make it to the hospital in Duluth?

"Ethan," Maddie gasped.

Ethan looked up in time to see Francis pull open the front door and stagger out into the storm.

CHAPTER 102

Lake Morikawa, Wisconsin
Tuesday, August 5, 2025

"**G**O," MADDIE WHISPERED THROUGH HER CRUSHED VOCAL CORDS. "I'm not leaving you," Ethan said. "We have to get to a hospital."

"It won't matter if Francis is out there." Tears came to her eyes. "Please, Ethan. Find him."

Ethan nodded. "Okay," he whispered as he ran a hand across Maddie's cheek, still plagued by Bell's palsy from the last time Francis had gotten his hands on her. Turning, he bolted for the door and burst out into the night, the rain loud and relentless. His Bronco had pinned the Range Rover in the driveway, preventing Francis from using the vehicle to escape. Ethan looked in all directions. A bolt of lightning brightened the night and allowed him to see a figure cut across the side yard toward the river. Ethan ran after him, slipping on the grass and stumbling over boulders as he raced for the riverbank. As he grew closer to Heaven's River, he saw that the current was angry and the rapids even louder than the rainfall.

He made quick work of catching up to Francis. When he'd cut the distance to a few feet, Ethan lunged onto the man's back. They tumbled down the embankment and splashed into the raging river. Ethan howled in pain from the bullet wound to his left shoulder as he and Francis wrestled in the water.

Climbing to his feet, he felt a blow that skimmed his temple as Francis swung at him with a large rock he'd taken from the riverbed. Ethan kicked him in the chest, sending Francis stumbling backward into the rapids. Like a fast-moving treadmill belt, the current sucked Francis away. Without thought, Ethan dove into the river, allowing the current to yank him downriver in pursuit.

Ethan knew the river well from having waded through it while brook trout fishing over the years. He understood the topography and knew that the torrential rain had lifted the water level so that the boulders, which normally poked through the surface, were now hidden beneath the water. He maneuvered himself into a sitting position as he crashed through the rapids. He lifted his legs so that he would easily bounce off rocks and avoid a foot entrapment.

Francis was farther downriver, and Ethan noticed that the man had no idea how to navigate the rapids. Francis bounced off boulders like a pinball until he finally went under. He emerged a moment later, Ethan barely able to see the man's head pop through the surface next to him as Ethan flew past. Ethan grabbed Francis's white T-shirt and, in tandem, they careened down a chute and through the rapids below.

When they emerged, the water level had dropped so that Ethan was able to stand. He still had Francis, waterlogged and exhausted, by the shirt. He delivered a sharp jab to the face and started to drag Francis to shore when a majestic bolt of lightning struck a tree upriver. The splintering of wood was deafening as the tree caught fire and fell into the river as if a lumberjack had sawed it at its base. The raging rapids tugged the fallen trunk from its roots on the riverbank and sent it careening toward Ethan and Francis. It took just a second for the tree to reach them. Ethan released his grip on Francis's shirt and dove beneath the water. Francis, Ethan noticed just before his head dipped beneath the surface, had not been as fast.

An eddy current spun Ethan in circles beneath the water. His foot found a boulder and he pushed off, freeing himself from the eddy and mixing back into the fierce current. The rapids sucked Ethan downriver and bounced him off rocks before finally spitting him out into Lake Morikawa. He swam perpendicular to the tide until he was in calm water, and watched for Francis to surface. The cold water had numbed his shoulder and taken away the pain. But he was treading water with only his legs and right arm, and wouldn't last long. The rain made it difficult to see and after a minute of watching the mouth of Heaven's River pour into the lake, Ethan headed for shore.

He crawled onto the rocks, heaving for breath as he squinted through the rain looking for Francis. But the river never delivered his father's killer into Lake Morikawa. Assuming he had been trapped under the fallen log, Ethan ran back up the riverbank to where the trunk had lodged against two boulders.

Water seethed around the wood and swelled over the tree trunk. Ethan had enough sense not to reenter the water. Fatigued from the battle, and with only one functioning arm, he would be no match for the river a second time.

CHAPTER 103

Lake Morikawa, Wisconsin
Thursday, August 7, 2025

ETHAN HAD MANAGED TO FIGHT THE STORM ON TUESDAY NIGHT AND get Maddie to the hospital in Duluth, which was a Level 1 Trauma Center. He had stopped to load Kai into the backseat of the Bronco, but knew it was too late. Kai was pronounced dead on arrival to St. Mary's. Maddie was rushed to surgery. Ethan was treated in the ER, admitted, and discharged Thursday morning.

He spent most of his time Wednesday in a hospital bed talking with police and detectives about the carnage that had taken place inside his beloved fishing cabin on Lake Morikawa. The blond-haired woman had been identified by the medical examiner as Harriett Al-shon and was confirmed to be the woman in the photos from the transport van's dash cam. Her body was found in Ethan's cabin. The medical examiner determined her cause of death to be exsanguination—blood loss from a puncture wound to the abdomen that pierced the inferior vena cava.

Ethan's left arm rested in a sling as he and Pete Kramer stood on the bank of Heaven's River. His cabin was behind them, roped off by yellow tape. The river had calmed but remained high. Divers from the DCI bobbed up and down as they combed the riverbed for Francis Bernard's body. Three DCI boats cruised back and forth through Lake Morikawa, dredging the bottom.

Finally, a diver surfaced with something in his hand. He removed his mask and SCUBA regulator.

"Got a shirt, boss."

Another agent met the diver on shore and dropped the shirt into a plastic evidence bag. He brought it over to Ethan and Pete. They examined it through the plastic. The shirt was stained with blood and badly ripped. Ethan remembered grabbing Francis by it on Tuesday night.

"Yours or his?" Pete asked.

"I wasn't wearing a shirt. I gave it to Maddie to dress her wound. It has to be his."

"We've dragged it twice," the agent said. "Nothing yet."

"The river was raging," Ethan said. "I wouldn't be surprised if the current spit him into the middle of the lake."

"We'll keep looking," the agent said. "And bring in sonar to assist."

Despite their efforts, though, by the end of the day Friday, Francis's body had still not been found.

CHAPTER 104

Cherryview, Wisconsin
Saturday, August 9, 2025

Despite his physical condition, Ethan finished his shift at the hospital. He had volunteered to cover an open slot, hoping to take his thoughts off the fact that they had not found Francis's body. The DCI had paused the search for the weekend, believing that in time Francis would float to the surface of Lake Morikawa as his body worked through the stages of decomposition. Eventually, intestinal gases would raise him from the bottom. Neither Ethan nor Maddie would get a decent night's sleep until they saw the man's dead and bloated body.

They were still gathering information and trying to understand the events that had unfolded during the last week. The only person who might have shed light on the mystery was Blake Cordis. Ethan had paid the man a visit the day before. Although Blake had never heard of Francis Bernard, he had come clean about his relationship with Lindsay Larkin—sleeping with her when he was her high school volleyball coach and then unceremoniously breaking things off when he fell in love with Callie. Blake and Lindsay had slept together again just recently. Blake told Ethan about Lindsay's bizarre behavior on Monday night, her knowledge of the prepaid Samsung phone Blake had used to communicate with Callie, and Lindsay's cryptic promise that Blake would soon be in prison. After he left Blake Cordis's house, Ethan started to assemble the puzzle.

A jilted Lindsay Larkin, heartbroken by Blake when she was a teenager, had discovered that he was in a relationship with Callie.

Lindsay had stolen the prepaid cell phone and used it to lure Callie to North Point Pier. There, out of jealously, Lindsay killed her best friend. According to Blake, Lindsay had tried over the years to revive their love affair, but Blake had never been interested. Having learned of Blake's relationship with Portia Vail, Lindsay abducted the girl in an attempt to frame Blake for the crime. And somehow, Lindsay had entered into an agreement with Francis Bernard, luring Ethan to evidence Lindsay had planted that would point to Blake Cordis as both Callie's killer and Portia's abductor. But Dr. Larkin had not planned on Francis escaping from prison and hunting her down. There was still much to learn, and Ethan was unsure if he'd ever know the full story.

He pulled up to his house and stopped the Jeep at the mailbox. Inside was a single envelope, which he retrieved before pulling up the driveway and into his garage. He dropped his keys into the bowl on the foyer table, placed the sandwiches he'd picked up for dinner on the kitchen counter, and grabbed a beer from the fridge.

Maddie was resting on the couch. The bullet that cruised through her abdomen had miraculously missed all vital organs and vessels. The biggest hurdle would be recovering from the bullet exploding through her abdominal muscle, which made it difficult to sit up, walk, or do anything that engaged her core. She was slated for physical therapy on Monday and was off work for two weeks.

Ethan leaned over the back of the couch and kissed her forehead. The stress of the last week had caused a relapse of her Bell's, and the left side of her face drooped and refused to respond when she attempted to smile. She placed her hand self-consciously over her cheek.

"It'll come back. Probably a couple of weeks."

She nodded.

"I grabbed sandwiches from the Old Fashioned."

"I'm not hungry."

"Okay. But you need to eat something eventually."

Maddie nodded again and lay back down.

In his scrubs, Ethan sat at the kitchen table and popped the top on the Spotted Cow. He opened the sandwich and took a bite as he pulled the lone piece of mail in front of him. It was addressed to

Special Agent Ethan Hall. Although he did not quite understand why, his insides fluttered with anxiety like a thousand butterflies were attempting to escape his ribcage.

He noted the postmark—Hachita, New Mexico. It was dated on Thursday. He squinted his eyes and then opened his phone to do a search, discovering that Hachita was located in southern New Mexico close to the U.S.-Mexico border. He put his phone to the side and lifted the envelope. He stuck his thumb under the edge and tore it open, removing the single page within and turning the envelope upside down so that the other item fell from inside—a silver key that rattled onto the kitchen table.

His eyes focused on the neat cursive as he began to read.

> *Dear Ethan,*
> *I hope you're well. Thank you for your visits over the years. You have no idea how much they meant to me. I understand they were something entirely different for you. You used our time together to exorcise your demons and promise that I'd never see the light of day outside the confines of a prison. By now you know how incorrect you were.*
>
> *I promised you the location of the girl's body, so here it is:*
>
> *45.2930° N, 88.6839° W*
>
> *I will miss our visits, Ethan. For me, they were a way to see a glimmer of your father. He was more to me than just the man I was convicted of killing. So much more. Every time I saw you on the visitation schedule, my insides filled with excitement. When I looked at you, I saw Hank.*
>
> *If you want to understand why your father excited me so much, use this key to find out.*
>
> *Lakeside Storage. Unit 223.*
>
> *—Francis*

CHAPTER 105

Cherryview, Wisconsin
Saturday, August 9, 2025

HE COULDN'T STOP MADDIE FROM COMING WITH HIM, AND ETHAN knew enough not to fight her on it. The Hachita postmark suggested that Francis had somehow survived the river and escaped to Mexico. But even with the man out of the country, Ethan wasn't about to leave Maddie alone. It took thirty minutes to find the location of the coordinates. Ethan finally turned the Wrangler onto a gravel road north of Lake Okoboji, not far from North Point Pier. The lonely road ran next to an abandoned building that had once been a power plant. His GPS glowed on the dashboard, and he followed the map until they came to the edge of a small lagoon. It was approaching 8:00 p.m. and the horizon burned lavender with dusk. He clicked his bright lights on, and the Jeep illuminated the water.

They climbed out into the evening. The temperature was a pleasant 72 degrees since the storm had dragged cooler air over the Midwest. Ethan and Maddie walked to the edge of the lagoon. Ethan shined a flashlight into the night.

"There," Maddie said, pointing out at the water.

Ethan stepped into the shallow water and spotted the red, 55-gallon barrel just below the surface about twenty yards from shore. It took thirty minutes for Ethan to secure the Jeep's winch around the barrel. He had to remove his sling to get it done and was soaking wet by the time they'd pulled the barrel to shore. It was resting on its side and spilling water when Ethan used a tire iron to pry off the lid. More water poured from inside. Ethan shined his flashlight into the barrel to reveal the grisly discovery. He knew he'd made the right decision to keep the location of Callie's body to himself and not share it with Governor Jones.

No parent should ever see their child in the condition they'd found Callie Jones.

CHAPTER 106

Madison, Wisconsin
Saturday, August 9, 2025

Lakeside Storage was located off Lake Mendota in a Madison suburb. Ethan and Maddie had spent two hours at the lagoon after they'd called in the location of Callie's body. Ethan answered questions from responding officers, waited to speak with detectives, and spent thirty minutes talking with Mark Jones when the governor showed up at 11:00 p.m.

It was approaching midnight when he and Maddie pulled into the storage facility and found unit 223. He parked the Wrangler in front of the bay door, keeping the engine running and the headlights on. He took his Beretta from the glove box, and Maddie climbed behind the wheel just in case a speedy exit was necessary.

"Keep your phone on," Ethan said, standing outside the driver's window.

Maddie held up her cell. "Check."

"And stay locked and loaded."

Maddie held up her Smith & Wesson SW1911 semi-automatic handgun. Her Glock 45 was in evidence. The Smith & Wesson was from her private stash.

"Check."

"Let me see what's inside," Ethan said. "I'll be out in a minute."

Ethan turned from the Jeep and approached the door to the storage unit. His clothes were still wet from his trip into the lagoon, his shoulder was aching, and he had yet to put his sling back on.

He inserted the lone key that had arrived in the mail and unlocked the door. It creaked when he pushed it open. He found a light switch on the wall and clicked it on, bringing the space to life. In the middle of the 20x20 storage unit was a table with a cardboard box resting on it. He walked slowly toward it, fighting against some invisible force that told him to stay far, far away from what waited on the table. As he inched closer he saw dozens of photos laid out on the surface and positioned neatly around the box.

The first image he saw brought Ethan to his knees—a glossy 8x10 that stole the air from his lungs. Ethan tried to stand, but his legs would not hold his weight. He fell to the ground, twisting as he landed on the seat of his pants. He pulled the cardboard box with him in the process, and its contents spilled onto the floor of the storage unit. Dozens of old-fashioned audio and videocassette tapes clattered on the concrete around him, in addition to scores of photos that rained down.

The photo that had started the chain reaction landed in his lap. Ethan lifted the 8x10 to his face. It depicted a sixteen-year-old Maddie Jacobson, unconscious and bound to a chair. On Maddie's chest, carved into her left breast, was a black heart. And standing on either side of her, smiling at their prize, was a young Francis Bernard and Ethan's father. Detective Henry Hall.

Summer 2026

Lake Morikawa, Wisconsin

CHAPTER 107

Lake Morikawa, Wisconsin
Monday, July 13, 2026

HIS HAIR WAS LONG AND WILD, AND A THICK BEARD HE TAMED ONCE a month covered his face. Dark bags drooped under his eyes from a year without a decent night's sleep. Every time he closed his eyes, Francis Bernard found him. In the worst of Ethan's nightmares, his father was there, too, holding the knife he had used to carve up women during the summer of 1993.

When the sleep deprivation became too much, and his life began to spiral, Ethan put in for a leave of absence at the hospital and disappeared. The governor had made good on his promise to erase Ethan's student loan debt, and when he found himself free and clear of that burden, he decided the only place he might be able to heal was up north. So he climbed into his Husky and took off for the backwoods of Lake Morikawa. It had not been lost on Ethan that both the passenger seat on the way, and the dock when he arrived, were empty. It had been the first time he could remember landing his Husky without Kai waiting for him on the pier.

He had arrived over Memorial Day weekend and spent the summer running a medical clinic for the Chippewa people. He spent his days seeing patients in the morning, fishing away the afternoons, and drinking too much in the evenings.

"It's infected," Ethan said as he stared into a Chippewa member's mouth and rooted around with a dental pick. He wore a head-mounted light and a surgical mask as he performed his exam.

"I can drain the abscess for you today and get you on antibiotics, but you're going to have to see a dentist soon."

"Do what you can, Doc," the man said. "I'll see the dentist next week."

"Tomorrow," Ethan said. "Or you'll lose the tooth."

The man nodded and opened his mouth as Ethan went to work. He saw ten more patients that morning and treated a host of ailments that included a man on the verge of a diabetic coma, an ulcer on a woman's heel, and a nasty hemorrhagic conjunctivitis. He finished charting, made calls to referring physicians in Ashland, and spoke personally to the dentist about the abscess he was sending over.

He closed the clinic, promised to be back Wednesday morning, and climbed into his Bronco for the ride home. His cabin had been gutted and remodeled since the previous summer. He'd hired a contractor out of Superior, Wisconsin to do the work and trusted that it had been done well, never making the trip up from Cherryview to check the progress. The first time he walked into the cabin over Memorial Day weekend, Ethan looked around and approved of the retooling. He was aware, however, that the esthetics could be changed in a single season, but the memories of what had transpired there would take much longer to fade.

Lingering paint fumes remained from the remodel, and he smelled them every time he returned to the cabin. He opened the windows and welcomed in the hot, humid summer air. One of the perks of the rehab was the addition of central air-conditioning. Ethan planned to set the thermostat to frigid that night. Perhaps it was the secret to a good night's sleep. With a lake breeze flowing through the cabin and carrying away the smell of paint and turpentine, he grabbed his Loomis spinning rod from the wall rack and headed down to his boat. He pulled the ripcord on the 50hp Mercury engine and took off across Lake Morikawa.

He killed off the afternoon hours, dropping two sixteen-inch walleye into the live well for dinner. He spent an hour hunting northern pike, finally tying into a forty-incher that he took on a Johnson Silver Minnow. Ethan brought the big fish to the side of the boat, netted it, and measured its length. Then, he carefully released it back into the water to fight another day. When the thrill of the catch was over, he packed up his gear and sat on the casting deck to take in the beauty of the lake.

Lodgepole pines filled his vision in every direction. An eagle cut through the air and skimmed along the surface of the water until it plucked a fish from the lake and flew back to its nest. A loon let out a long tremolo from the middle of the lake before disappearing under the surface. He remembered his many hours on the water with Kai, and missed his friend.

As usual, Lake Morikawa worked its magic. For a couple of hours Ethan had forgotten about the pictures of Francis Bernard and his father posing with Maddie and the women they killed during the summer of 1993.

The audio and video recordings, however, were harder to forget. Ethan didn't have the stomach to watch all the videos. But he had watched enough to know that Francis and his father had documented each of their victims, including Maddie. For a couple of months after he'd visited the storage unit, all he did was obsess over the videocassettes. Eventually, he stopped watching them. Eventually, he stopped listening to the hours of audio that Francis had recorded of himself and Ethan's father discussing their next victim and obsessing over Maddie Jacobson.

But there was one item Francis had left in the storage unit that Ethan could not disengage from. Francis had written Ethan a final letter, and with it was an audio recording of Francis's final interaction with Ethan's father. Ethan had become unhealthily fixated with it.

He yanked the ripcord on the Mercury outboard, clicked the motor into gear, and started the trip back to his cabin. It was time to start his nightly routine of drinking too much beer and listening to the audio recording of his father's last words.

CHAPTER 108

Lake Morikawa, Wisconsin
Monday, July 13, 2026

NEARLY A YEAR AFTER HE'D FOUND THE LETTER IN THE STORAGE unit, it was weathered and worn from having been read so many times. He opened his first beer of the night and began reading.

> *Dear Ethan,*
>
> *Prison takes just about everything from the incarcerated. But the one thing it provides is time. Without the interference of the Internet or television or books—or anything, really, to distract my thoughts—prison allowed me time to plot and plan. If things have gone according to how I had organized them in my mind, then I am a free man right now. Maddie Jacobson, the only woman to have escaped from your father and me, is dead. She's been a burning passion of mine for over thirty years. The one that got away. The one I can't forget.*
>
> *Before I head for parts unknown, I thought I owed you an explanation. The less humane part of me revels in the idea of tormenting you with the photos of your father. But another part of me is delighted to tell you the full story of how your father and I got started together.*
>
> *Despite a well-maintained façade, Hank Hall was an unhappy man. Discontent with his life in every sense. Hopeless in his marriage. Disheartened with his family. And bitter about his career. The only time he found joy, he told me, was when he*

and I were on the hunt for our next girl. And when we found
her, he lit up with anticipation. When Maddie Jacobson came
around, I'd never seen your father so excited. And we had fun
with her. But when the time finally came to bring her to the
shores of Lake Michigan, things went tragically wrong. She
managed to escape us, and our relationship fell apart from
there.

If you want to know what happened the day I killed your
father, listen to audiocassette number 18. As I did with nearly
every interaction with your father, I recorded our final conver-
sation because I knew where it was headed.

I know you'll find no peace knowing that your father is gone
and I'm still out there. But peace is something you earn. It is
not free.
—Francis

Ethan dropped the tattered letter onto the kitchen table, took a
long sip of beer, and pressed *play* on the audiocassette player he
had purchased the year before. The thirty-three-year-old recording
was staticky. Ethan had listened to it so many times over the last
year that the tape had warped, making the voices it held nearly in-
audible. But by now Ethan had the entire conversation memorized.

He sat back and listened. Ethan assumed the audio had been
taken secretly. Judging by the muffled voices, Francis had likely
placed the audio recorder in his pocket when he answered the
door the night Ethan's father showed up at his house. The recording started with the sound of a lock disengaging, and then a door
squeaking open.

Henry Hall: We need to talk.
Francis: I figured.
Henry Hall: My department is already speaking with her at the
hospital.
Francis: There's nothing she can tell them.
Henry Hall: We don't know that. We don't know what she remem-
bers.
Francis: I want her to remember. We'll wait until she's back home

and then send her a reminder. Send her an audio clip of her scream-
ing in terror. It might be better that she got away. This will be more
fun.

Henry Hall: No. The forensics team will analyze something like
that, and it'll lead back to us. We shut this whole thing down. Now.

Francis: You mean, shut it down as in no more girls?

Henry Hall: That's exactly what I mean.

Francis: That's not happening, Hank. You know it and I know
it. Neither of us can exist without this.

Henry Hall: You don't know how these people work. The forensic
teams, the detectives, the psychiatrists. They'll pick that girl's body
and mind apart until they find what they need. And by the time
they're done, she's going to lead them back here. You need to leave
town. Get far away from here.

Francis: I'm not going anywhere.

Henry Hall: Yes you are! We're done! No more girls.

Francis: I don't want any more girls. I want the one that got
away.

Henry Hall: That is not happening. I won't allow it.

Francis: It's not up to you.

Henry Hall: The hell it isn't. My life is on the line here and—
BANG!

Despite the fact that Ethan had listened to the recording hundreds of times, he still jumped at the sound of the gun being fired.
The recording continued for another hour, although Francis never
spoke again. It was left to Ethan's imagination to fill in the details
of what he heard. But he knew enough to paint a realistic picture
of what was happening during the recording.

Francis shot his father in the face and then spent an hour packing
up the basement where they had brought their victims to torture
them and brand them each with a black heart. Then, with Ethan's father dead in the front foyer and the video and audiocassettes packed
up for Ethan to find thirty-two years later, Francis lit his home on fire
to erase any evidence of what had transpired there.

Ethan finished his beer in one, long swallow. Then, he rewound
the tape and listened again.

CHAPTER 109

Lake Morikawa, Wisconsin
Monday, July 13, 2026

IN THE EARLY EVENING, ETHAN FIRED UP THE GRILL AND COOKED THE walleye he'd caught, along with potatoes and onions. He popped the top on a can of Schlitz, which he purchased at the small convenience store in town. The Schlitz was a salute to his father, and a trip down memory lane. Schlitz had been the maiden beer he and his dad shared together when Ethan was sixteen years old and his father brought him up to the cabin for the first time. It tasted as bad now as it had then, but Ethan discovered that if he drank enough of them, they dulled the reality of his father's new identity that had taken root in his mind.

He finished the beer in a few long gulps. Foam covered his bushy beard. He took the fish and potatoes off the grill and brought them inside. Sitting at the kitchen table, he popped the top on another beer and was about to eat when he heard the distinct sound of an amphibious floatplane approaching. He stepped out of the cabin and stood on the front porch as he watched the plane approach from the south. The Cessna 182 touched down in the middle of the lake before taxiing to the dock in front of Ethan's cabin.

The cargo door opened, and Mark Jones stepped from the plane.

CHAPTER 110

Lake Morikawa, Wisconsin
Monday, July 13, 2026

"**W**ANT A BEER?" ETHAN ASKED WHEN THE GOVERNOR MADE IT up the long flight of stairs to the cabin's front porch.

"No thanks. But I need a word."

"I figured. But you could've called. The whole landing on the lake and all that is a little dramatic."

"I *have* called. Eight times since Friday. No answer. And I've left a message every time."

"Don't be offended," Ethan said. "I haven't checked my phone in weeks."

"And it looks like you haven't shaved in a year."

"I haven't."

"Can we talk inside?"

Ethan opened the door to the cabin and waved the governor in.

"Sure you don't want a beer?" Ethan asked after they were inside.

"I'm good."

Mark sat on the couch. Ethan took a spot in the adjacent chair.

"So, Governor, what brings you all the way up north?"

Mark pulled a folded newspaper from his back pocket and dropped it on the coffee table.

"Sunday morning's *Journal*," Mark said.

Ethan lifted his chin to get a look at the headline.

After Thirty Years, the Lake Michigan Black Heart Killer is Back

Ethan slowly reached for the paper.

"A body showed up on the shores of Lake Michigan Friday morning. The woman's throat was slashed, and a black heart was tattooed on her breast."

Ethan skimmed the article.

"The story's on every local newscast and starting to get picked up nationally," Mark said.

Ethan looked up from the paper. "You think it's Francis?"

"Yes. And that's why I'm here, Ethan. He left something with this woman's body to let us know it's him."

"Other than the black heart tattoo?"

"Yes. The medical examiner found this in the victim's mouth."

Mark handed Ethan a photo. It was of a crumpled piece of paper that was flattened and resting on a metal autopsy table. Neat block writing flowed across it.

I KNOW YOU'LL COME LOOKING.
DO BETTER THAN YOUR FATHER, ETHAN.

"I'm creating a task force. I want you to head things up."

Ethan looked up from the photo.

"I want you to take the lead, Ethan. Francis has made this personal, and I want you to find him before more bodies start dotting the shoreline."

Ethan ran a hand through his disheveled hair, and then down along his long beard. The taste of Schlitz hung in his throat. The photos of his father posing with Francis Bernard and the women they'd killed flashed through his mind. And his father's voice from the recording echoed in his ears. For an entire year, Ethan had struggled to process what he'd discovered in that storage unit. Despite the irrefutable proof, some part of his mind refused to believe that his father could have been Francis Bernard's partner. He had locked up the storage unit the previous summer and kept the contents to himself. But now he was at a crossroads. In one direction was denial; in the other was a collision course with the truth.

Images of the life he had created played through his thoughts. Memories of medical school and the ER where he had carved out a promising career and a happy existence. Where he was admired by the staff, respected by his colleagues, and beloved by his patients. No one had to know about the photos of his father. No one had to see the videos or listen to the recordings. He could take the photos and the cassettes and burn them. He could go back to the hospital and leave the past behind. Perhaps he had left his old life at the DCI for reasons greater than the ones he thought he understood. Perhaps leaving had been a subconscious way to preserve the memory of his father.

Ethan shook his head. "I'm just an ER doctor, Governor."

"You're the best investigator we have, Ethan. In one summer you solved my daughter's case—a case that had been cold for a decade. And right now, we need you."

Ethan took a sip of beer and shook his head. "I don't think I'm the right man for the job, Mark."

The cabin door opened, and Maddie walked in.

"You're the *only* man for the job. And I need you to say yes to this."

CHAPTER 111

Lake Morikawa, Wisconsin
Monday, July 13, 2026

THE HORIZON WAS CHARRED WITH THE GINGER GLOW OF SUNSET THAT bottom lit a network of clouds drifting over the lake like frayed cotton shredded across the sky. Ethan and Maddie stood out on the porch and looked down over Lake Morikawa. Mark Jones had finally taken Ethan up on his offer and sipped Schlitz while he sat on the couch inside the cabin.

Ethan looked at Maddie and ran a finger along her left cheek.

"Told you it would come back."

Maddie smiled, each side of her face responding, the Bell's palsy invisible to anyone who didn't know it had once existed. She reached up and placed her hand on his wrist.

"I don't know what happened last summer. I don't know what you found in that storage unit that sent you into such a spiral. And, honestly, I don't care. I don't need to know why you ended things with me. I don't need to know why you quit your job. And I don't need to know why you ran away. All I need to know is if you'll come back and help me with this. I've been put in charge of the investigation by the Milwaukee PD. We've called in the DCI to assist us. If you come back, you and I would be leading the charge on this, Ethan. And I need you by my side."

Ethan swallowed hard. A fish swirled near the pier and broke the surface of the water. An elk bugled from somewhere in the brush. Ethan wondered when he'd be back here again. He wondered if this place would ever be the same for him. He wondered how many more women would die if he refused Maddie's request. He wondered the same thing if he accepted.

"Ethan?" Maddie asked.

Ethan looked at her. His gaze shifted to the lake in the background, and the lodgepole pines all around him. Slowly, he nodded.

"I'll do it."

ACKNOWLEDGMENTS

A big Thank You to everyone who had a hand in making *Guess Again* what it finally became.

Thanks to everyone at Kensington Publishing—from the art department that created such a stellar cover to Vida Engstrand in the PR and marketing department and everyone else who played a role along the way. Special thanks to my editor, John Scognamiglio, who not only helped make the story better with his insights and suggestions, but who also came up with the title in the eleventh hour!

Thanks to Marlene Stringer at StringerLit. Holy crow, Marlene!

Thanks to Amy and Mary, who always read first and always help me make a good story better.

Thanks to Capt. Rich Hills who helped me get Ethan Hall safely to his secluded cabin on Lake Morikawa. I've flown in seaplanes many times, but I've never operated one. Although Ethan's piloting skills are not perfect, Rich helped me make them believable.

Thanks to my old college friend Mike Ross, MD, who shared insights about emergency medicine that helped Ethan find a way to take the summer off to peruse Callie's case, stitch up a nasty gash, and triage a gunshot wound. I didn't follow Mike's advice perfectly, but close enough.

Thanks to Jen Merlet, who is always kind enough to take a final read through my manuscripts to look for errors everyone else missed. No one can find them all, but Jen comes damn close. Any errors in this novel are, of course, Jen's fault. So PLEASE email her about them.

And thanks to the readers and the bloggers and the reviewers and the influencers. This little writing journey is nine thrillers long now and I have you all to thank for spreading the word.